PLAYING WITH THEIR HEARTS

MCKENZIE BROTHERS #6

LEXI BUCHANAN

HFCA Publishing House

Ireland

www.lexibuchanan.net

First Published 2015

This Edition 2024

Cover Design: Alison Chaffin Higson

Editor: Sirena Van Schaik

Proofreader: Kellie Montgomery, Eye Candy Bookstore

BETA Readers: Carla, Celia, Emma, Jane, Joy, Lisa, Nadine & Tricia

SYNOPSIS

Ramon McKenzie offered Noah his heart, but he rejected him. Noah has been silent for nearly two years, but he has returned, determined to beg Ramon's forgiveness.

So where does that leave Sylvia? She is not only Michael and Sebastian McKenzie's personal assistant, but also the woman Ramon is dating.

The lives of the McKenzie brothers are anything but simple, and Ramon McKenzie's is no exception.

This is the sixth novel in the McKenzie Brothers series and may be read as a standalone.

Please note that this is an M/M romance with explicit scenes.

1

Ramon

PACING BACK AND FORTH IN THE HOTEL ROOM WHERE I'm supposed to meet the contact Eric set up is grating on my nerves. The security at the Lexington site is constantly on my mind, and my confusion about Sylvia only further aggravates it. What the hell am I doing with her? To make matters worse, I can't stop thinking about Noah, which is extremely annoying.

Sylvia wants a lot more than I can give her right now, and I should give it to her. She's been here for the last two years, but Noah hasn't, and no one has heard from him since he left. One day—my birthday, to be exact—everything was fine, and the next, he'd disappeared. There was no explanation or hint of where he was going. Not to me and not to his sister Carla, who is now married to my brother Sebastian.

Right now, I feel as though everything is crashing down around me. Nothing is going right at the site I'm managing. One thing after another has gone wrong, and I'm afraid someone is going to get killed working there if something doesn't happen soon.

None of us have ever had this problem before, so it's pissing me off right now.

I hear a tap at the door, peer through the security hole, and see a guy standing on the other side. He's hunched over with his face averted, as though he's aware that I'm watching him. He's dressed like the dozens of other workers on the site—blue jeans, T-shirt, fleece, and a blue baseball cap—but there's something about him that nags at me. I feel like I've seen this man before. The man bangs on the door again, harder this time.

I take the security lock off and open the door wide, letting him walk in. His face is still averted as he moves into the room. He stands with his back to me. But as he starts to turn, the blood in my body turns to ice.

No fucking way!

I feel the blood drain from my face as I drop into the chair beside the table, holding my travel bag.

No matter how many times I blink, he's still standing before me, looking just as shocked to see me as I am to see him.

"Two years," I whisper.

He shuffles back and falls onto his butt against the bed when his legs hit the side.

In a nervous gesture, he turns his cap backward. "I don't know what to say." He buries his head in his hands, then looks at me again. "I knew it would be a shock for you to see me. Even though I knew this meeting was with you, it's still shocking to be in the same room with you after all this time." I was planning on heading back to Lexington to find you when Eric approached me about this job. I need to explain, but I have no idea where to start."

"The beginning is usually a good place to start, although nothing will change the fact that you left without any explanation." Where's my anger when I need it? "We spent the night together celebrating my birthday. You bought two tickets." I stand up, feeling my anger like a hot flash running through my blood. The chill of shock has disappeared, replaced by this strange heat. "To a Bruins game in Boston! There wasn't any sign that you didn't want to be with me."

I find it difficult to stay where I am, but I don't move toward him. I don't know whether I want to punch him or sleep with him to show him what he's been missing by not being with me.

My fists clench at my sides as I watch his eyes travel the length of me, probably noticing the change in my appearance. I've always been muscular. All the McKenzies are, either from our job or from the gym. But I've changed since I was with Noah—in a good way. At least, I think I have. I'm more toned, and my jaw is more prominent now that my hair is cropped close to my head. The Ramon with the soft touch and overly long, dark hair is gone. In his place is someone who won't let Noah walk all over him again. He tore my heart to shreds. I'm not going to let him do that again.

Yet, as I watch him, I can't help but feel a spark of worry for him. Damn it! As much as I don't want to admit it, I still care about him. Really looking at him, I see Noah drop his head into his hands and notice them shaking slightly. I realize that these past months must have been hard on him for one reason or another.

His face is raw with emotion, as though he's been through hell since he left. His dark hair, which he wears slightly long like I used to, is desperately in need of washing. What has he been doing to look like this? His green eyes are dull, unlike the way they used to spark to life the moment he looked at me.

"I'm sorry. I didn't want to leave you." His voice is heavy as he looks up at me, his eyes pleading. "You have no idea how many times I've wanted to come back to you. How much I've missed you. I've missed talking to you, or just fucking sitting and watching TV. I even bought a ticket to the Bruins game just for a glimpse of you, because I'm broken without you. You took Ruben with you."

I seriously don't know what to say to him. He's confusing the hell out of me.

"If what you say is true, then why? Why did you walk out on me?" I slumped back in the chair, all my anger draining away as numbness took its place.

"I can't explain now. I promise I will when I can." Noah stands up and comes over to where I'm sitting. He stands in front of me. "I'm coming back to Lexington with you. Once I've seen Carla and made sure she's as happy as I hope she is, then we'll talk. Just give me a chance, Ramon. Please. I can't live my life without you in it anymore."

Shaking myself out of the haze of lust that washed over me when he got close—I'm now at eye level with the bulge behind his zipper—I jump to my feet, causing Noah to take a step back.

"I've spent years trying to get you out of my head and heart, so why would I let you back in when you've proven that you can't be trusted?"

Before I can respond, he has me pressed against the door, his aroused and angry body flush against mine. "You aren't listening to me, as usual," he hisses. "If I could have stayed with you, I would still be with you in Lexington. Let there be no mistake about that."

We're both breathing heavily, our mouths mere inches apart. There's no mistaking the truth behind his words.

"Why the fuck did you leave?" I whisper, wanting to push him away but desperate for answers.

Instead, I find my hands sliding over his hips and ass, pulling him closer. Our hard dicks press together through denim. He reaches up and fists my short hair. He brings his mouth close, so our lips are hovering above each other's.

"If I'd stayed, you'd be dead." I barely catch the anguished words as he closes the gap between us and seals our mouths together in a kiss that tastes of lust, passion, hunger, and, most of all, home.

This can't happen. Not now.

I push him away and wipe my mouth, even though

all I want to do is lick my lips to savor his lingering taste. I can't let him do this to me again. What the hell did he mean?

"You need to either tell me what you meant by that or leave. Either way, I'm not doing this again with you. I have someone else," I blurt out.

His head whips around to stare at me. He's trying to gauge whether I'm lying.

"You've been with someone else?" he asks, his fists clenching at his sides.

I nod, unable to lie to him. I have been seeing Sylvia, and although she wants more, I haven't slept with her. I can't, and the reason why is standing in front of me.

"Fuck you!" he shouts, his eyes flashing with fury. "I guess all your talk about love was bullshit. How long did it take you to be with someone else after I left?"

I don't answer, looking everywhere to avoid his gaze.

"Fucking tell me," he roars, getting in my face.

I shove him back. "What the hell is your problem? Have you forgotten that you left me? You left me! Without a word, for two years! Did you expect me to pine away and wait for someone who I thought would never come back?" I glare at him; the anger is coursing through me so fast that I feel like I'm shaking. "And you still haven't answered my question about 'I'd have been dead if you'd stayed.'"

His eyes narrow, and he ignores my questions. "My problem is that you slept with someone else when I stayed true to the man I loved. Who I thought loved me, but I guess I was wrong. Well, I'd better make up for lost time," he practically spits at me. He's so damn angry.

Yanking the door open, he storms out, slamming it loudly behind him.

What does he mean by "make up for lost time"? Is he going to find someone to sleep with? Over my dead fucking body!

I can't get his words or the hurt in his eyes out of my head. He hasn't been with anyone since he left, just like me. I keep telling myself that I should focus more on his comment about me being dead if he'd stayed, but all I can hear is that he remained true.

Noah

If Ramon can sleep with someone else, then after over two years of celibacy, I certainly can. The opportunity has arisen in the past, but I was, and still am, so tied up with Ramon that the idea of sleeping with someone else makes me want to puke.

My life has been a struggle since I left, but knowing that one day I'd have the chance to talk to Ramon and explain things has kept me going.

But all this time, he's been sleeping with someone else. Does the "someone" live with him? Is this person male or female? I grimace at the thought, and I'm not sure if I'd be angrier if it were a woman or a man. I know Ramon liked both, or at least he did. A few months after we met, he lost interest in women and only wanted me.

I push through the doors of the bar and wonder why he couldn't wait for me. He had no idea why you left or that you intended to come back. Trying to reconcile my desire with the facts, I drop into the only vacant seat at the bar and point toward the Jack Daniel's behind the bartender.

The bartender starts to pour the Jack Daniels over my glass when I hold up three fingers. He raised his brow but continued to pour.

"Bad day?" he asks.

"You have no idea," I reply.

The bartender watches me drain the glass, and when I slam it down on the bar, he fills it again without being asked.

As I watch him pour the golden liquid, I realize how young he is. The fact that he's tending bar tells me he's at least twenty-one, but not much older. With his baby face and the slight shake to his hand as he pours my drink, he looks fresh out of high school.

I'm not interested in anyone so young, but the thought of Ramon catching me chatting him up causes a small smile to slip across my lips. If Ramon comes after me, that is. Oh, he'll come after me.

Since leaving Lexington, I've kept a low profile, moving from town to town. I never stayed long wherever I ended up, and I only worked for cash paid out daily so that I could leave town as quickly as I arrived if needed. I hoped that all the shit and threats I left behind wouldn't follow me.

Two years ago, all I could think about was keeping Ramon safe. Now that the threat is over, I want to pick up where we left off. I grimace into my drink, the irony not lost on me, before taking a long swallow. I'd expected a warm welcome. I thought Ramon was waiting for me and that, the moment he saw me, everything would be like it was before I left. I realize now how stupid that was.

The dream that kept me sane is gone, so what the hell am I supposed to do?

I drain the glass again and cover the top with my hand when the bartender goes to pour. "No, I want more, but I just need the edge off for now."

"Whatever you say." He turns and puts the bottle back before leaning on the bar toward me. "So, what's your story?"

It's clear he's gay. With the look he's giving me, there's no way he's anything else.

"You don't want to get involved with me, kid." I hold his gaze and notice his lashes flicker slightly when I call him "kid." He doesn't like that. He probably plans to hustle me—plying me with drinks and robbing me blind when I can't see straight.

I've seen it happen more than once, which is why I never drink excessively anymore, no matter how much I want to.

"You're interested," he insists. "I can tell."

"Hmm, is that so?"

"It is. Do you want to know how I can tell?"

"I might as well." "Go on."

"I've been watching you since you walked through the doors. Your eyes have followed me around the bar." He points behind him. "I can see everything through the chrome."

Great!

You're too young for me. I think you should move on." I wave toward the blond guy nursing a tall glass at the end of the bar.

I toss enough cash on the bar to cover my tab plus tip. I smile to myself when he quickly grabs the cash and pockets some so fast that I'm sure he's skimming his employer.

Who cares? He can do whatever he wants because the last thing I want or need is trouble from him while I'm trying to figure out how to get Ramon back.

With my head starting to throb, I move away from the bar toward the door. I push through the thickening evening crowd and notice three tall, overweight guys around the dartboard staring at me.

I slip outside and start to make my way to the motel office to try to get a room. I might not be drunk, but driving on these roads after only one drink isn't advisable. One false move, and I could go through the barrier, end up in a ditch, or even worse, at the bottom of a mountain. Even if I were lucky enough to walk away, I'd always wonder about that drink I had. Not worth it.

Shaking my head, I take a deep breath and push

through the doors into the lobby. Just then, the doors to the bar open behind me. I turn to look back over my shoulder when I hear loud music. Two of the guys who had been watching me leave exit the bar and glare in my direction. Where's the third guy?

My gut tells me I need to get out of here right now. Glancing through the door I was about to open, I realize that I won't have any help from that direction when I see the person behind the desk, who looks to be over eighty years old. A quick look around tells me that my only escape is up the alley to the side of the motel.

I can probably run faster and for longer than the unfit bastards who are now heading in my direction with smirks on their faces.

I turn and run smack into someone, bouncing back slightly. From the snickers I hear behind me, I realize they expected me to retreat down the alley. Struggling to break free from the third thug, I bite back the bile rising in my throat. Damn, this guy is reeking. I twist, managing to turn and look at the other two men when my attacker's grip loosens slightly.

My body hums to life, and the world slows down around me. I can feel the man behind me move as I gather my strength and prepare for a fight. I've been in much worse situations than this, and these three yahoos aren't going to break me. I slam my head backward and smile slightly when I hear his nose break. Blood splashes against my neck, but his grip falls from my arms, and I slip completely free.

Shaking off the sickness that overwhelms me, I pivot and drop my leg back before bringing it up hard and fast into his groin. The man gurgles as blood rushes into his mouth. He grips his groin and slumps to the floor, whimpering in pain.

As I hear footfalls approaching quickly, I twist and manage to block the second attacker's blow as my fist swings up and under his jaw. His eyes flutter, but the uppercut doesn't take him out. He and his friend tackle me to the ground.

Ramon

I glance at the clock and groan at how slowly time is passing. I've been pacing back and forth in my room for an hour, wondering what the hell I'm going to do. The last person I expected to see tonight was Noah.

After he left, my first reaction was to reach for my

phone and call Eric. I wanted to ask him what he thought he was doing setting up this meeting, but then I paused. Eric knows I was in a relationship with another man, but I never mentioned Noah to him. Unless he figured it out.

My stomach is still rolling with shock, and I'm fighting the urge to go after him and explain that I lied about Sylvia.

How would I feel if Noah had admitted to having sex with someone else? I'd want to beat the shit out of anyone he'd touched.

I run my fingers through my hair, regretting getting it cut. I tug at the short strands and tell myself that I need to stay put. Anything we had was over two years ago. The only problem is that my heart isn't listening to my head. Maybe it would if I actually believed that we were really over.

No matter how much I wish it were otherwise, I can't just switch off my feelings for him, and that fact scares me a little. I'm not sure my heart could withstand being broken by him again.

I flopped down on the bed, grabbed the remote, and started flicking through the channels, but nothing held my interest for long. I drop my head onto the bed and sigh. I can't leave it. Fuck! I toss the remote to the floor, get to my feet, grab my car keys and cell phone from the desk, and yank the door open, letting it slam shut behind me.

I'm not sure what I'm going to say to him or if I'll even find him. But when I do, I'm not letting him go until I get the answers I deserve. He's been too damn vague, and that's got to stop.

I run down the outside stairs of the motel and stand for a minute to look around. I figure he'll have a car close by because he won't fly. He hates not being in control. He also has a thing about large vehicles. I notice the same old black SUV he had when we were together sitting in a parking spot on the other side of the motel.

As I start heading toward the SUV, I hear a scraping sound, followed by a couple of thuds as though someone has been hit. The sound comes from the alley to the side of the motel block. My instincts scream to walk away and avoid the confrontation, but my conscience wins out when it becomes obvious that someone needs help. "Hell!"

I quickly turn and run toward the alley. I pause when I see a guy on the floor getting kicked. Before I can stop myself, my feet carry me forward.

I grab one guy by the scruff of his neck, catching him off guard, and slam him to the ground. My fist connects with his jaw with an audible crack, sending him sprawling to the ground. As he lands, another guy tries to catch me off guard, but I'm quicker. My fist connects... one... two... the third thrusts into his stomach, crumpling him over. As he recovers, I knee the third guy in the groin and watch him drop.

The guy on the floor isn't moving. As I stand over him, I realize it's Noah. Seeing him so beaten makes my anger surge, and I turn back to the bastards who are now making their escape. I'm torn as to whether I should let them go or chase after them. In the end, though, Noah wins.

I check the alley to make sure we're alone, then drop to his side, unsure where to touch him. His face is bloody, and swelling has already begun. There is blood around his stomach. As I lift his soaked shirt, I discover a shallow gash across his ribs. I didn't see any weapons, but I did notice a large ring on one of the guys' fingers.

Cursing under my breath, I realize that I need to get him to safety before they come back with reinforcements. My heart pumps with adrenaline.

"I'm sorry for this," I whisper as I slide my hands under him and pull him up. I stagger slightly under his weight, but I manage to get my legs moving.

At the corner, I scan the area to make sure no one is waiting to ambush us, and then I quickly dash to my room. I hope I won't regret heading for my room instead of the truck, which would put miles between us and the roughnecks.

Noah isn't a lightweight, so by the time I push into my room, I barely make it to the bed before dropping him on it. He doesn't move or make a sound when he lands.

I quickly turn to make sure the door is secure before rooting through my luggage for the medical kit I always carry.

When I look back at the bed, I see the man lying prone on the dingy cover. It hits me that I'm going to have to undress him before I can do anything. He isn't going to like that. In fact, judging by the way he left the room, I'd even say that if he wakes up while I'm undressing him, he'll attack me.

I take a deep breath and reach for his ruined shirt. Gripping both sides, I tear it the rest of the way up. At the neckline, I pull, and the shirt parts easily.

I pull the sides apart and gasp at the full extent of his injuries.

He should be in the hospital.

"I'll live," he hisses.

My eyes shoot up to his, and it hurts to see Noah's face lined with pain. I have a feeling that not all of his pain is from the beating he just received, and that some of it has to do with our sharp words from earlier.

"I don't know where to touch you." I sigh in frustration and point toward his torso.

"No hospital. I think I'm going to pass out, so knock yourself out."

As I watch, his eyes close, and he passes out.

Before he comes around again, I quickly start removing his clothes as carefully as possible, dropping them in the trash before opening the medical kit.

2

Noah

As I stretch, an intense pain rips through my body, causing the air to rush out of my lungs.

What the hell is wrong with me?

I force my eyes open and blink rapidly at the brightness coming through the slats of the blinds. It leaves me unable to focus. When I turn my head away, I manage to keep my eyes open and realize that Ramon is asleep in a chair in the corner of the room.

What is he doing here? Come to think of it, nothing looks familiar as I look around.

I try to push myself up, but my head spins, and the pain around my ribs sends me back to the bed.

Then it hits me.

What happened last night?

"Fag… homo… queer!"

I close my eyes as the words become a vivid nightmare in my head. They are a chant running through me as I remember that night, those bastards shouting and running up behind me.

Feeling sick, I open my eyes and stare at the ceiling, trying to remember the rest of the night. Then I realize that Ramon must have come after me.

I'd wanted him to.

I hadn't wanted him to find me the way he did, but I'd wanted him to come after me. In an ideal world, he would have come after me and told me that he still loved me and had never stopped. But we don't live in an ideal world, and I'm positive he came to find out what I meant by saying he'd be dead if I'd stayed.

Ramon won't rest until I've told him everything. Maybe that's what I have to do.

Glancing at Ramon, the man who still holds my heart, causes a hitch in my breathing. Ramon is still a stunning man.

His muscular build and Spanish heritage make him stand out in a crowd. Anyone would be lucky to have his heart, and for a while, he had eyes only for me. Even in Canada, when we sweet-talked women, his eyes were always on me. Every time he came, his eyes were on me, not the other woman.

So, hearing him tell me that he had someone else tore my fucking heart out. We used to be so in tune with each other that, even though I was the one who left, I feel as though he's committed the ultimate betrayal.

Watching him now, I miss his long hair, which used to fall to his shoulders. In fact, I miss everything about him. I miss the feel of his face against mine, against my skin, my thighs, my stomach—you name it. I miss having his long legs wrapped around mine while we slept. I miss waking up to his morning wood pulsing against my ass or my own cock.

I try to shift into a more comfortable position, my dick hardening as I reflect on my past with Ramon. I try to think of something else to stop my desire, but it's persistent.

My relationship with Ramon wasn't just sex, although that was part of it. I loved spending all my free time with him. We'd talk about books, hockey, and softball. We'd also eat at small restaurants outside of Lexington to avoid his family. He's my other half, and I need to work damn hard to make him see that. I have no intention of walking away from him again.

The first time was more painful than I ever want to experience again.

Stroking my shaft, I feel the first drop of arousal release from the tip, and I stifle a groan. It's been a long time since I've taken care of myself, and I haven't let anyone else do it since Ramon.

As much as I need a release right now, I'm not sure I have the strength to follow through. I'm certainly not going to ask Ramon to suck me off. Yeah, that would go over well given the mood I left him in.

I need to think about something other than having his lips locked around me. Fuck—not helping!

I suddenly notice a glass of water on the bedside table and reach for it. My fingers slide over the cool glass, and it slips from my clumsy grip. With a crash, it falls to the floor and shatters.

"What the fuck?" Ramon shouts, jumping from the chair. His hair is sticking up, and his eyes, though alert, are still heavy with sleep.

His sleepy eyes glance around the room and come to rest on the mess I caused. He grabs some towels and tosses them onto the spreading puddle of water.

"Sorry," I mumble, my voice hoarse.

"No problem. Let me get you another one."

Ramon shoves his hands through his hair and

heads out of the room. It's a habit he had when he had long hair. He looks like he's still trying to wake up.

While I wait for him to return, I try to assess my injuries. My throat feels dry, and my stomach growls with hunger, making me smile. I know my groin area is uninjured. Thank God. I have a slight headache, which could be from lack of food. From what I remember, they mainly attacked my stomach and ribs, which is why my rib cage hurts so much.

As Ramon walks back into the bedroom, I devour his appearance with my eyes. He's rumpled from sleeping in a chair, yet he looks sexy as hell. His black sweatpants hang low on his hips, and he's shirtless— my favorite outfit. He's tantalizing enough to make me want a glimpse of what he's hiding.

The movement of his sweats makes my eyes widen, and I look up and search his eyes. The blaze of heat coming from him causes me to harden.

He smirks and, stepping forward, pushes a straw between my lips. "Sip," he growls.

I do.

The cold water slipping down my throat feels amazing. The more I drink, the more refreshed I feel. All I need to do is figure out how I'm going to empty my bladder when moving hurts so much.

"You want some more?" Ramon asks as he moves the empty cup away.

I shake my head and immediately regret it as pain lances through my head. "I'm good for now. Thanks."

Ramon puts the glass on the windowsill and turns to face me. He doesn't say anything, he just holds my gaze. For once, I'm not sure if I'll be the last man standing.

Ramon scares the shit out of me like this. It's as though he's looking into my soul, his body still and his gaze locked on me.

Wanting him to stop, I ask, "How long have I been out, and where are we?"

He blinks and moves back to sit in the chair he'd been sleeping in.

"Three days. I've rented this cabin just outside of town. I figured it was more private than the motel."

Fuck. At least I'm safe for now.

"Hospital?"

"You begged me not to take you."

I did.

"You've been in and out of consciousness since I stopped them." He drops his head against the back of the chair, closing his eyes. "You scared the fuck out of me, Noah," he whispers. "Seeing them... seeing you... I wanted to kill them."

His eyes snap open, and the anguish he feels is clear. I don't know what to say, so I stare at him for a few minutes, trying to think. Rather than delving too deeply into my feelings when I can't show him through action or words, I tell him what happened that night: "I was in the bar, trying to drown the pain of knowing you have someone else. I'd been flirting with the bartender, hoping you'd walk in and see me." I laugh, but there's no mirth behind it. "I had had enough to drink, so I headed out. Within a minute, I was ambushed, and you know the rest." I sigh. "They must have been watching me at the bar to realize that I was gay."

Ramon curses and sits forward. "They attacked you because you're gay."

It's a statement, not a question.

"I figured that, and I'd hoped you'd tell me I was wrong."

"I wish you were wrong."

The attack three nights ago wasn't the first time I've been attacked for being gay. I hope it's the last. "Thank you, Ramon. Thank you for taking care of me. I don't deserve your kindness after the way I left you..."

"Did you really expect me to turn my back and leave you there?" He shook his head. "I still care about you, Noah. I wouldn't have left anyone in that alley, least of all you. But we once belonged to each other, and I guess I'm still struggling to accept that we don't anymore. Otherwise, I would have ignored you and taken you to the hospital. In fact, I nearly did. I was worried about internal bleeding given the condition you were in. After talking to Ruben, he told me to check your urine. You should be fine if there's no blood."

"I was a mess, huh?"

"Yeah," Ramon sighed. "I didn't know what the hell I was doing."

The fact that Ramon is talking to me and still has feelings for me fills me with hope that we can rebuild our relationship. I want nothing more than to spend the rest of my life with him. I used to think that's what he wanted, but after his "have someone else" comment, I'm not so sure. I guess I'm easily forgotten. What can I expect? I left him two years ago.

"Noah, will you tell me what you meant by your comment about my life...or death?"

I glance over at him and see Ramon sitting forward with his hands clasped together.

I can't go there yet. "I'm not ready," I whisper.

Ramon narrows his eyes, and then his jaw tightens in anger. He stands and gives me a glare that makes my heart drop. Then he walks out of the bedroom and slams the door behind him.

Fucking hell!

I rub my temples and curse the whole situation—the one I found myself in over two years ago—the same one that is still messing with my life. It all started with my sister's ex. Thank God Carla didn't marry him.

When they first got together, Gary seemed like a decent guy, and he was really into Carla. Then he got involved with the wrong crowd, and something inside him snapped. Drugs do that to a person.

Carla was scared and had no one else to talk to, so she came to me. I'll never begrudge her that. I've taken care of her since she was a teenager; we lost our parents in a house fire.

Maybe it was the loss that brought us closer, but I always looked out for her. No one frightens my sister, especially not the way Gary did. Keeping that in mind, I kept everything to myself and went to a friend on the drug squad. Then my world fell apart, and the trouble followed me to Lexington. One decision I made to help my sister resulted in a death threat against Ramon. I'd ruined their lives and business, so they set out to ruin me. They almost succeeded.

Luckily, the guy behind the threats was careless and killed himself with a drug overdose, so I was free to head back to my guy.

Now, all I have to do is convince Ramon that I'm worth a second chance and that the woman he's with means nothing to him. He has to believe that. I can't bear the thought of Ramon not letting them go for me. It kills me to think about him making love to anyone but me.

Shifting, I groan at the ache in my body. I can tell that I'm healing, but three days in bed have created new aches that probably weren't there after the beating. I need to move and get my battered body into the shower because I'm tired of thinking.

Ramon

I'm extremely frustrated by Noah's refusal to talk to me. He won't tell me what he meant by what he said the other night. I hate not knowing something that involves me, especially when it was serious enough for Noah to leave me.

I need answers, and before we leave this cabin, I'm

going to get them. For now, though, I'll try to be patient, as much as it frustrates me. I'll try not to badger Noah for information while he looks so beaten up, but I won't be able to hold out for long.

Some of Noah's decisions have been ruled by his stomach in the past, so I'm hoping that if I supply him with breakfast, he'll feel more like talking after he's eaten. It's a start, I suppose.

I grab the toast as it pops up and coat it with butter before splitting it between the two plates. I lean against the countertop while waiting for the eggs to scramble in the microwave, smiling when I think about Noah's hard cock while he was lying in bed. There was only a sheet between us, so the hard ridge was obvious. It caused an uncomfortable twitch in my sweats.

Noah's dick has always lain flat against his stomach when fully aroused. Mine sticks out and away from my body when I'm fully aroused. Like it has started to do with thoughts of a naked Noah. Shaking my head, I sighed. This really has to stop.

If Noah is to be believed, he hasn't been with anyone since me. No matter what I told him, I haven't been with anyone else either.

This brings my thoughts to Sylvia and my complicated feelings for her. I could hear the hurt in her voice when she answered the phone the other day. She was clearly upset when I immediately asked to speak to Sebastian to let him know that I was delayed. I didn't want anyone to worry, but I should have stopped to talk to Sylvia for a bit.

Sylvia complicates things because I'm attracted to her, and that makes me nervous. Every time I think of her, my body reacts, but I don't feel the thud in my chest that indicates love. Not like when I think about Noah.

On the night of the gala, I thought about taking her back to my place, but then I remembered that Noah's things were still there. I thought about inviting myself to her apartment, which I knew she would have gone along with, but something held me back. That night, my body wanted release from all the heartache I'd suffered since Noah left. Sylvia was so beautiful that my body was hypersensitive to her touch. My cock ached to dip between her thighs. But something stopped me. The disappointment Sylvia couldn't hide made me feel like a first-class jerk.

I've been a coward ever since, partly because I'm confused about my feelings, and partly because I don't want to see the hurt on her face. I've done my best to avoid her, but that won't last forever. I need to head back to Lexington soon. I've already been gone too long.

First, though, I need to deal with the man who's screwed me up for anyone else.

Hearing the shower turn off, I quickly grab a T-shirt from the back of the chair and pull it on. I saw his eyes linger on my body earlier, and although I don't mind the heat in his eyes, we need to talk without distractions. I just wish my dick were as easy to hide as my chest.

With that in mind, I quickly pull together break-fast and slam it on the table before dropping into a chair just as Noah enters.

My mouth drops open and my dick springs back to attention. I swallow around the lump in my throat, but nothing clears the lust overtaking my body.

Small droplets of water trickle from his damp hair and fall onto his naked chest, beckoning me to lap them up and taste him. He leans against the door-frame wearing only the sweats I left out for him. His sculpted chest is even more defined than before, though the black-and-blue bruising along his ribs remains vivid. The sweats hang loosely on him, leaving little to the imagination. The longer I stare, the more the outline of his dick grows larger, and I realize that I'm staring as though I haven't eaten in a long time.

I close my eyes and inhale, filling my nostrils with his scent, which causes them to flare. I exhale the scent as I open my eyes, but I avoid looking at Noah as I try to find my strength. My cock throbs beneath the table, and I need a distraction from Noah. I take a hefty mouthful of eggs, bite into a slice of buttered toast, and swallow it down with a gulp of fresh orange juice.

"Eat before it gets cold." I point to the food opposite me.

He shuffles forward and sits in the suggested chair. Our eyes meet before he offers me a wry smile and starts eating.

Us sitting together like this should feel uncomfortable, but it doesn't. I feel settled, as though I'm where I'm supposed to be. Judging by how at ease Noah is, I think he feels the same way.

"Who do you have?" Noah asks out of the blue.

I'm not surprised by the question, but I am surprised by the timing, given that he won't answer my questions.

I place my fork on my plate and take a long swallow of coffee before saying, "If I tell you what's going on in my life, you have to tell me everything that's been going on in yours. And I mean everything —starting with why you walked out, what you've done for the past two years, and why you're suddenly here. If you lie to me, I won't forgive you."

I keep a straight face, hoping he doesn't see the lie in my eyes. The truth is, I'd probably forgive him for lying to me unless it involved another man. I don't need to worry about him being with a woman because he isn't interested in them. Before, when we had a woman, I was the one doing the fucking while I sucked him off. The women found it hot, and Noah would get excited seeing my wet dick slide in and out of them. All that changed after he let me inside him.

One minute, Noah was in the driver's seat of our relationship; the next, we'd switched places. After that night, Noah gave me an ultimatum: I could either never fuck a woman again while I was with him, or he would leave and I would never see him again. Giving up women never bothered me because I was turned on by him watching me, not by the woman. With him, I've always been able to be myself, unlike with my family—that's another story.

We ate in silence, but I noticed we were both glancing at each other. After he finishes eating, he wipes his mouth with the yellow napkin I placed next to his fork and meets my gaze.

"I wanted to wait to talk, but it's better if every-thing is out in the open, with no more secrets between us."

I nod.

"Are you okay sitting in the living room, or do you need to go back to bed?" I ask, my voice filled with concern as I watch him. He'd been pale while eating. I originally attributed it to the topic of conversation, but now I'm not so sure.

"I'll be fine. I think it will be better if I'm upright for this conversation."

I agree with him and pour us both another cup of coffee. I carry them through into the living room.

3

____

Noah

KNOWING WHAT WE'RE GOING TO TALK ABOUT AND
that my ribs are aching makes it hard for me to get
comfortable. I sit on the edge of the sofa, hoping
Ramon will be the first to start.

After being gone for so long, there's a lot to say.
Part of me is afraid that we'll get tired, and I won't
find out anything about what Ramon's been up to.

"Sylvia."

"Pardon?"

"You heard me. Her name is Sylvia."

His tone is flippant, as if he doesn't care, but I
know Ramon—he does care about what he's saying.
Sylvia must mean something to him.

"Man, Noah, I missed you, and she was there, looking so damn sweet. She wasn't going anywhere, so I started taking her out." He runs his hands through his short hair, clearly agitated. "We had dinner and went to movies. Sometimes she'd come to family functions with me to keep Mom from shoving unmarried women at me."

So she's good enough to meet his family, but I never was. I know I'm being unfair, but hearing him say that she's met his family hurts. It hurts a lot.

"But I let you believe we had an intimate relationship, which is wrong."

What is he saying?

"I've never had sex with her, Noah. I'll admit I cut it close not too long ago. But by the time I took her back to her apartment, I'd come to my senses and realized she wasn't the one I wanted." He laughs. "I was craving someone who'd made it clear that he didn't want me."

The room falls silent as Ramon finishes admitting his feelings about Sylvia. I thought I'd have more time to get my thoughts in order. I don't. Whatever I was going to say is gone, replaced by the fact that Ramon isn't in a relationship with someone else. No matter how much I told myself he had the right to be with someone else, it would have killed something inside me if he were.

"Please say something," he pleads.

"I'm surprised you'd admit that to me without hearing my side, but I'm relieved." I laugh. "You have no idea how relieved I am."

"I think I do. Your turn." Ramon forces a smile.

I have no idea what he's thinking, and it causes butterflies to flutter around my stomach. I used to know what his next move would be and what he was thinking at any given time. It was as if we had the same thoughts, but not anymore.

With a heavy sigh, I explain about Gary. It isn't easy, but I feel relieved to be able to leave out some parts since he knows a lot of it from Carla and Gary going after her. When I finish, Ramon says, "You haven't explained the threat that sent you running."

I shake my head. "We're still talking. I haven't finished."

He raises a brow in question.

"The repercussion of going to my friend in the drug squad was that two guys approached me. Apparently, their boss wasn't happy about Gary's loss or its effect on his business. Basically, I ruined their lives and set their business back, so they're going to try to ruin me. They threatened you and Carla." I sink back into the chair, exhausted by everything.

"I would never have left you if I'd had a choice. As soon as I heard the threat was over, I made plans to head back to Lexington after finishing my current job. That's how I met Eric."

"I wondered how Eric managed to set up the meeting in Denver because he had no idea about us," Ramon pauses, "or did he?"

I shake my head. "No, he knows nothing about us. I didn't tell him I knew you, even after he told me about the job he wanted me to be involved in. I needed to see you first and talk. He's part of your family, and I didn't know how much you'd told him, if anything. I wasn't sure if you'd told him about our relationship or if you'd just said we were friends, so I stayed quiet."

He didn't know anything about us. He knew someone had hurt me. That's how I explained going slow with Sylvia whenever anyone asked. No one knew."

"Knew?" I asked.

"My family knows about us, except for Michael and my parents." He pauses, then thoughtfully rubs his chin. "Well, Michael might know, since Lucien has a big mouth. But I doubt my parents do. My brothers will leave that one for me." He smiles.

After all of our time together, I find it hard to believe that he finally told his brothers about me when we're not even together anymore. There's something wrong with that picture.

Not really wanting to know the answer but unable to keep it inside, I ask, "If I hadn't disappeared, would you have told them about me?"

Ramon blushes and refuses to meet my gaze. His lips tighten around a word, but he doesn't let it slip. I have my answer. It hits me like a sledgehammer to the chest.

Slowly pushing to my feet, I head toward the bedroom. Stopping in the doorway, I glance over my shoulder at Ramon. He's facing the window, his eyes averted from me, and I notice the slump of his shoulders. He looks as wrecked as I am. I still haven't explained how I met Eric.

Ramon

I'm not ashamed of my past relationship with Noah. Even if I took another chance on him, I wouldn't be ashamed.

The fact that I'm an adult should make it easier for me to come out to my parents. The way I'm acting, you'd think I were a teenager again. That has to stop. I didn't miss the hurt that flashed in Noah's eyes when I remained silent.

I rub my chest over my heart, sigh, and follow Noah into the bedroom to finish our talk. I need to know what's going to happen now. I can't leave things between us unresolved. I can't let Noah think I'm ashamed to be with him.

To my surprise, Noah isn't in the bedroom or the bathroom. My heart starts to pound as I wonder where the hell he's disappeared to. He couldn't have left. But then, I see his shadow through the curtains.

With my blood still pounding in my ears, I open the door to the porch and lean against the doorframe when Noah turns to look at me.

His eyes widen with surprise. "What's wrong with you?" he asks, taking a step toward me.

"I thought you'd left."

His lips tighten. "I'm not going to do that to you again. If I'm leaving, you'll know about it."

I nod, pull myself together, and drop into one of the two rocking chairs on the porch.

After a brief pause, Noah sits beside me.

"You still love me."

My head whips around in surprise at his bold statement.

He grins and repeats, "You still love me."

My frown shuts him up.

"You do, right?" he asks, the surety draining from him as quickly as his smile.

"I don't know how the fuck I feel." That's a lie, though, because I still love him. I change the subject, saying, "Tell me about Eric," needing more time to come up with a plan of action before heading back to Lexington.

He'll come back with me. He doesn't have much choice, and I'm not about to give him one.

Resting his feet on the porch railing, he slowly rocks in the chair. He looks relaxed until I glance at his hands. They're flexing against his thigh—a sure sign that he's stressed.

He isn't the only one.

My first instinct is to lean forward and touch him.

His bare chest and the sprinkling of hair trailing over his nipples and down past his navel have my mouth watering. I want to follow that trail further south with my tongue, past the elastic of his sweatpants, to something I'm longing for. I crave his taste and touch more than ever. It's been a long time since I've been with Noah.

My cock agrees, jumping in my sweats and tingling with arousal.

Noah has always been able to arouse me to unbearable heights with the slightest glance. Hell, just looking at him can make me ache for his touch, and my body ignites at the slightest embrace. His absence has made me crave him even more.

"You sure you want me to talk about Eric?" he asks, breaking into my thoughts. His eyes are on my groin.

I close my eyes to gather my strength and answer, "Yes."

"Hmm..." He pauses, giving my groin a pointed stare before meeting my gaze and continuing, "I met Eric in a bar in North Carolina." He laughs. "I'd been working on a building site not far from the bar, and some stealing had been going on. I happened to be in the right place at the wrong time and caught the thieves red-handed. That was the job I was finishing before heading back here. After they were caught, the guys took me to a bar to celebrate. We weren't exactly quiet. At some point, Eric introduced himself, and we talked. By the end of the night, he'd asked me to help him out on your site. How could I refuse?"

He pauses. "I kept quiet about my history with you because I wanted to see your face when you first saw me. I didn't want you to be prepared. I wanted to see your reaction when you realized it was me and that I was standing before you. I'd been prepared to see you again, but actually, I wasn't prepared at all..." His voice trails off, and he stares out at the yard. "God, I missed you," he growls.

"Oh boy. What the hell are we going to do? I want you on the McKenzie site.

And in my bed."

From the burning glance he gives me, he knows what I want to say.

"Do you have a place to stay in Lexington?"

He hesitates and then answers, "Not yet."

"You can stay with me, but in the guest room."

He frowns, and I see a flash of stubbornness as his jaw tightens. He doesn't like that idea. His eyes focus on everything but me.

"Okay," he whispers after his silent battle with his pride. "I deserve that, and I certainly don't expect you to accept me back just like that." He laughs. "Even though I wish you would."

"I'm not the same guy you walked out on, Noah. I'm not the pushover you were used to." I get to my feet and start pacing back and forth.

I come to an abrupt halt when Noah stands in front of me, stopping my sharp pacing.

"I never took you for a pushover," he says, poking me in the chest. We were both in that relationship. You're the one who kept it hidden when I would have shouted it from the rooftops."

Noah turns away. I reach out to grab his arm, but I miss, and my hand grazes his hip instead. We both catch our breath and freeze.

Unable to stop myself, I step into his space. My front presses against his back, and a shudder runs through Noah. I lean forward and press my lips to the top of his spine, slipping my hand further around his hips. I nudge the crown of his erection with my fingertips and pause, wanting to take one more step closer to paradise. One encouraging move from Noah is all it will take for me to reach into his sweats and stroke him.

My throbbing erection presses against the cheeks of Noah's ass. My body screams at me to give in to what we both need. Unfortunately, my brain won't shut down, and it doesn't want to risk messing anything up by jumping straight back into sex with him. No matter how much our bodies disagree, I have to think with my brain.

I breathe in his unique scent. I place a kiss on the back of his neck and gently rub the leaking tip of his cock with my finger before forcing myself to step back.

Noah runs an unsteady hand through his hair and disappears back into the cabin without saying anything. I watch him go, fighting the urge to follow him. It isn't until his flavor bursts on my tongue that I realize I'm sucking my finger as though I can't get enough.

I turn and grip the porch railing so tightly that my knuckles turn white. I drop my head and breathe through the pain of my own raging arousal.

4

Ramon

As I walk through the door into the outer office, I feel nervous because I know Sylvia will be sitting behind her desk.

I wish I could have put off coming to the McKenzie offices until later, but I've been away too long. However, I've been away too long for any excuse to make a difference.

The door closes softly behind me, drawing her eyes to mine. I stand face-to-face with Sylvia.

She's beautiful, as always.

I don't miss the once-over she gives me.

Today, I've exchanged my usual jeans for black slacks and a black shirt, as I have no intention of visiting the site. The dark colors of my clothing against my tanned skin make my heritage stand out. Or so Noah tells me. The only color against the black that I have on today is my blue eyes.

As I watch Sylvia start to fidget, I move forward to put her at ease.

"You look good, Sylvia." I step into her space, place a lingering kiss on her cheek, and Eric walks into the office and witnesses it.

He stops and glares.

"Ramon?"

I pause, unsure how to take Eric's abrupt use of my name.

I squeeze Sylvia's hand and straighten up.

Meeting him in the middle of the room, we exchange a quick handshake, then clap each other on the back. I'm not sure if it's my imagination, but the handshake seemed tighter than usual, and the smile seemed forced. Acting as though being caught kissing Sylvia's cheek were an everyday occurrence, I notice Eric's smile turn into an angry frown.

What is his problem?

"How are you doing?"

"Fine," Eric mumbles.

"Fine, right?" I sit on the corner of Sylvia's desk

and watch the emotions playing across Eric's face, but I can't read them.

Eric glares right back at me, leaving me more confused than ever. We lived together before, so what the hell is going on?

I hear the buzzer on Sylvia's desk go off and glance at her. She smirks and says into the microphone, "You need to come out here."

Within seconds, Sebastian's door opens, and he strides out. He studies me before his gaze shifts to Eric. He frowns and goes back to his office. "Let's go in here," he suggests. "Sylvia, would you mind getting us some coffee?"

"I'm on it."

Noah

Today, I woke up in the apartment where I used to live. It would have been even better if I had woken up beside Ramon in the bed we used to share. However, I intend for that to happen sooner rather than later.

Before he left for work, Ramon told me about the cabin he built on his family's land by the stream that snakes around the main house. He was evasive when I asked why he wasn't living there and was still in the city apartment.

Ramon hates the bustle of city life and can't wait to escape to his parents' ranch house or, better yet, his cabin. Of course, I could never visit him there. After all, I'm his dirty little secret.

I resolve that I'm not going to be anyone's secret anymore. It's all or nothing, and if I've read Ramon correctly, that's what he wants.

Having Ramon's touch on my skin again after so long has rekindled my passion for him. It had lain dormant for so long that I'm surprised how quickly it engulfed me. Now, I have to fight hard to keep my hands to myself.

This morning, he looked so handsome that my heart nearly jumped straight out of my chest. My dick went from zero to a hundred in five seconds flat when the scent of his cologne drifted toward me.

No sooner had the apartment door closed than I was in the shower, masturbating and pretending it was Ramon's hand wrapped around me. I closed my eyes as my hand slid over the wet flesh. The image of him dressed all in black filled my mind, and I couldn't help but smile at the memory. He'd had a noticeable bulge behind his zipper. Oh, yes. He responded to my lust, which was clear as day on my face.

Ramon knows me and knows the signs of when I'm highly aroused. I don't just mean having a hard-on, but all the subtle cues I give.

Adjusting to my arousal, I tried to concentrate on the passing countryside outside my SUV's window. I guess I should be thankful that Ramon drove me most of the way back to Lexington. By the time we were halfway there, I was ready to drive, which got us home sooner than Ramon had planned.

My first priority today is to visit my blissfully happy sister, Carla. When I called her after getting back to Lexington, she was so overwhelmed by hearing my voice after so long that she couldn't talk. Her husband, Sebastian, wasn't impressed and made that clear.

Carla is the one who made me cry. Until I heard her voice, I hadn't realized how much I missed my sister. My only family. Who abandons his only family?

Someone who wants to protect them.

I keep telling myself that. Most of the time, it works, but other times, I don't believe my own hype. I was protecting them, but I sometimes wonder if I was protecting myself more.

With a heavy sigh, I follow Ramon's directions so I can surprise Carla.

Sebastian knows I'm on my way to visit his wife. Although I got the impression he wasn't happy about my wanting to meet up with her without him, he understood that I needed to.

The way he protects her warms my heart, and I'm thankful she found him. All I've ever wanted for my sister is to find someone who puts her above everything else, and Sebastian does just that.

Carla certainly sounds like she's given her heart unconditionally to Sebastian, and she couldn't stop talking about him when we finally had a brief conversation. I'm almost giddy with excitement over seeing her.

Hopefully, she won't be too angry. I've never seen anyone with a temper like my sister's.

As I come to a stop outside Carla and Sebastian's home, I admire their large cabin. It's a sprawling wooden building with a wraparound porch. The flowers on display are undoubtedly my sister's doing. She's had a green thumb since first grade. I smile at the memory of her lectures to Mom about the proper fertilizer and the ideal time to plant the sunflower seeds she loved so much. Mom always had a black thumb, so my sister was the family's resident gardener.

I'm glad she hasn't lost her touch. It's clear that she has put her knowledge to use, surrounding her home with color.

Carla has a colorful personality, and her home reflects that.

As I climb out of my vehicle, I spot her on the porch, watching me.

When she realizes it's me, her whole demeanor changes. Within seconds, she drops the watering can, races across the porch, and jumps into my arms. I wrap my arms tightly around her and hold her while she clings to me and cries.

Her sobs continue, and my emotions start to get the better of me. I take her to the porch steps, drop down onto them, and pull her into my lap.

I keep my arms around her as she rests her head against my shoulder. I bury my face in her neck and let my tears mingle with hers.

She's a grown woman, but she'll always be my baby sister. Having her back in my arms after almost two years of no communication causes my heart to flood with emotions I tried to forget to make our separation easier.

"I'm sorry," I mumble against her.

"Don't." She pulls away and gets a tissue from somewhere. She wipes her face before passing me a fresh one. "Let's put the past behind us. You're here now, in one piece. I never want to go through that again, so this is your only warning—if you do that to me again, you'd better stay gone."

I pull her back into my arms. "I promise not to disappear like that again." I kiss her on the forehead and help her up.

She slips her arm around my waist, and I wrap mine around her shoulders. I let her lead me into her home.

Ramon

I'm having trouble concentrating while Sebastian drones on about the business at the site. Eric seems angry with me, and I get the feeling it has something to do with Sylvia, although that makes no sense.

Sylvia looks gorgeous, and I notice that she's gotten her hair done. It's a splash of color in her already luxurious shades, and there's definitely more style cut into her long locks. She's always perfectly put together, and I can't fathom why she ever accepted dates with me.

I told her from the start that I was looking for friendship, not a relationship. But somewhere along the way, she got under my skin—as I know I did hers.

The thing is, I don't know what to do about it. My heart belongs to Noah. But there's something about Sylvia that calls out to me. It's been years since I've been with a woman, and I didn't miss it when Noah was around. But once he left, things started to change. When I first started seeing Sylvia, I attributed my interest to missing the wetness of a woman's vagina. As time went on, though, I realized that I didn't miss that at all, and that my interest in Sylvia was about more than just lust. Not only that, but Noah is the one who makes me feel completely fulfilled after sex.

Sylvia, however, is unique. Sometimes she's old-fashioned, and other times she acts as though she's experienced a lot more than I ever have.

Truthfully, I've really missed seeing and talking to her. This brings me to the fact that I've been a jerk to her. I've avoided talking to her since the gala. I know I hurt her badly that night, but I'm such a coward that, instead of apologizing, I ran at the first opportunity.

Seeing Eric glaring at me when I thought we were friends confuses me. I know he's angry with the world right now after receiving a medical discharge. But what happened to our friendship?

"If you two could stop sulking and actually listen to me, this meeting would be over by now," Sebastian points out, exasperation clear in his voice.

"I'm listening." I grin.

Sebastian glances at me and gives me his "yeah, right" look.

I grin, knowing he's trying to be professional, even though he's usually the one giving Michael a hard time.

"I've been listening, if Ramon hasn't," Eric adds.

I glance at him, startled by the hostility in his tone. That's it. I've had enough. My jaw tenses with anger. "What the fuck is your problem? If I've done something to piss you off, I'm used to you calling me out on it instead of acting like a dick."

He stands and glares at me.

I match his stance.

"Oh, hell no. Not in Michael's office," Sebastian says, jumping between us. "If you two want to beat the shit out of each other, I suggest you go down to Yuri's gym."

Eric grins, his face full of predatory rage. It's clear

he'd love to spar with me at Yuri's. He's definitely mad at me about something. I rack my brain, but I seriously have no idea what it could be. Then it hits me: Sylvia. I remember the look on his face when he walked in and caught me kissing Sylvia on the cheek.

Is he jealous?

"That won't be necessary." His grin turns into a frown. "Call me if you need me," he tells Sebastian before opening the office door.

"Hey, we need to talk," I shout after him, making to follow.

The man standing in the office talking to Sylvia stops me midstep. All thoughts of Eric fly straight out of my head. "Noah?"

Upon hearing his name, he turns, and his face lights up with his secret smile.

A thump on my back brings me abruptly back to the present.

I never thought I'd have the opportunity to introduce Noah, my ex-lover, to one of my brothers. But it looks like that's about to happen, with Sylvia and Eric looking on.

Fuck!

"So you're my brother-in-law," Sebastian says, beating me to the introduction.

"Sebastian, it's good to meet you. My sister

wouldn't stop talking about you this morning. I think she mentioned you in nearly every other sentence."

Sebastian frowns. "She's missed you like crazy."

Pain flashes in Noah's eyes, and I want nothing more than to soothe it away.

"I missed her as well. More than I'll ever be able to tell her."

It seems that Noah has spoken the words Sebastian was waiting to hear. The tension snaps apart, though I hadn't noticed it before. Sebastian relaxes and says, "Welcome to the family. This is our cousin, Eric."

Eric nods in acknowledgment, then glances at me. He's well aware of who Noah is, as he set up the meeting. It's clear that he's also figured out who Noah is to me. I'm grateful he's keeping his mouth shut for now. Sylvia needs to hear it from me.

"And this is Sylvia," Sebastian continues. "She's the only reason my office isn't littered with papers."

Noah's eyes widen when he's introduced to Sylvia, but he recovers quickly and winks at her, causing her cheeks to blush.

After the introductions, an uncomfortable silence falls.

Eric's loud curse breaks it. "I'm out of here."

He leaves but doesn't bother closing the office doors.

Sebastian looks between the three of us and smirks now that Eric has left. "I'll leave you to it."

"Bastard," I mumble, hoping only he can hear me.

His laughter rings in my ears as he closes his office door.

"What are you doing here?" I finally ask.

"On my way back to the city, I decided to see if you wanted to grab lunch...for old times' sake."

Sylvia's head bobs between us. I have no idea if she knows anything or is trying to figure it out.

"I could eat." I choose the easiest option.

Anything to get him out of the office.

"Shall we?" I gesture toward the elevator waiting across the hall from Sylvia's open, double doors.

"Sylvia, it was nice meeting you. Perhaps I'll see you again."

"Bye, Noah."

"I'll call you later," I assure her.

"Okay, I'll be waiting. Have a good lunch, Ramon."

As I follow Noah to the elevator, my eyes land on his ass and the way the denim molds to his buttocks. With every step he takes, my dick twitches in the tight confines of my pants, growing tighter with each passing second.

Noah doesn't turn to me as he presses the elevator button, but his arousal is obvious through the slightly mirrored door.

I step close to him and let my erection throb against his ass. I whisper into his ear, "This elevator goes directly to the underground parking garage."

He shudders at my words.

The doors open. We step inside, and the bulge in my pants aches for his touch.

Noah keeps his back to the door, giving me a view of his arousal, the fire in his eyes, and the hard ridge of his cock pressing against the front of his jeans.

I lean against the back wall. As the doors shut, I see Sylvia watching us, but I don't care.

Being enclosed in the small space with Noah isn't helping my libido. As the elevator slowly starts to descend, my breathing increases, and I finally make eye contact with Noah.

Fuck this!

I reach out for him at the same time he lunges forward.

His hands hold my head in place as our bodies press together, wanting and needing more. His lips are hard and demanding on mine. I open my mouth for more of him. When our tongues finally tangle and Noah sucks mine into his mouth, my orgasm nearly explodes. I hiss, fighting to control my body as I pull away. I know that if I don't stop, I'm going to climax.

"No," Noah growls.

He pulls my shirt out of my pants, and then his hands slide up my bare chest.

I shove him forward and slam my hand down on the stop button while he's trapped in my arms.

"We have three minutes before the emergency override kicks in." I pant the words before slamming my mouth down on his. I can't get enough as our teeth and lips bump together. Finally, our groins meet as we grind against each other. It feels so good, but I need more.

Ripping my mouth away again, I shove Noah's T-shirt up and latch onto one of his nipples with my mouth and teeth. I use my other hand to unbutton his jeans and release his manhood, which is heavy and solid in my palm. His legs quiver, and I understand without words. I know he's close.

Before I can make my next move, Noah knocks my hand away and is on top of me. I'm pushed back against the elevator wall, and he shoves his hand into my pants.

This is bad.

"I'm gonna come," I groan as Noah latches onto one of my nipples and bites it.

I wrap my hand around his cock and stroke him. I want him to come with me. As Noah's fingers fondle my scrotum, I feel the fire igniting under my skin.

"We're going to make a mess."

Why does he have to make sense right now?

My dick is still confined in my pants. Although I'll be uncomfortable until I can get home to change, I won't make as big of a mess as Noah is about to.

Growling, I grip his wrist and pull his hand from the front of my pants. His touch along my throbbing length is enough to make me come, but I fight the need to maintain control, although I'm going to have blue balls afterward.

Before he can complain, I drop to my knees and take him in my mouth.

"Fuck... Fuck... Ramon."

Noah holds my head in place as he fucks my mouth. I moan around him as my dick pulses in time with the suction of my mouth on his cock.

Holding his hips still with my hands on his ass, I spread his cheeks and imagine fucking his tight ass or having his thick shaft slide in and out of mine. Moaning, I come in hot bursts of pleasure in my pants.

Ripples of pleasure fill me as I swallow around him. Noah groans long and loud as his seed fills my mouth and slides down my throat.

Once he's finished, I slowly massage his cock with my tongue, making sure to get every drop, before pulling away.

That felt good!

But damn, I just sucked him off in the elevator. Shit. So not good.

Then, the elevator starts heading down.

I quickly got to my feet and glanced down, wincing at the large wet patch on the front of my pants. Thank God my shirt was long enough to cover it.

Noah is a bit better off than I am. He zips up his jeans and straightens his shirt. The door slides open on the parking level just as he finishes, and he waits for me to exit first. Neither of us speaks until we reach our vehicles.

"Meet me back at the apartment," I demand, not waiting for his answer.

The fuse has been lit.

As I drive out of the garage, Noah follows behind me in his big vehicle.

5

Noah

I DON'T KNOW WHAT'S WRONG WITH ME. IN MY THIRTY-four years, I've never acted like a sex-starved man.

I've never hidden the fact that I'm gay, but I've also never made a point of letting people know. Taking the chance of being caught in the elevator with McKenzie wasn't smart for either of us. That sure as hell wouldn't have gone over well.

But damn, it felt good. Ramon's mouth wrapped around my hard dick felt a million times better than anything I'd ever felt before.

In my younger years, I'd been with a lot of women before realizing they didn't really do it for me. At first, I fought what came so naturally to me, trying to come up with excuses for why I wasn't attracted to women. I know now that it isn't something I can choose.

I get excited the minute Ramon touches me. I hope that as soon as I get off the elevator at Ramon's apartment building, we'll pick up where we left off.

Now that Ramon's back in the picture, my cock certainly wants more action. He should have been in it all along.

As I step off the elevator, Ramon is leaning against the wall across from it. I pause mid-step and let my eyes caress his body. He's taken off his jacket, and his dark shirt is open, giving me a view of his perfectly chiseled chest. My mouth goes dry, and my gaze is pulled to the bulge behind his zipper. I can see the damp patch from earlier, which makes me want to unzip him and take a taste.

I search Ramon's eyes for a sign that we're moving forward and that he doesn't regret what happened in the elevator not too long ago. To my relief, I don't see regret; however, I do see doubt. My heart thuds when I realize I'm the one who put that look on his face. I'm going to have my work cut out for me convincing him that I'm here to stay. I'm not going to walk out on him again.

He says he isn't the same man I left behind. I don't

believe him. He may be hiding behind a shield, but the Ramon I fell in love with is still in there somewhere. Hopefully, when he starts believing in me again, he'll be able to lower his guard and let me in.

I keep my gaze locked with his as I start walking. When I'm in front of Ramon, I reach out and caress his cheek.

I smile when he exhales sharply.

I caress his neck and collarbone before moving down over his chest. I rub his nipples and move in closer, swallowing back my rising passion when I feel Ramon's hard groin against mine.

"We need to fuck," he groans.

I smile, knowing it's my mouth on his skin that caused his loss of thought.

Finally, Ramon touches me and holds my head against his chest as I swirl my tongue around one of his nipples.

I raise my head to meet his heated gaze, taking great delight in watching him try to pull himself together. I've always been able to wipe his mind of everything but me. The slightest of my caresses can cause him to lose track of his thoughts. I'm glad that hasn't changed.

"We need to go inside," he says, inhaling deeply.

Gripping his hips, I walk him backward into the

apartment and kick the door shut with my foot. Reaching behind me, I pull the deadbolt into place.

While I'm distracted with the door, Ramon moves away, leaving my arms and heart empty.

"Is this how it's going to be between us from now on?" I call out to him, unable to hide my emotions in my voice. I know he'll hear how desperate and hurt I am by his pulling away.

Ramon's temper is starting to kick in. His jaw looks like granite, and his eyes have darkened, as they do when he's aroused or angry. "You're the one who put doubt in my head, so you have no one to blame but yourself. You also need to stop reading too much into my actions." He runs his hands through his dark hair. "Fuck, Noah. I came in my pants in the elevator," he snaps. "I want a shower." He sighs.

Shit!

He turns around, his shoulders drooping before he straightens up and heads to his room. At the doorway, he whispers, "I'll see you in the morning," over his shoulder before disappearing behind his now-closed door.

Well, I blew that.

Rubbing my chest where my heart aches, I turn and head into the guest room.

As much as I want to continue living with Ramon,

I can't. Being around him will be too painful when all I see reflected in his eyes is indifference. I don't believe he actually feels that way, but for whatever reason, he wants me to believe it.

I deserve it. I know I do. I just didn't expect it to hurt this much. I thought I was tough enough to handle anything Ramon threw my way. But I'm not. Anyone else, yes, but not from the man I love.

I don't have anywhere else to go. I'm used to living in motels, so what's one more?

I grab my duffel bag and shove my few belongings inside, then hesitate.

No matter how indifferent Ramon is to me, I'm not sure I have it in me to just disappear like that. I promised I'd never do that again.

With a heavy heart, I head into the living room to find the pen and pad of paper Ramon always has lying around. I stop when I see Ramon standing with a drink in his hand, staring out the window. He's back in his favorite sweats, and his hair is still damp from his shower.

Do I have the strength to walk away from this man? I'm not sure.

My duffel bag slides to the floor as I drop heavily into the closest chair, alerting Ramon that he isn't alone anymore.

He turns, and his gaze pauses on my duffel bag before landing on me.

In that moment, I see surprise and pain flicker in his eyes.

Ramon

I grimace when I see Noah sitting behind me with a duffle bag at his feet. He's leaving again, despite his promise not to. The pain rips through me, and I feel more broken than I did when he left the first time. My eyes sting with the tears I'm holding back. I know I blew it with him before. If I hadn't been such a jerk and let him get under my skin by thinking I was pulling away from him, then we would have had sex in the hallway. Hot, sweaty sex.

As soon as I realized he thought I had second thoughts, I got pissed off. Considering how long it's been since we were last together, I'm allowed to have second thoughts.

My body was ready for him, but if I'm being honest, I'm not sure my heart is ready to let him in again. I know I love him. I'm not going to disrespect myself by lying. However, having sex with Noah in our bed and then having him walk away again would kill me.

I'm strong, and I can argue and fight with the best of them. But Noah is my Achilles heel, and it pisses me off to see how weak I am with him. Before he left, I never doubted myself. I never doubted my strength. I knew he was my weakness, that I needed his touch and his glance to fill me with desire and make me feel whole, but I had to fill that void when he left. I filled it with a fear of being hurt like that again. I don't know what I would do if he left me again.

When I saw his packed duffel bag, I thought I would collapse. I felt the hole open and the fear come raging out, filling me with weakness. I may have given the impression that I was indifferent, but that was just me hiding behind a wall of indifference.

"You're leaving?" I asked, my voice as strong as I could make it, lying for me in the face of that fear swallowing me.

"I can't do this. I thought that if I came back with you, it would only be a matter of time before we got back together. I believed that if you could see my love for you and that it was still there, you'd jump all over it." He sighs. "Like before. But I was wrong to think that way. No matter why I walked away, you hate me for what I did. I can't stay here with you hating me. I can't look into your eyes and see the accusations in them. I did what I thought was right, but I can't be around you if you can't accept my reasons."

Baring my soul right now won't help me, even though I know it will help Noah feel better. I'm not sure I'm ready for him to know how deeply I feel about him, because then I'm opening myself up to more pain. Can I really keep him at arm's length? I'm not sure if I'm strong enough. I need him close by so that I know he hasn't disappeared.

I move to join him, drop onto the sofa, and stretch out with my feet on the coffee table.

I lean my head back and stare at the ceiling, collecting my thoughts and emotions. Then I admit, "I moved into my cabin a few months ago. It doesn't feel like home yet because I'm still spending most of my free time here or with one of my brothers. But it's there, sitting on the riverbank, close to my family home." I smile. "It's so close to the river that you don't need to leave the wraparound porch to cast a line."

Opening my eyes, I sneak a look at Noah and see the same tiredness overtaking his body as mine. My heart flips in relief—he won't be going anywhere.

"Is your cabin the same design we discussed?"

I nod. "Yes."

We used to discuss the design at night in the comfort of this apartment. Noah would tease me, saying that I needed to add a hot tub to the master suite or, even better, to the porch. I've always led him to believe that I had no use for one, but he'll discover the truth when I take him to the cabin, if not sooner.

"Why are you telling me this, Ramon? I thought you wanted me gone."

"I don't want you gone," I admit. I sigh and run my hands through my hair. "It's going to take time for me to trust you again."

I straighten up and rest my hands on my knees. "My fear that you're going to leave without saying anything isn't going to disappear overnight. You realize that, right?"

Noah nods, but I can tell by the way his shoulders slump that he's hurt. "Yeah, I understand what I lost by walking away." He sounds so damn sad that my armor cracks slightly.

Even though it's the middle of the day, I'm so tired that I could sleep for a week.

Before I can change my mind, I get to my feet and move toward Noah. I hold out my hand and wait for him to grab it. When he does, I pull him to his feet. "I'm tired," I say, hesitating, but deciding to go for it. "I need you back in our bed."

His eyes widen in shock.

I continue, "No sex. At least, not yet. I just need to know that you're close. Perhaps I'll actually get a night's sleep."

Noah stares at my hand grasping his, but he doesn't call me out on what I'm saying or not saying. I'm grateful for that.

Until I'm ready, the words of love that I used to easily profess to him will stay hidden. He knows how I feel, but it's different to hear the words.

I tighten my hold on his hand and lead him to our room. I let go of his hand so he can remove his clothes.

Not wanting anything to weaken my resolve to avoid sex, I turn away and climb beneath the covers.

Seconds later, the rustling of the sheets and the dip of the bed tell me that he wants to be with me like this.

He doesn't reach for me like he used to, making me wonder if he's waiting for me to make my move.

I want—no, I need—to feel him snuggled up against me. Only then will I be able to relax and fall asleep.

Lying here and listening to our breathing isn't helping me fall asleep. It makes me feel like a young boy experimenting with another guy for the first time.

Just as I'm about to roll onto my side to face him, Noah says, "Fuck this," and the words echo around the room as he suddenly moves. His hands are on me, pulling me close as he spooning against my back.

I sigh into his embrace, unable to hide what he makes me feel. As his hand slips to the front of my sweats, my cock pushes against his palm.

My breath catches in my lungs. I want him to continue and disregard what I said about no sex. But I know Noah well; he'll do as I asked.

His hand withdraws, allowing me to catch my breath.

"Just checking to make sure I'm not the only one affected," he whispers into my ear. The words send shivers down my spine and to my dick.

I shove back into him and smile when I feel his pulsing cock between my ass cheeks. I grasp his wrist and pull him tighter against my back. Finally, before drifting off to sleep, I feel his fingers entwine with mine.

6

Ramon

I SLOWLY COME AWAKE AND LIE STILL, NOT WANTING TO move. I can't remember the last time I slept uninterrupted. Usually, I toss and turn because I have something on my mind, but last night, I slept like a log.

Noah.

The weight of his leg over mine reminds me that he's still in bed with me. I smile. He hasn't left.

Yesterday, I gave him mixed signals because I couldn't decide what I wanted. I know what I want, but I'm afraid to reach out and grab it.

Seeing his duffel bag packed and knowing he was about to leave had me panicking, which is why I

79

brought him to my bed. I needed to know he was still there.

I've been away from the site longer than I should have, but having Noah back in my life makes me want to throw everything away. But I know what we need. I need to take him to my cabin. Over the weekend, we'll have dinner with my family.

The thought of taking Noah to Sunday dinner doesn't frighten me like it once did. I don't know if it's because my brothers know about my relationship with Noah or because I want to show Noah that I care about him enough to be honest with my parents. I'd like to think it's the latter, though.

My love for Noah is going to override all my common sense. I trusted him once, and I know I'll end up trusting him again.

For our relationship to work, I need to compromise and show him that I want to try again. My only hope is that he won't break my heart again. Today needs to be about us, about Noah.

Once I'm up, I'll call Eric to see if he can cover for me on the site. He probably knows more about what's going on anyway.

Testing the waters with Noah this morning, I roll over and bite back a groan when our hard dicks touch. We might be wearing sweats, but the contact has my dick throbbing for so much more.

"I guess we're both awake." Noah stretches and pushes against me.

I straddle his hips, not closing the space between us, and rest my hands on either side of his head. The lust on his face matches mine.

We both need this.

I grab his sweats and yank them from his waist, starting to shove them down. When he tries to take mine off, we get tangled up.

Laughing, I quickly roll off him, shove my pants down my legs, and watch Noah do the same.

As soon as I'm free of my sweats, I'm back on top of him, giving him my weight this time. My legs quiver from the sensation of him fully against me. Skin to skin. I groan into his mouth as our tongues slide together, just as our cocks are doing.

His hands grab my ass cheeks as he rubs his dick against mine. Then, I feel his finger probing my ass. Arousal drips from my crown onto his groin as I push back against his finger. But he teases me, refusing to give me what I want.

"You're not coming yet." He bites my jaw, and as I arch my back, he uses his position to lick and nip my nipples. His wet tongue arouses me.

I drop my head and look down, catching my breath. Our dicks are pressed together, leaking like crazy from our excitement.

Noah gently rotates his hips, releases my nipple, and drops back down to the bed, groaning as his hands quiver on my ass.

"Make me come, Ramon. I want to feel your hot mouth on me...please."

How could I refuse when that's what I intended from the beginning?

I kiss my way down his body, taking my time to get to know him again. I know him better than anyone, but being without him for so long has made me afraid to risk my heart again. Being with Noah makes me feel alive. Having him lie under me and show me his trust brings tears to my eyes.

Before they can fall, I push them back and use my tongue to trace the V leading down to his heavy cock and sac. He's trimmed the hair surrounding his shaft, which turns me on. He's gone bare before, but I much prefer the trimmed look. There's nothing sexier than seeing him in jeans or sweats that dip low, hinting at a teasing glimpse of hair.

Noah arches up as I rub my nose against him and sneak my tongue from between my lips.

I smile.

I take my time licking his balls before sweeping my tongue along his swollen cock and lapping up the taste of pre-cum leaking from his crown.

As his taste bursts on my tongue, my own dick swells more than I thought possible. I press into the mattress, trying to ease the ache he's caused, but it only arouses me more.

I slip my hands beneath Noah and hold his ass, keeping him against me as I slide my mouth down the length of his cock.

"Fuck...Ramon!" he growls.

Slowly, I let him slide back out before taking him deeper again.

"Oh, fuck." He arches into me. "No," he roars, pulling me off of him.

I raise my head to meet his burning gaze.

He closes his eyes. "I'm seconds from coming. Seeing you over me like that isn't helping me control the urge." He breathes heavily. "I want to make you come with me."

I smile and say, "Oh, I will," then lick his quivering dick like a Popsicle, teasing him.

"Ramon... oh... God," he groans long and loud.

Music to my ears.

Grasping his thighs, I open him further and rub my dick against the mattress, desperate for release.

I take him fully into my mouth and feel his hands slide against my scalp as he looks for hair to grab onto. I wish I hadn't cut all my hair off.

Refusing to let up, I take him deep, pressing against the sensitive spot on the underside of his cock with my tongue.

I reach up, stick my finger in his mouth for lubrication, and nearly lose my load at the feel of the wet warmth surrounding my digit.

Groaning as my dick twitches on the bed, I slowly slide my fingers between his legs and find the entrance to heaven.

I push my lubricated finger inside him. He hooks one of his legs over my hip and starts fucking my mouth as my finger plunges deep inside him.

While he's lost in what I'm doing to him, I rock my hips against the bed, creating an unbelievably hot friction. Noah makes a gurgling noise in the back of his throat and starts coming. Feeling his hot release in my mouth sends excitement coursing through me, and I thrust my hips against the bed to control my own need.

As soon as I've lapped up all his release, I quickly straddle him. The minute his hand wraps around my dick, my release shoots out, coating his stomach, chest, and even the headboard.

Groaning and panting for breath, I push his hand away and slide down to the bed beside him. Noah grabs the sheet and uses it to clean himself up. I feel him wipe my cock.

This causes my cock to rise again, so I pull him between my legs and lie with his head on my chest. He wraps his arms around my waist and holds me close.

My mind is racing, trying to figure out what's going through his. Does he regret what we've just done? Does he think I've forgiven him for walking away, no matter the reason?

As my fingers play with the hair at the nape of his neck, he sighs against me. I feel his lips on my chest. He settles back down and whispers, "You have no idea how much I've missed you. And I don't just mean the sex."

"I have a feeling I do."

He tilts his head to look at me. I cup his face in my hands and pull him closer to meet my lips.

There isn't an explosion of lust, but a tender feeling fills me as soon as our mouths connect. We both keep the kiss gentle, and when we finally separate, I hold him close.

"Will you come to my cabin for the weekend?" I ask the question that has been on my mind since yesterday. Noah stays silent, so I continue, "It'll give you more time to heal before we have to act like boss and employee at the site on Monday."

"It's on your family's land, right? Won't that be difficult if your family drops by?"

"No," I say, closing my eyes and praying for strength. "I'm planning on introducing you to everyone at lunch on Sunday."

His grip on me tightens, the only sign that he's affected by my words.

Noah

"Okay."

All I can manage is a whispered agreement as I try not to get my hopes up. Ramon has told me in the past that he's ready to tell his parents about us. But when the time comes, something else comes up. Usually, something work-related happens, and Ramon leaves quickly, as though he's relieved to have a distraction. Saved by work.

I want to believe that this time is different. It's certainly starting off differently, with the invitation to his cabin. When we used to spend Sunday mornings reviewing the plans he'd drawn up, it was one of my favorite times. I loved seeing the pure enjoyment on his face as he shared his dreams with me. I loved how he listened to my suggestions, adding some to his plans and explaining why others wouldn't work. It always seemed like we were building our dream home together.

I'm curious to know if he kept my ideas after I walked out without saying anything. I'll understand if he didn't, though. I know myself, and it will hurt. A lot.

"What are you thinking?" Ramon asks. He reaches out, caressing my shoulders, and then slides his hands into the hair at the nape of my neck.

"I'm wondering about your cabin." I move one hand from under him to his butt, caressing his hip and buttock.

Ramon grunts as his cock pulses into another erection.

I smile, knowing that I still have the power to arouse him with the slightest touch.

"What are you wondering?"

"Whether or not you kept the ideas I came up with that you incorporated into the original plans."

"You'll have to wait and see."

I smile against his chest.

"When do you want to head out?" I ask, my stomach grumbling loudly.

He chuckles. "I think I'd better feed you first. Come on, we'll head out after breakfast, provided I can get ahold of Eric. I want him to check a few things on the site over the weekend, assuming he's going to be around."

I roll off Ramon and sit on the edge of the bed. Glancing back, I realize all I want to do is climb back into bed with the sexy, rumpled man looking at me with heat in his gaze.

He stretches, and his hardened cock bounces with the movement.

I jump from the bed before I can reach out to him, and he smirks. He damn well knows what he's doing to me.

Ramon wraps his hand around his shaft and pumps a few times. My cock swells and pulses with need as I watch the show he's putting on. It wouldn't be the first time we've jerked off while watching each other.

I slide my hand down my own shaft and cup my balls, then nearly jump out of my skin when I hear a voice shout, "Ramon, are you up?"

It's almost comical. Ramon meets my gaze, then

looks at his shaft, and scrambles to get into his sweats. He points to the bathroom.

I quickly disappear and hear mumbled voices as Ramon leads his visitor away from the bedroom door he just exited.

I'd guess it's one of Ramon's brothers in the next room. I mean, you don't just walk into someone else's apartment, right? I won't let my mind wander and wonder if Ramon lied to me about not having any sexual partners while I was gone.

Shaving can wait. I jump in and out of the shower in minutes because I'm curious and want to know who's in the apartment. I know it isn't his father because the voice sounded much younger.

As luck would have it, Ramon's built-in closet is right outside the bathroom. I open the doors and am shocked to find that Ramon's clothes are not there. Instead, I find the clothes I left behind. They're all hanging neatly and color-coordinated.

I smile, letting my fingers caress the fabric, knowing Ramon spent time rearranging my clothes. A wave of emotion hits me, nearly sending me to my knees, but the voices in the living room motivate me to move, so I grab some clothes.

As I shove my legs into a pair of jeans, I realize they're low-slung, not my usual choice, but whatever.

I yank a T-shirt over my head, leave my feet bare, and head out of Ramon's bedroom looking for coffee. And, if I'm honest, to find out who he's talking to.

As soon as I step out of the room, Ramon and, I think, Rubén turn to stare at me.

Ramon doesn't look too happy to see me and clenches his jaw. Ruben, however, turns away to pour some coffee, which makes me laugh.

If Ramon is to be believed, then Ruben knows about my history with his brother. Judging by Ruben's expression, seeing me come out of Ramon's bedroom is the first time it's been more than a rumor.

"Sorry," I say, apologizing for interrupting. "But the coffee was calling. Anyone want a refill?" I hover with the pot in my hand.

"No," Ruben clears his throat. "Um, thank you."

"Fuck!" Ramon curses, and both of us look at him.

"Ruben, this is Carla's brother, Noah." Ramon waves his hand around, and I nod to his brother. "And Noah, my brother, Ruben." He pushes away from the counter and starts pacing in the small room.

I seriously don't know what the big deal is, since Ruben already knows about my relationship with Ramon. However, I'm kind of pissed that Ramon introduced me as Carla's brother. So much for him taking me to meet his family on Sunday. As much as I wanted to come back here and be with him, I'm not sure it's worth the heartache to come. If he's going to deny our relationship, then I'm not sure I can be with him.

I want an open relationship with him—not one where I'm afraid to make the wrong move in case one of his family members is watching. I want to be with someone who has no problem introducing me as their boyfriend. I don't want to be someone's dirty secret, which is how Ramon makes me feel, especially right now.

I've only spent a couple nights in his apartment, one of which I spent in his arms. It would be nice to go back to how things were before I messed everything up, but I'm not expecting any grand declarations. I just don't want to be hidden anymore. I guess Ramon needs to get used to the idea because I'm not going anywhere.

"—Sylvia," Ruben trails off, and I realize that, while I've been thinking about Ramon and getting angry with him, they've continued talking.

Sylvia is the one Ramon's been seeing and taking out. We haven't talked about her since I met her yesterday, but we will. Right now, I'm upset that I missed what Ruben has been saying, especially when I catch the look Ramon gives me out of the corner of his eye. It's as though he's warning his brother to keep quiet about her in front of me.

"I know about your relationship, Ramon, and it doesn't bother me." Ruben turns to me. "Sorry, my brother can be a dick on occasion."

Ramon snorts. "Look who's talking."

"You're still not going to get away with ignoring the Sylvia problem."

"What Sylvia problem?" I ask.

"She was all over Eric in the club last night. If I hadn't interrupted, they would have had sex up against the back wall."

As Ruben talks, I watch Ramon closely and notice the emotion flashing across his face. He's definitely surprised, but he's feeling something else as well...maybe jealousy at the mention of Sylvia and last night.

"What was Eric doing?" Ramon asks.

"Eric was the one holding her pinned to the wall. Seriously, Ramon, we all thought—he glances at me again before continuing—well, you know. You and Sylvia. At least we did until we heard about Noah."

I keep my distance from Ramon, who keeps glancing at me. I watch and listen, wondering if I or Sylvia am the problem here.

"Ruben, I have no idea why you're here telling me

about Sylvia. We're only friends, and she's known the score from the beginning."

Ruben's eyes widen, but I think he's misunderstood Ramon.

Ramon shakes his head. "I mean, I told her from the beginning that I was only looking for friendship. She doesn't know I'm gay."

Hearing him admit he's gay out loud to his brother without any hesitation makes my heart feel slightly lighter. I try to ignore the fact that Ramon is refusing to meet my gaze now that he's spoken the words.

"Well, whatever you told her didn't go over too well because Eric thinks she only made out with him to get to you. Sylvia told me not to tell my brothers about her making out with Eric because it has nothing to do with you. Basically, I don't know what to believe, and now I wish I'd listened to Rosie and ignored all of you."

"I think I followed that, and I think you need a vacation." Ramon smirks.

Ruben grumbles, "God, I feel like a fucking girl."

"You are a girl." Ramon shoves him. "Are you going to be at Mom and Dad's on Sunday? I thought I'd take Noah."

Ruben chokes on his coffee. "Okay," he gasps, his eyes watering. "Sorry. Down the wrong way."

"That doesn't bode well," I observe dryly.

"No, don't let me put you off. Mom and Dad are more open-minded than most people their age. Mom might start talking about how you two won't be able to give her grandbabies, and Dad might stare at you silently, but they'll support you. They raised us to accept anyone, and I truly believe they'll accept you as my brother's boyfriend."

I glance at Ramon and see the emotion he's trying to keep at bay. He turns away and walks over to the floor-to-ceiling windows with their magnificent view of the Lexington skyline.

When I turn back to Ruben, he looks uncomfortable.

I hold my hand out to him. "Thank you for saying that. I look forward to seeing you on Sunday."

He shakes my hand. "I won't miss that." He winks. "I'll see you both then. I'm going to get back to Rosie."

After watching Ruben leave, I turn back to Ramon and notice that he has disappeared.

But not for long.

Before I can go find him, he walks out of the bedroom, fully dressed.

Frowning, I asked, "Are you going out?"

"I'm going to see Sylvia."

"Why?"

"She was with Eric."

"I heard, but why do you have to go talk to her? I don't get it."

"Look, Noah, you don't have to understand. Sylvia is more than a friend to me, and I can't just abandon her after what Ruben told me. I'll be back later."

He grabbed his car keys from the table by the door and left me standing in his apartment, wondering what the hell was going on.

Why am I so easily replaced by someone else?

Ramon

Seeing Sylvia walk out of her bathroom naked stuns me. With her back to me, she bends over, giving me an amazing view of her shapely rear end. She starts to towel-dry her blonde hair.

A groan gets stuck in my throat, sounding like a gurgling noise. Sylvia quickly spins around and stares at me.

"What are you doing in here?" she gasps.

I stay quiet, which seems to make her angrier. She stomps over to me and pokes me in the chest.

"What are you doing in my room, Ramon?"

"Your friend let me in on her way out," I admit distractedly.

"Oh."

I find that I can't take my eyes off her body. Her large breasts, with cherry-red nipples, are on display, quivering with anger. I'd be lying if I said her nude body wasn't causing a twitch in my pants, but she isn't Noah.

"Ramon," she whispers.

I reach out and place my hands on her shoulders, slowly caressing her skin with my thumbs.

I gulp. "You need to put your clothes on."

Those words were a mistake. I see the challenge in her eyes as she takes a step closer. Her nipples press into my chest, and my hands quiver on her shoulders. It's a telling sign that she's making me nervous.

"Kiss me, Ramon?"

"I can't," I mumble.

"You can't or you won't?" she asks. The sound of her disappointment is clear in her voice.

"Sylvia," I say, caressing her shoulders and allowing my hands to slide up her neck. Staring into her beautiful eyes, I say, "I don't know what to do about you." I drop my forehead to hers.

She presses closer, and I let out a groan.

"You're beautiful, Sylvia, and you're tempting me like no other woman." I breathe heavily as my hands move of their own accord. I slowly caress her collarbone, and then my hands drop lower until I cup her breast in my palm.

She grabs my arms for support when my thumb rubs her nipple.

"Sylvia." I dip my head, avoiding her lips, and seal my mouth over her plump breast.

But when Sylvia stiffens in my arms, I feel guilty, and I can only think of Noah. I shouldn't be doing this with Sylvia. I shouldn't even be here with her.

I lift my head and meet her sad gaze. "Neither of us wants this, Sylvia." I take a step back and look around. Seeing what I need, I grab her robe from the only chair in the room and open it. "Here." I help her into it.

Once she has fastened the belt, I meet her gaze and finally admit, "There's someone else."

She offers a wry smile.

I continue, "They've been a part of me for a long time. When I started asking you out as a friend, it was an attempt to move on with my life. But it didn't really work. I've enjoyed our time together. I don't want you to think otherwise. It's just that I can't give you what you need. That's why I'm here."

Sylvia nods, but she doesn't say anything. I can see the hurt and the challenge in her eyes as she waits for me to continue. I open my mouth to speak, but then I stop. How do I bring up Eric?

Just go for it.

"Eric," I say, narrowing my eyes.

"Did Ruben tell you about last night?" she asks. She won't look at me now that I've spoken Eric's name.

"Sylvia, that isn't you. What the hell were you doing?" I demand.

"I'll admit that I don't want you in my bed anymore," she confesses.

"Ouch." I laugh, realizing she's just as relieved as I am.

"What I do doesn't have anything to do with you, Ramon," she says softly to soften the blow of her words.

"I'd like to think that we're friends." I hold out my hand, and she takes it. I sit down on her bed and pull her down beside me.

"We are friends, Ramon."

Then listen when I tell you that Eric isn't someone

you want to get involved with." I sigh. "He's my cousin, and I'll be the first to say what a great guy he is, but only as a friend. He likes his freedom, and he won't commit to any woman. I really don't want to see you get hurt. Regardless of what did or didn't happen between us, I don't want to see you get hurt because of him. Just think of me as a big brother."

She chuckles. "Jeez, I've been dating my brother."

Groaning, I let a smile play on my lips. "Just be careful, okay?" I nudge her shoulder.

"I will." She offered me a wry smile. "What about you and the woman you're involved with? Who is she?"

I feel myself pale at her question and turn away before I can meet her gaze.

"It's complicated," I admit.

Sylvia rests her head against my shoulder. "The relationships worth having usually are."

"Speaks the voice of experience." I wrap my arm around her shoulders.

"My parents," Sylvia admits. "They're still happily married, but their story makes my heart pound. I think my dad messed up more times than he cares to admit."

"Guys are stupid when it comes to relationships."

"Ramon, that's funny coming from you."

"It's the truth."

"Yes, it is."

I clear my throat and excuse myself. "I better get going. I left a friend to come talk to you. I didn't explain why I had to leave so quickly, so I should probably go explain."

"Okay, you better head back. Thank you for being concerned about me. I can assure you that I may be small, but I'm capable of looking after myself."

"I believe that." I kiss her on the top of her head. "I'll always be here for you, Sylvia."

"I know."

7

Ramon

I'M ON A ROLL THIS MORNING, AND IT'S NOT EVEN 11 a.m.! Sylvia is finally off my mind, although I'd be lying if I said I wasn't worried about her being with Eric. I certainly didn't see that coming.

When I spoke to Eric on my drive back to my apartment, I asked him to be careful with her. I just hope he listens. The good news is that Eric is going to watch the site while I stay at my cabin with Noah this weekend.

I intended to make it difficult for Noah to be back in my life, but I can't be that cruel. Noah and I were always meant to be together.

Waking up tangled with Noah felt right this

morning, and we probably still would have been in bed if not for my hotheaded brother.

As I pull up outside my apartment building, I'm still wondering what got Ruben so upset this morning that he just let himself into my apartment. He's never just walked in before.

Strange.

I grab my cell phone, switch the engine off, and climb out. The heat of the day hits me as I walk toward the building's entrance, eager to see Noah.

I didn't miss the hurt expression that crossed his face when I left. Had I stopped to think, I would have reassured him, but at the time, I was more concerned for Sylvia. I'll admit that my priorities were misplaced as soon as I see him.

Stepping into the elevator, I rub my temples, feeling a headache approaching. At least I'll be able to tell Noah that Sylvia and I realized we both need something from other people, not each other.

Seeing Sylvia naked had been a shock. I'm not sure what I was expecting when I walked into her bedroom. I definitely hadn't been expecting that. I knew she was beautiful, but she has an amazing body. My body came to life when she bent over to dry her hair and again when her large breasts pressed against me.

I didn't lie to her about her beauty. If there hadn't been a Noah in my past or present, I might have taken her up on the obvious invitation. But I'd have felt like a heel after realizing she wasn't really into me anymore. I might have even been hurt. Not too long ago, I'd considered taking our "friendship" to the next level, which I'm sure she wanted as well.

Off the elevator, I walked toward my door with a smile plastered on my face. If Ruben didn't exaggerate about what happened last night in his club, Sylvia is going to drive Eric to distraction. Eric has always been a private guy. Everything behind closed doors. But it looks like petite Sylvia has awakened something in him. It should be fun to watch.

My hand hovers over the keypad to my apartment as I wonder what kind of reception I'm going to get from Noah.

Our relationship—or whatever it is we have right now—is fragile, and I know I messed up this morning. Once upon a time, we could say or do anything to each other because we were secure in our relationship. Now, I'm second-guessing myself, hoping Noah won't leave when I'm not thinking.

"What the—?"

I stumble into the apartment when the door is yanked open.

"I've had enough of waiting for you to come in."

"Um, okay." I move away from the door, dropping my car keys onto the tray, and turn to look at Noah.

He's found all his things that he left here when he took off. I tried countless times to throw them out, but I couldn't do it. He didn't leave much, but I've kept the things he did leave hidden and to myself all this time. I'm glad he's here wearing them.

His faded, low-riding jeans hug his hips, and I lick my lips in excitement. These are the jeans he always wore to tease me. They had a way of dropping as he reached for items from the kitchen's overhead cupboards, leaving me with a tantalizing view of his pubic hair. This would get my blood boiling, and nothing has changed.

I'm unnerved by his penetrating gaze, as though he can see inside me, into my deepest thoughts. I'm relieved right now that he can't see them.

"I know I messed up what we had, but you leaving to be with someone else isn't going to fly, especially after we woke up together." Noah stalks toward me, but I hold my ground.

My nostrils flare with irritation, but a small part of me is excited by this behavior. "I wanted to make sure she was okay." What a lame reply, even if it is true. "Look, I feel really guilty about Sylvia." The irritation drains from my body, and I sigh. I don't want to talk about Sylvia anymore. "I need a coffee, and then we'll head out to the cabin."

I pour a large travel mug full of the thick, dark coffee Noah prefers and hand it to him.

He smiles and takes it, our fingers caressing as he does so. "You mentioned Sylvia earlier. Tell me what's really going on," he says, sitting at the breakfast bar and not letting me forget about Sylvia.

I was hoping to avoid this, but lying has never gotten us anywhere.

I pour myself a coffee and walk around him to stand on the opposite side. "I was jealous," I admit.

"I knew it." Noah jumps up and slaps his hand down on the countertop.

I reach out and hold his wrist down. "I wasn't jealous of Sylvia, although at first, I thought I was." I hold his gaze. "Please sit back down and listen."

After a pause, he sits down.

"At first, I thought the jealousy I was feeling was because of Sylvia being with Eric. But when I got there, I realized I wasn't jealous. I was worried that I was going to lose a friend." I start to pace back and forth. "I care about her. I don't want to lose her friendship. But there's nothing sexual between us." I blush and avoid meeting his gaze.

"What aren't you telling me?"

My eyes snap up to his, and it's as if he can read my mind.

"I know you well, Ramon, so tell me, because I'll find out."

And that's the truth.

"She didn't know I was waiting for her in her bedroom. She'd just gotten out of the shower and walked in stark naked." I laugh, embarrassed. "I touched her breasts and realized she wasn't what I wanted. I felt relieved that, because of whatever Eric has done to her, she doesn't want me. I realized that I had left the person I wanted at my apartment without explaining why I was leaving so quickly. I'm sorry."

Noah

I'm not happy about his confession of touching Sylvia, but I can accept it if it means he's free of her. "What about other women?" Ramon only ever swore off women when we were in a relationship. I don't know what type of relationship we have right now.

"You're not hearing me. The only person I've ever

wanted is you." Ramon sagged against the wall behind him. "I know us being together again is going to take some getting used to, but that's really what I want, and I thought that's what you wanted."

I swallow around the lump in my throat. "That is what I want."

Ramon lets out a loud sigh of relief. "Good...good." He smiles cockily and holds his hand out to me.

I don't need to be told twice and reach out to clasp his hand. When our fingers touch, they entwine. Ramon gives a slight tug, pulling me flush against him.

I raise our joined hands and keep them above Ramon's head on the wall behind him while slipping my free hand beneath his T-shirt. His stomach quivers at my touch, setting off a similar quivering in my jeans. It doesn't take much. It never has with Ramon.

He returns my caress, but his hand dips lower, grazing the hair of my groin hidden just below my jeans.

"I love these jeans," he whispers.

I smile. "Why do you think I'm wearing them?"

His fingers slide lower, touching the head of my rapidly rising dick. He rubs back and forth along my slit, causing pinpricks of pleasure to ripple along my throbbing length. My arousal is evident, as is Ramon's.

Craving his taste, I dip my head and softly caress his mouth with my lips as I push into his hand, which is now cupping my scrotum. His mouth opens, and I accept his invitation as my hand wanders down to press and squeeze along the length of his erection.

Our moans mingle as our tongues dance in a blaze of want and need.

Breathing heavily, I pull my mouth away from Ramon's, but I can't stop what's happening between us. I nibble down his whisker-covered jaw and back up to his earlobe. I suck down hard on one of his pleasure spots and slip my hand inside his jeans to wrap around his cock. Suddenly, the fucking doorbell rings!

"I need to see who that is," Ramon whispers, sealing his lips to mine.

I shove my hands into the back of his jeans, push them down, and drop to my knees. Looking at his beautiful dick, I nearly come.

The top part of his impressive erection is visible, his jeans stuck around his hips. I guess I should have unfastened them first. But seeing him like this is a big turn-on.

Leaning forward, I swirl my tongue around the

leaking head and moan when his flavor hits my taste buds. I lick and lap at his arousal, feeling his frustration when I refuse to unbutton his jeans. I knock his hands away when he tries, and continue teasing him.

Not again—the doorbell rings.

"Fuck... I need—"

"My mouth on your cock," I finish for him.

He offers an unsteady laugh. "I was about to say 'get the door,' but you'd be more accurate."

I get to my feet and pull his jeans back up. With our lips inches apart, I whisper, "We'll finish this at the cabin." I quickly kiss him before disappearing into his bedroom to hide my arousal.

I'm damn uncomfortable with the denim cutting into my dick. I rip the zipper and button open and sigh in relief when my hard-as-fuck dick springs free. There's no way I can go anywhere until I take care of my throbbing problem.

I hear voices in the living room and quickly head to the bathroom, locking the door behind me.

I chuck my clothes to the side, step into the shower, and turn on the water before reaching for the shower gel. I wrap my hand around my dick and sigh in relief as I start to caress its length. I was so close in the kitchen that this won't take long.

I quicken my stroke, widen my stance, and lean

against the shower wall with my other hand. The pleasure slowly works its way from deep in my stomach toward my balls, boiling into an inferno. Before I can catch my breath, my dick thickens, and the fire explodes from my cock.

Growling, I drop to my knees as the cum continues to coat my hand and the shower wall.

Fuck me.

Ramon should have been in here with me—or better yet, I should have been inside him. Feeling my dick rise again, I stop that train of thought and get to my feet, quickly rinsing off.

I turn the shower off and step out. My eyes catch sight of my jeans on the floor. I smile as I remember letting them fall there. After towel-drying my legs and junk, I yank the jeans back on. I figure I can find a more appropriate shirt in case I meet more of Ramon's family before the day's out.

Feeling tired but refreshed, I open the bathroom door and come face-to-face with a smirking Ramon.

"That sounded good," he comments.

I walk past him to the closet. "Yeah, it was. It would have been better if you'd been in my tight ass when I came." I look back over my shoulder and grin when I see the stunned expression on his face.

"Grab your stuff. We're leaving in ten," Ramon

announces as he leaves the bedroom. "And," he pauses, "it would have felt amazing to have you come in my ass."

The door closes behind him.

That was one hell of a parting shot from Ramon, and it's going to become a reality before the weekend is over.

8

———

Ramon

AS I WAIT FOR NOAH TO FINISH HIS THIRD LAP AROUND
my cabin, I admire the view of the river running
across the back.

The large, wraparound porch has double glass
doors that open onto the outside on three sides of the
cabin, as well as a large, double front door for
visitors.

When my parents visit, their favorite place to sit is
in the two rocking chairs to the left of the cabin. As
my mom instructed, a small coffee table rests
between the two chairs.

I have a feeling that Noah's favorite spot is going
to be the same as mine. The back porch. It is two feet

113

wider than the other three sides because I set the hot tub back and still wanted room to walk around my entire cabin without a giant bathtub in the way.

I haven't told Noah that I haven't used the hot tub since it was installed. No matter how much my muscles have ached, I've always used the tub in the bathroom to ease the pain.

The addition to the porch was an extravagance that Noah suggested. There are a few things around the cabin that he suggested. Even after he left, I couldn't bring myself to remove them from the plans. My injured heart had hoped that Noah would return one day, and he has.

Although it was my idea for us to spend the weekend here, I'm not sure how I feel about having him in the cabin I built for us. If Noah is serious about being back with me and picking up where we left off, seeing this cabin will fill him with hope as it does me. I'm fighting to keep my emotions in check, but all I want to do is join him inside and christen the master suite.

"Son, I didn't know you'd be here this weekend," my dad says, delight clear in his voice. He steps onto the porch and hugs me before I can process the fact that he's here.

"Why didn't you tell us you were coming up? Your

mom would have gotten you some supplies," he chides gently.

I tell him the truth: "I didn't know. It was last minute," and then I go for broke: "I've brought a friend with me."

He raises a brow.

I cringe because the look on his face tells me he's thinking it's a girl.

"Your mom will be pleased."

"Ramon, that's one fucking bed—" Noah cuts off when he sees that I'm not alone. "Um, sorry."

I shake my head and introduce the two men: "Dad, this is a good friend of mine and Carla's brother, Noah."

My dad looks stunned.

"Does she know you're back?"

"She does," Noah replies.

"In that case, welcome to the family." My dad pulls Noah into a bear hug; he's never been one for formalities. "Call me Elias."

"I can do that," Noah agrees, taking a step back.

Dad looks between the two of us before grinning. "You two come up to the house for dinner. Pippa will be happy to finally meet you, Noah."

I groan.

Dad chuckles.

Noah looks lost.

I fill him in: "Mom will take it upon herself to find you a woman to have babies with."

"Hell no," he blurts out. "I mean, um, no disrespect, but hell no." He shudders.

I can't contain my laughter anymore, and it bursts forth.

Dad chuckles and turns toward the steps. "I just came up to say hi, and I should get back to the house." He takes a step off the porch before turning back to us. With a wicked smile, he says, "She'll have a couple of women out here so quickly, you won't have time to get into your truck."

Noah glares at me, making it clear that he isn't impressed with the outcome of this meeting.

"Um, Dad," I shout.

"Son."

"Not tonight. We have something else planned, but we'll be at the family lunch on Sunday."

"Hmm, okay."

I watch my dad disappear through the trees separating our houses and try to come up with an explanation for Noah as to why I wasn't completely honest about our relationship.

Nothing comes to mind. The fact is, I just wasn't ready.

"Noah, I should have told him. I'm sorry."

My words are inadequate and are met with silence.

When I glance over my shoulder, he isn't there. I quickly turn around, but he has disappeared.

Shoving away from the porch railing, I head inside. I dash through the kitchen and come to a stop when I find him standing at the living room window, looking outside.

"Your father wants you married off as much as your mom," he says.

He knows my dad well.

"My parents want all five of their sons to be married with kids. My mom thinks that once that happens, she can rest easy knowing that we won't be alone." I shrug. "You heard what Ruben said this morning about our parents."

I take a chance and slowly invade his space.

My hands rest loosely on his hips. I smile when I notice his fists clench.

"We can't have children, but as long as I have you, I won't be alone," I whisper in his ear. "I know my parents will be happy as long as I am. I'm just having trouble finding the words."

"They can't stay down forever, Ramon." He drops his head to the window.

I lean in, press a kiss to the nape of his neck, and let my lips hover. "I know. I told you I'd tell them at lunch, and I will."

Noah turns and thrusts his fingers into my short hair. "I want to go back to how things were before," he says, dropping his forehead against mine. "But I refuse to hide how I feel about you behind closed doors."

My heart feels lighter knowing what he wants. I just wish the nervous butterflies in my stomach would disappear. I'm a grown man. It shouldn't be so hard to say, "Hey, folks, I'm gay." My insides twist into a tight knot when I think about it.

"You're freaking out," Noah accuses, pulling away.

I cringe. "Not exactly."

He raises a brow.

"Okay, yeah. Yeah, I am. The thing is, I can't figure out why." My brothers are cool with me. I'm not sure if one of them has told Michael, but the others know and haven't given me a hard time about it, so I don't know why I'm afraid to tell my parents." I pace back and forth. "They're just as laid back as the rest of us."

"Ramon." Noah sighs and sinks into the sofa with an air of defeat. "They're your parents. No matter their age, all kids want is their parents' approval. I wish I was the one with the problem—the one whose parents needed to be told that I'm gay." Noah drops his head into his hands.

I move over to him, drop to my knees, take his face in my hands, and make him look at me. I search his eyes for something—any sign—but all I see is sadness.

After placing a soft, lingering kiss on his lips, I offer him a wry smile. I sit next to him on the sofa, take his hand, and entwine our fingers.

"I wish you had the same problem," I admit. "Not just because you'd know how difficult this is for me, but because it would mean you still had your family." I squeeze his hand for comfort. "You and Carla are part of our family now, Noah. Nothing can change that."

Noah kisses our joined hands before letting them rest in his lap.

"I'm tired, Ramon," Noah admits in a heavy voice, as though he has the world on his shoulders.

"I know."

Hearing him sound so lost, I need to give him hope. Relaxing my body against the sofa, I tell him the truth: "I want you, Noah...so much it scares the fuck out of me. We had an amazing relationship before, and I want that again. I'm not going to lie and say it's going to be easy. I still have that fear in the back of my mind, the one that took root when you walked away before. I'm afraid that something else will happen, and instead of coming to me, you'll walk away again."

"You know why I did that," he answers, sounding upset.

I can't look at him right now; otherwise, I won't be able to say what I need to.

"I spent two years thinking you didn't care about me. Two years of hurt because you walked away. And until you came back, I had no idea why. I've wondered over and over again what I could have done differently to make you stay. I can't do that again."

Silence follows my statement.

The emotion running through Noah is evident in his death grip on my hand and his soft, shaking sobs beside me.

I've only seen Noah cry once before, when Carla's ex hit her. He was distraught that his sister had been hurt and that he hadn't been there to defend her.

My tough guy doesn't normally cry, so this says a lot about his true feelings.

I sit beside him for as long as I can before I can't sit any longer.

I pull my hand free from his and turn to pull him between my spread thighs. Lying back on the sofa, he climbs on top of me, wraps his arms around my waist, and rests his head against my chest.

"This," he hesitates. "This right here, with you, is what I've always wanted."

Suddenly, I feel the courage I need to admit to my family that I'm gay and in love with Noah.

I'm finally ready to do this.

Noah

I hate that Ramon has the power to reduce me to tears, yet I sense a change in him.

He's finally laid his cards on the table. He hasn't said, "I love you, Noah," but he's told me what he wants. He's also told me about his fears, which I can understand.

What hurts the most is that, in trying to keep him safe, I've lost his trust. It's something I'll be able to earn back, but it hurts to hear him admit it.

My intentions toward Ramon have always been serious. Perhaps in the beginning, when we messed around, it wasn't as serious. After the first woman we shared, I realized how jealous I was of Ramon being inside someone other than me. I didn't participate much with the woman, but Ramon ended up giving me a blowjob while he was inside her, and he came at the same time I did. We're so in tune with one another.

Neither of us would work with anyone else, even though that had been my biggest fear when I walked away—that Ramon would find someone to replace me. But he hasn't.

My head is full of two years' worth of pain and heartache, which I finally feel easing as Ramon caresses my back. His fingers rub the back of my neck and the base of my skull.

The more I relax into him, the more aroused I become. His embrace was comforting, but now that I'm relaxed, his touch arouses me, and the hot tub is at the forefront of my mind.

When Ramon showed me the porch, I was over-joyed by the large hot tub in the corner, but I avoided letting him know. Much as I wanted to show my appreciation, I knew that, from the moment I suggested it to Ramon, I had imagined us making love inside it.

Now, as my erection presses into the sofa, it throbs with thoughts of being inside Ramon while the water bubbles around us.

I shift my hand to the front of Ramon's jeans and rub the outline of his cock.

His hands tremble on my back as I unbutton and unzip his jeans. Reaching inside, I pull it out and hear him curse when I swirl my tongue around the leaking head.

Smiling, I press his shaft against his stomach and gently rub the sensitive underside up and down. I take great pleasure in the fact that more pre-cum leaks out and wets his belly.

Hot tub.

Kneeling between Ramon's spread thighs, I free my own dick from the uncomfortable confines of my jeans.

I hear Ramon gasp as I wrap my hand around my length and stroke it while watching Ramon's cock bob in excitement. Ramon loves watching me touch myself, just as I love watching him.

Ramon reaches out and stops me. "Not this time." He gulps. "This time, I want you in my ass."

Beautiful words.

"Hot tub?"

His eyes widen, and then he laughs. "Fuck! I'm not sure I can wait for it to be ready."

Truthfully, I'm not either, but I whisper, "The

anticipation will make it hot," against the head of his dick before nibbling the tip.

Ramon arches his hips, and the tip slips between my lips.

I feel his shaft quiver with need as his hands tighten into fists.

I gently suck him further into my mouth and lap at the crown with my tongue before letting him drop free.

"We'll finish this in the hot tub." I have a sudden thought. "Is it safe with your family being so close?"

"Yes," he mumbles.

I glance at him and laugh. "Really?"

"Fuck...probably not...but I don't give a shit. Let me up, and I'll take care of the tub."

If Ramon doesn't care about being caught with me outside, then I sure as hell am not going to worry about it.

I clamber to my feet and try to shove my junk back into my jeans. I'm not sure that's going to happen, though. My hard-as-fuck cock won't be contained.

Ramon snickers but is faring about as well as I am.

What the hell!

I kick off my shoes, and my jeans and T-shirt follow.

"What are you waiting for?" I stand with my hands on my hips, wondering how I'm managing to stay in place while Ramon's eyes eat me alive.

Ramon slowly leans forward, using his index finger to trace the vein from my balls to my crown. I groan as my dick aches for more of his touch.

"Tub," Ramon croaks.

We move to the back porch to turn on the hot tub, and while Ramon adjusts the temperature, I admire the view.

Not that view!

Ramon really did choose an amazing spot for his cabin. The back of the cabin sits on the riverbank of his parents' property, and the trees on the opposite side provide plenty of privacy. I know for a fact that Ramon's cabin is on the far edge of the property, so the only way someone would see us is if they were planning on coming to the house.

"Is it nearly ready?" Ramon interrupts my thoughts.

"Mmm," I moan as he moves behind me and caresses my ass in long, sensuous strokes.

"I'm kind of liking this view right now." He spreads me open, resting the length of his dick in my crease before gripping my hips. He thrusts back and forth while I wrap my hand around my dick and match his movements.

I don't want it to end this way. I don't want to come again until I'm buried in his ass, with my hand on his dick.

I break free of his hold by wrapping my hands around his wrists and gulp when I watch the essence trickle from his slit down the length of his dick.

Of all the men I've been with, he's the only one who loses so much pre-cum. I find it incredibly arousing.

"Set the jets in motion while I go get supplies."

Ramon disappears back inside, and I do as he asks before climbing into the warm water.

I sigh as the water soothes my muscles. God, it feels good. I didn't realize how sore I still was from the attack.

I wade to the opposite side, find the seat with my feet, and sit down with an even deeper sigh. The jets immediately start working on the kinks in my body. I move to the side, spread my thighs, and groan. I drop my head to the back of the tub in pleasure as a smaller jet pulses against my sacrum.

"Mmm," Ramon snickers. "You found my surprise."

"God, yeah!" I moan, feeling the pleasure harden my dick even more than I thought possible.

Ramon chuckles, and I sense him climbing into the water. Then, I feel his foot slowly creeping up my thigh.

I crack my eyes open and peer at him through my lashes, catching my breath. He's the most handsome man I've ever seen, and knowing he's still mine excites me beyond anything else.

I'm so aroused that I'll probably come the minute Ramon surrounds me. But no matter what, my need to pleasure him first overpowers all my senses right now.

I inhale, exhale slowly, and slowly move toward him, straddling his thighs. Ramon's hands immediately go to my hips, keeping me in his lap.

I lean into him, letting my hands caress his torso and rub and pinch his nipples. He sighs as his dick jerks against mine. I have to resist the urge to rub against him. But I didn't lie when I said that I want to come inside him this time. It's been a long time.

Meeting his lust-filled gaze, I slowly lower my mouth and capture his lips. He's always ready for me and never disappoints. His mouth opens, and our tongues immediately seek and find each other. The kiss quickly becomes heated as Ramon shifts against me. His hands slip down my chest, and then he grips both of our penises. I groan long and hard against his mouth, pushing more of my length into his hand.

Our teeth bump and grind. I can't get enough of him.

Feeling my orgasm building in my balls, I break free from his mouth and gasp for breath. I drag his hand away from my dick, breathe heavily, and move to sit beside him.

"You wreak havoc on my intentions," I confess.

He offers me a frustrated grin. "I need to come so fucking badly," Ramon groans.

"I know." So do I.

I'm about to do something I've only ever done once before—to Ramon.

I move in front of him, place my hands on his thighs, and smirk when I feel them quiver.

He knows what's coming.

After taking some deep breaths, I duck beneath the water and slide my mouth down his penis.

The water ripples around me as Ramon reacts as though he's just received an electric shock.

I bob up and down a few more times before surfacing to catch my breath.

"I don't know how the fuck you can do that underwater."

I smirk. "In high school, I held the record for the longest time underwater."

Get ready.

I submerge again and massage his sac with my fingers as I slowly slide down the length of him. The head pulses against the back of my throat. Just when I'm about to suck, he frantically tugs at my head. Unhappy to be forced to stop, I suck as I'm pulled off, cheeks hollowed out.

As the first drop of cum hits my mouth, I'm yanked free.

The fingers in my hair loosen, and one hand goes to his dick, covering the crown with his palm as he releases.

When I surface again, I realize I'm gasping for breath from the hardest dick I've ever had.

It soon starts to wither.

"Mom... um... Mom," Ramon stammers, his face flushed.

Fuck! This isn't good.

I mean, witnessing your son—who you don't know is gay—getting his cock sucked isn't on anyone's agenda. And knowing that Ramon is reluctant to admit he's gay...

"Fuck!"

"Ramon, stop catching flies." She turns her attention to me. "You must be Carla's brother, Noah. I'm Pippa, your sister's mother-in-law."

I have no idea how I'm supposed to respond. Does she know what I was doing underwater? It's hard to see with all the bubbles, but it's not rocket science to figure it out.

I feel a kick under the water.

"Um, yeah." I shake her outstretched hand. "That's me. Noah. Carla's brother. Noah."

Ramon starts to laugh, which relieves some of the tension surrounding us. "Sorry, Mom. He's not usually so short on words."

"That's all right. He probably wasn't expecting to meet me in the hot tub." Pippa frowns and asks the question I was hoping she wouldn't: "What were you doing under the water?"

Thinking quickly—for a change—I held up my hand and flashed my finger. "My father's wedding band slipped off."

Ramon's eyes sparkle with mirth.

It was a close call, but luckily, she seems to believe me, so I don't have to show her how loose it is. This ring will only come off if it's cut off. It's the only thing of my father's that I carry with me everywhere.

"It obviously holds a lot of sentimental value." Pippa raises an eyebrow and continues, "You should go get it resized so you don't lose it." Pippa turns back to Ramon. "Can you come into the house? I'd like to speak with you."

Ramon is startled. "Um, yeah. Okay."

Neither Pippa nor Ramon moves.

"Mom, I'll follow you inside."

"Oh, oh. Of course. Sorry." She twirls and scurries through the door.

Ramon closes his eyes, then stares directly into mine. Neither of us says anything, but I don't think either of us has anything to say.

"This isn't over." He climbs out of the tub, splashing water all over the porch.

He wraps a towel around his hips and follows his mom inside, leaving me wondering what the hell just happened.

There's no way Pippa is as clueless as she seems. Where the hell did Ramon put the lube and condoms he searched for before joining me? I should have paid more attention.

Ramon

As I watch my mom leave, I finally start to breathe again.

Even if I live to be one hundred, I don't think I'll ever get over the shock of opening my eyes and finding my mother standing over me while I'm receiving the best blowjob of my life.

I had clenched my jaw and shut my eyes tightly while trying to stave off my orgasm. I'd been so close to exploding. The pleasure Noah was wringing out of me was exquisite. Then, I sensed I wasn't alone.

When I opened my eyes, my concentration was shot to hell, and I exploded when I noticed my mom. Not my finest moment.

My only saving grace was that there were too many bubbles for her to see below the water's surface.

I rubbed my chest where my heart was finally slowing down and made my way back outside, only to find Noah relaxing in the tub as though my mom hadn't just caught us in the middle of a sexual act.

"Is she gone?" he asked without opening his eyes.

"Yeah."

"Well, that was a first," he comments.

I start to laugh.

"Fucking embarrassing." I drop onto one of the rocking chairs.

"It was kind of hot."

My eyes widen. What does he mean by that?

His eyes snap open. "I don't mean having your mom catch us, you idiot. I mean sucking you off underwater and catching your cum as you shot your load."

I groan, sit forward, and rest my wrists on my knees. "Don't remind me."

He smirks. "Yeah, bad timing on your part."

"My part?" I shake my head. "If you hadn't sucked when you did, I might've had a chance of holding it in."

"Yeah, right. We both know the only reason you came when you did is because you were fighting to stay loaded. As soon as you lost your concentration, you lost control over your body's response, and—wham!"

I feel myself blushing as I listen to him.

"I hope my mom doesn't tell everyone what just happened. She might have been clueless, but the others will damn well know what we were doing."

"I'm sure your brothers have been caught in compromising situations before," he comments.

"Yeah," I smile. "They have." Then, I start laughing. "But I don't think they've been caught quite like that."

I fix my gaze on Noah and feel my heart fill with love for him. So much love.

"After what happened with Mom, I think we should lock up and move to the bedroom."

Noah pauses, then climbs out of the tub.

He moves to stand in front of me, quickly kisses me, and pinches the towel from around my hips.

"I'll be waiting."

He strides into the cabin and out of view.

I retrieve the condoms and packets of lube that I'd hidden on the built-in shelf near the top of the hot tub and turn the jets off.

I'm damn lucky Mom came at us from the side she did and not the other, because she would have most certainly seen what was on the shelf.

I wipe my mom out of my head and follow Noah into the cabin, locking the door behind me.

I'm the only one with a key to this place, so there won't be any unexpected interruptions. The fact that Mom managed to sneak up on us before tells me just how deep I was in it to not have heard her approach.

That's damn dangerous.

After making sure the locks on the front door are in place, I head through the house to the master bedroom. Knowing that Noah is waiting for me naked has my arousal slowly coming back.

I reach down and lightly wrap my hand around my swelling shaft, giving it a few pumps. But then I realize it isn't necessary. The moment I look into the bedroom, my cock goes rock hard within seconds.

Noah is lying on the bed as expected, but he's masturbating and looks to be really into it.

"Took your time," he comments, forcing himself to slow down.

"Looks like I was about to miss the party." I stroll into the room, climb onto the bed, and drop the condoms and lube beside us. I crawl across the bed and sit astride him.

His eyes fill with heat as I lean over and swirl my tongue around the tip of his cock. "You taste good." I trace the slit with my tongue.

Before I can take him fully into my mouth, Noah flips me onto my stomach, trapping my pulsing dick between my stomach and the bed. Noah lifts my hips and widens my legs before starting to massage between them.

I groan and push back against his hand, cursing when the head of my dick rubs against the bed. I want the friction to heighten my pleasure, but instead, I grip the quilt with my hands to force myself to stay put—to not move.

Looking down, I see not only the pre-cum leaking uncontrollably from my dick but also the wet spot it's making on the bed. The head bulges red, and I need... I need... something.

Then, Noah breaches the ring of muscle in my ass, and I nearly fly forward. He quickly reaches around and grips the base of my cock to stop me from moving. But it doesn't stop the pleasure rippling along my length.

"Fuck, Ramon. I need to get inside you before I come...or you do."

"Yes," I groan.

"I need to watch you, Ramon. Sit on me." Noah removes his fingers from me and slowly releases my dick.

Lying on his back, he passes me a condom.

I rip it open with my teeth and take the rubber, torturing him by slowly rolling it down his length before coating him with lube. Tipping forward, I position him at my entrance.

Noah wraps his hand around my dick, and pleasure ripples through me. Gasping, I slowly push down, moaning as Noah gives me all of himself.

Once I'm fully seated on him, I can't move. The excitement of having him inside me is overwhelming. The feel of his solid length filling me will make me come without any more stimulation. My cock is so excited that it's leaking all over Noah's stomach and his thumb as he rubs against the slit.

I need to move.

As I rock forward, Noah's hand tightens around my dick. "This is going to be really quick," I growl as he pumps my cock.

"Yes...finish us, Ramon," he begs.

Rising slightly on my knees, I start to rock back and forth, and the faster Noah's fist moves on my cock, the faster my hips rock.

There's no way I'm going to last any longer. As I feel the explosion building in my balls, Noah thrusts up into me, hitting my gland. My eyes roll back, and just like that, I start to come. I hear Noah curse as he holds me still, gripping my hip with one hand while continuing to grip and stroke my overexcited dick.

Opening my eyes, I meet Noah's burning gaze and watch him come down from the high. He smiles softly and glances at his hand on my semi-hard shaft.

I grin.

His stomach, chest, and hand are covered with my semen.

"I like that look on you," I comment.

"Me too." His smile fades. "I've missed you, Ramon."

I lean down, not giving a shit about the mess between us, and kiss him. "I missed you as well." I smile. "Let's see if you still think you missed me after we've had lunch at my parents' house tomorrow."

Noah

Hearing Ramon talk about his family and being in the same room with them are two different things. I obviously never did the math, because standing in the corner of the room while they catch up with each other is overwhelming.

"You'll get used to it," Carla whispers, coming up on my right.

"Hmm."

She nudges me.

"Okay, what's really going on with you, Noah?"

I shove the beer bottle into my other hand, freeing myself to wrap my arm around my sister.

I kiss her on the top of her head. "Don't worry about me. I'm fine." I smile. "I'm better than fine."

"Oh, yeah."

"Oh, yeah," I chuckle.

"Pippa likes you," Carla comments, noticing her smile at us. "She's really big on family, so having you here with us, especially with me, is making her happy."

I wish I could be sure that's the reason for her smiles. She makes me nervous.

"Noah," I say, turning around upon hearing Ramon's voice. "I'd like you to meet my brother, Michael, and his wife, Lily."

I smile and return their greeting.

My first impression is that Michael is the serious McKenzie brother. But then he looks at his wife, and his whole face changes. He also seems to be having trouble keeping his hands off of her.

Lily is smaller than Michael and looks radiant, her pregnancy quite obvious.

"Carla, it must be heartwarming to have your brother home," Lily comments.

"It is." Carla cuddles against me, and I realize how badly I hurt her when I left without saying goodbye.

Was I selfish to leave without saying anything? Without telling anyone my reasons? Would it have made a difference? I'll never know.

"I'm not going anywhere," I announce, smiling when I see the spark in Ramon's eyes.

Holding his gaze, I admit, "Everything I want is here in Lexington."

Michael warns, "About that, I think you should be warned that Mom will consider you part of the family, which means she'll try to set you up with one of her daughters."

"I already have someone, so her help would be misguided."

Lily looks between Ramon and me with amusement, and it's clear that she knows what's between us.

Michael, on the other hand, has no idea. "You should have invited her for lunch. Is it not that serious?"

Since when do guys stand around asking questions you'd expect from your mother?

I stare at him, trying to collect my thoughts. He's still waiting for my answer. Shaking my head, I grin. "Oh, it's serious...just different. At least for today."

He frowns. "Hmmm."

Ramon gives me a secret smile before turning and wrapping his arms around a pretty redhead.

"Ruben's fiancée, Rosie," Carla whispers.

I put my empty bottle behind me. Looking down at my sister, I caress her face. "I really missed you. I'm sorry." I rest my forehead against hers.

"Sorry to interrupt, but we're heading out to the patio to eat," Pippa says. "It's easier to clean up the mess out there."

I chuckle.

Carla pinches my side. "Hey, don't you think she's joking? Michael and his brothers sometimes act like children when they're together." She rolls her eyes.

"I have to see this."

I follow her outside and look around for Ramon, whom I spot talking to Rubén.

"Sit here." Sebastian doesn't give me a choice and shoves me into the seat, drawing curious looks from others.

Ramon breaks free, moves closer, and drops into the vacant seat beside me. He grins. "Seb knows this is where I always sit."

"Is it wise for us to sit together?"

He frowns, and I want to kick myself for such a stupid remark. I want everything to be out in the open, so why did I open my big mouth? You know why. I'm terrified that Ramon will have the courage today to announce our relationship to everyone, and I'm sick to my stomach because I know everything is about to change for the worse. Although I've never hidden who I am, in a way, this is like my coming out as well.

Feeling Ramon's hand on my thigh, I reach under and hold onto him for strength. I should be the one offering Ramon support.

While I've been lost in thought, everyone has taken their seats and started helping themselves to the food.

After squeezing Ramon's hand, I let go and take some chicken, potato salad, and a large slice of home-made bread.

"So, Noah," Pippa begins. "I've written down the name of a jeweler so you can have your father's ring resized. You don't want to lose it again."

Ramon starts coughing, so I thump him a few times on the back without thinking. It ends up as a caress. I quickly pull my hand back and pass him his glass of water.

He takes it and drinks quickly.

"You okay?"

He nods.

The table grows silent as everyone looks between us.

I haven't the slightest clue how to answer such an innocent question without opening myself up to more questions. Carla knows that our father's ring fits my finger like a glove.

I go with, "Brief." "Um, thanks."

"Why do you need to alter Dad's ring?" Carla asks.

I scowl at her. "I just do." I change the subject as I bite into the bread. Chewing and speaking around a mouthful, I say, "My favorite is homemade bread, and this is delicious." I smile at Pippa.

After a pause, she returns my smile. "It's my mother's recipe. I've never found another that comes close."

"You still haven't answered about Dad's ring."

Why can't she leave it alone?

"It slipped off in the hot tub. He was looking for it yesterday," Pippa adds.

Ramon curses under his breath.

"Hot tub," Ruben snickers, getting an elbow in the ribs from Rosie.

"I was playing with it, and it slipped off into the water."

"Has anyone heard from Lucien or Sabrina lately?" Lily asks, to my relief.

"Yes." Pippa turns away and focuses on Lily. "I spoke to them this morning. Sabrina is doing well, but she's tired. Lucien hopes to bring her back to Lexington within the next few weeks."

"I'm glad. It'll be fun to have my best friend back," she says, pointing to Carla and Rosie. "But don't think you two are getting out of listening to me moan all the time. You'll be able to compare my moaning with Sabrina's."

Rosie laughs. "You love being pregnant, and Carla and I don't believe you."

"I do. I can't wait to see what our new son or daughter looks like." Lily rests her hands on her stomach. "We're both relieved that I'm not having twins again." She smiles softly at her husband. "I wouldn't have minded too much, but it would've been difficult with Charlotte and Jr. being so young."

"You would have managed," Carla comments.

I have a feeling it won't be long before Carla and Sebastian announce that they're expecting. I hope it's sooner rather than later. I wouldn't mind having a niece or nephew.

"Do you have a place to live now that you're back?" Michael asks. "There are a couple of condos near the lake that have recently become available, in case you don't." He continues eating.

"I have a place, but thanks for the offer."

While I'm working on the McKenzie site, I have an apartment across the street from the location. When I'm not working, I plan to spend time with Ramon, either at his apartment or at the cabin. Now that I'm back in his life, I'm not going anywhere without him.

"You're family, so think nothing of it," Michael adds. "If you change your mind, just let Sebastian know, and he'll set it up."

I nod.

I sit back with an empty plate and start to relax. It feels good knowing I'm now part of this.

The large table seats all of us, and with the sun shining, it's perfect.

Michael now has his hands full with the wiggling children who just woke up from a nap, while Lily finishes her dinner. The love these two share makes me want to share the same with Ramon and have it out in the open.

Ramon's nervous twitch catches my attention.

Ramon

It's now or never.

At least, that's what I've been telling myself since we sat down for lunch.

It's just harder than I thought to say what I need to say. Most of my family already knows, so it shouldn't be such a big deal, but these are my parents.

Oh, fuck it!

"I'm gay," I blurt out.

Silence follows my statement.

I clear my throat and repeat, "I'm gay."

Sebastian and Ruben roar with laughter, but it slowly dies down with one look from Dad.

Michael looks back and forth between Noah and me. Yeah, he's figured it out.

"I know, son. Or rather, I didn't know for certain until you introduced me to Noah."

Although my heart stops beating so frantically in my chest when I hear my dad say he knows, I'm not completely at ease. My mom still hasn't said anything, and while I wait with the rest of my family, Noah slips his hand into mine on my thigh.

"Oh, my goodness." Mom places her hands over her mouth in surprise. "You weren't looking for your ring," she says to Noah, who looks like a deer caught in the headlights. Her face fills with an embarrassed blush. "You really were playing—"

"Pippa," Dad hisses, thankfully cutting her off.

"Excuse me a minute," Sebastian mumbles, dashing inside the house.

"I'll go see if he needs help," Ruben laughs before dragging Rosie up with him and following Sebastian inside.

Dad glares at Michael. "Do you need to join them?"

"No way am I missing this." He sits back down with his son on his lap. His son is trying to grab his sister, who is sitting on Lily's lap.

"I'll go get my husband under control." Carla glances between Noah and me while getting to her feet. As she heads inside, she looks back over her shoulder and winks just before disappearing into the kitchen.

Bringing my attention back to my family, I admit, "I was with Noah before he disappeared, and now he's back in my life. I don't want to hide our relationship from anyone." I smile at Noah, knowing my next words will shock him: "I love him."

His eyes widen, and he opens his mouth to reply, but nothing comes out.

I squeeze his thigh and look back at my parents.

They still haven't said anything other than expressing their surprise at the beginning.

Dad has always been a man of few words, so I'm not sure what I'm expecting. Something would be good, though, to help ease my anxiety about being honest.

I watch as my dad stands and moves toward me. I stand and find myself pulled into a tight hug. "Nothing will ever change the fact that you're my youngest son, nor will anything change how much I love you. As long as you're happy, then so am I." He steps aside and looks at Noah, who stands up.

"Welcome to the family, son." He pulls Noah in for a hug. "I want you to feel like this is your home, too. You're welcome to come and go from the house just like the rest of the family. Do I make myself clear?"

Noah swallows a few times. "Yes, sir."

"Good. Now, if you'll excuse me, I need to go sort your brothers out."

I grin and join Noah as we drop back into our seats.

Mom still looks confused, but Michael looks thoughtful.

I stare at my brother, wondering what he's thinking. I don't have to wait long.

"I want to know what Mom caught you doing in the hot tub," he snickers. This tells me he's okay with everything.

"I wasn't expecting this today," Mom begins, "but I'm always happy to have someone one of my children loves join the family." She stands and kisses me on the top of my head, then does the same to Noah.

"You can both rest assured that I have no intention of visiting you at the cabin unexpectedly again." She heads inside.

"I'm dying to know about the hot tub."

I glare at Michael, who starts laughing.

"I'm sure I can show you what I think they were doing," Lily suggests.

"We can let Ramon and Noah babysit," he says, wiggling his brows at Lily.

She smacks his arm. "Let's go join the rest of your family inside and feed these two." She smiles at us both. "I'm glad about everything, Ramon. Welcome to the family, Noah."

"Thank you, Lily." Noah returns her smile.

I watch them disappear inside, then turn to my guy.

"I'm kind of feeling let down." I frown, but it quickly turns into an uncontrollable grin.

Noah laughs. "You'd have preferred them to be pissed off instead of accepting?"

"No, but their reaction makes me wonder why I haven't said anything before. And don't you dare say 'I told you so.'"

He chuckles. "Okay, even if I did."

I try to scowl, but I end up laughing.

"I have to say, though, I hope your mom doesn't keep bringing up the hot tub."

"She won't, but you can bet my brothers will."

"Are they seriously all right with us?"

"Yes."

I know where he's coming from. Although some of my brothers told me they were okay with it, I had a hard time accepting it at first.

"Are you all right?" He rubs my shoulder.

"I'm good and grateful that my family is a lot more accepting than I thought they would be. I'm still waiting for Dad to say he was joking or for Mom to tell us to leave." I shrug. "Deep down, I know my parents aren't like that, but I'm still a little afraid. My grandparents raised them to believe that everyone is equal, and they raised my brothers and me the same way. I just feel deflated, somehow. I got all worked up for nothing. I'm glad, though."

"What do you want to do now?"

"Join our family inside."

Noah stands up, takes my hand, and pulls me to my feet. Once we're both standing, he steps closer to me.

I don't even flinch at the thought of anyone catching us.

"You said you loved me. Did you mean it?"

"I meant every word. Our secret is out; no more hiding."

He leans forward and teasingly kisses my lips. "I love you, too. I never stopped."

10

Ramon

"FUCK," NOAH CURSES FOR THE THIRD TIME IN AS MANY minutes.

I smirk, keeping my back to him so he can't see the amusement on my face.

He's been trying to tie his purple cravat for the past five minutes, but he hasn't had any luck.

I keep my back to him so that I won't be tempted to touch him.

His dark gray morning suit slacks fit him like a glove, and the fabric caresses his ass perfectly.

Today is finally here: Ruben and Rosie's wedding day. I never thought sweet Rosie would tame Ruben, but I guess she took my brother by surprise.

Since telling my parents about Noah and me twelve weeks ago, things have been pretty damn perfect. I've felt as though my life is finally falling into place—family gatherings, with Noah by my side. He plays just like my brothers when we head to the backyard at my parents' house to play a game of rugby or football.

My heart fills with pride when I see him being accepted with open arms by all my family. We've had to endure the occasional crude joke from Sebastian, but he gives as good as he gets.

My only regret is that, outside of our family, no one can know about us. Noah stays in an apartment across the street from the construction site I'm managing during the week to make it seem plausible. The last thing we need is for word to get out that he's my lover, boyfriend, or whatever you want to call it.

We're both starting to get frustrated. It's been nine weeks since Noah started working on the site, and so far, nothing has come of it. He has made some connections, but none of them have panned out. Nothing out of the ordinary has happened on the site since he started working there. I hope it's not the calm before the storm because I don't believe that all the bad luck has stopped. My only hope is that the culprits are caught before anything else happens.

I just have a bad feeling that something needs to happen first.

Shaking off the day's stress, I quickly finish fastening my cravat before finally turning to Noah.

I let out a laugh and move toward him. I place my hands on his shoulders and turn him toward me. "You look good in purple," I comment, knocking his hands out of the way.

With a few twists, I fasten his cravat. Smoothing my hands along his arms, I can't stop touching him. He feels good under my fingers, and the way his muscles flex tells me he's enjoying my touch as much as I'm enjoying giving it.

But we don't have time.

We don't have a lot of time together, so we value what time we do have. Weekends.

I sigh heavily, not wanting to burden Noah with my depressing thoughts. He's doing what he's doing for my brothers and me, but I don't like having him away from me. Part of me wishes the people messing with us on my site would make their move so this could all be over, but I don't see that happening anytime soon.

"Hey," Noah says, holding my chin and forcing me to meet his gaze. "Why the heavy sigh?"

"It doesn't matter." I try to step back, but he follows me.

"Yes, it matters." He steps into my space, resting his hands on my hips as he leans in to kiss me.

He intended to give me a quick kiss, but I had other ideas. I slid my hands into his hair and held him in place while my mouth took over.

Our tongues dance and our teeth clash. I can't get close enough. My heart pounds in time with Noah's, and all I want is to be naked, to feel his hard dick rubbing against mine with nothing between us.

I groan when I feel Noah's hand on me as he pulls the zipper down and slides his fingers into the opening. My dick aches to have his hand wrapped around it. But the fucking alarm on my phone starts going off. We both freeze.

Fuck!

Noah drags a finger along my length before zipping me back up, disappointment clear on his face. I'm not faring any better.

"We should hurry," he says, but doesn't move.

I do what I've wanted to do since we started getting ready today and wrap my arms around him. My nose rubs against his neck as I breathe in his scent.

Noah wraps his arms around my waist, holds me tight, and sighs in pleasure.

My alarm on my phone goes off again. I kiss Noah on the neck and reluctantly step back.

"We need to leave." Even though today is my brother's wedding day, I want to stay here with Noah.

"I should have listened to you last night instead of wanting to taste you," Noah comments with a sexy grin.

He'd certainly tasted me, and it had taken hours for us to be satisfied enough to sleep. That's why we hadn't driven to my cabin. That would have given us more time this morning to get dressed, get ready, and do other things.

"Perhaps you'll remember next time." I smile and grab my morning coat from the hanger.

My brothers and I have been asked to wear dark gray slacks and morning coats. Our vests are a slightly paler gray, and we're wearing lilac shirts and purple cravats. My heart felt full when Ruben told me to make sure that Noah was dressed the same way. I think he was choked up as well.

Lily, Carla, and Sabrina are wearing purple brides-maid dresses, so of course we had to match. I'm surprised they've gotten away with not having a huge affair. But Rosie and Ruben were adamant that they only wanted family and very close friends, so Mom had to be satisfied with that. In fact, I don't think she was too bothered. She's just happy that Ruben's getting married. It took four weeks to make all the arrangements for today. One minute they were happy being engaged; the next, a wedding was being planned.

I wasn't the only one who noticed how excited Mom was. No doubt she's thinking there's a reason for the quick wedding—like another grandbaby on the way. I'm not so sure, though. My brother is besotted with Rosie, and she feels the same way, tenfold.

Finally ready, I picked up my car keys from the door and turned to Noah, who took my breath away.

He's completely unaware of my reaction to him. He's so fucking handsome that with one look, my cock hardens and tingles, and with one touch, I'm ready to come.

Today is going to be stressful with all the extended family around. Sylvia is going to be there, too. I've avoided her since our talk in her bedroom, but Ruben told me that she was caught in a compromising situation again, this time with Eric. He won't be here today because he's working somewhere—he's been very secretive—so we'll see how Sylvia really feels. I also want to tell her about Noah before someone else does. I'm surprised she still doesn't have a clue. According to my brothers, they haven't said anything. I do feel guilty for not being completely honest with her.

As I run my hand through my hair, which has grown out since I cut it all off, I open the apartment door. As I watch Noah walk through the door carrying our overnight bag, I can't resist sliding my palm over his ass. The slacks fit him like a glove.

The look he throws at me is so heated that it causes a growl to rumble in my throat. I want this man, and before the day is over, I'm going to have him.

Noah

The McKenzie family is overwhelming. At least, that's the conclusion I've come to while hiding in a corner of the living room. I have been introduced to all of the McKenzies, which is rather daunting. Apparently, only three of the cousins are present; one has brought his fiancée. I'm not sure what she said to Pippa, but fairly soon after being introduced, Pippa winced and excused herself.

I grin when I catch movement out of the corner of my eye and see Sebastian slowly moving toward me, looking relieved.

"Wicked witch," he comments after following my gaze.

"She has claws, huh?"

"Oh, yes. I'm glad I have a sweet, loving woman. I'm not sure Mateo's all that pleased with her." He looks around and motions toward a server. "I wish I had eaten before arriving here. I thought Mom was going to put out a spread before the wedding." He laughs. "This is it."

A server arrives with a tray laden with canapés.

A marquee has been set up in the back pasture, where we'll be eating and dancing in a few hours. I don't dance well, so I'd like to disappear somewhere quiet with Ramon. I'd be happy if we disappeared for just a kiss or a hug. I'm craving his touch, but for some reason, he's keeping his distance now that we're at his parents'.

He wants to tell Sylvia about us first, but that conversation will only take five minutes, so his desire to stay quiet is grating on my nerves.

"Where's Ramon?" Sebastian asks. I'd forgotten he was standing with me, quietly eating the canapés.

"I'm not sure." I frown. "Your dad called him away not long after we arrived, and I haven't seen him since."

"Oh," he grins around a pastry. "Dad will have him helping set something up. I'm on to him now, so I always make myself scarce. You'll get the hang of it." He claps me on the back.

Changing the subject, I ask, "Ramon never mentioned having cousins until recently. What's with that?"

A serious look crosses his face. "My dad had a falling out with their dad after their mom died. She was my dad's sister. I'd never seen my father so angry, and I don't think I ever have again. We used to hang out a lot as kids. Because of their falling out, I guess we all suffered. Lucien kept in touch with Dante, and through him, Eric came out to Lexington. Our parents still aren't talking, but I'm glad Ruben invited our cousins to the wedding. Eric, Diego, Aiden, and Kasey couldn't make it, but I'm glad the others made the effort."

Before the McKenzies came into the picture, Carla and I only had each other, so being around a large family makes me nervous. Carla seems to have adapted well, though, and Sebastian dotes on my sister. She needed love and a family, and I'm glad she found that. I'm also glad that I'm becoming part of the family. I missed her when I left. I didn't see her often before, but not being able to drop by and visit her in Canada hurt. Being gone showed me how much I value having her and Ramon as my family.

Ever since I met Ramon, he has been my home, which is why I hate getting out of bed every day to work on the construction site. I've always worked in construction, which is how I met Ramon in Canada. However, not being with the man I want to be with every day is wreaking havoc on my concentration. I've been away too long to stay away now. I don't know what to do because I can't keep going the way I am.

I have a sixth sense about Ramon, and as if I knew he was coming, I turn and watch him head toward me. Our eyes meet, and it's as if there's no one else in the room.

After hearing a throat cleared, I keep my eyes on Ramon and tell Sebastian, "Go find my sister."

He laughs. "You wish."

"Don't you have something better to do?" Ramon grumbles to Sebastian.

He roars with laughter. "Noah said something

similar." He pats us both on the back. "Just remember there's a room full of guests, even though they're family." Sebastian walks toward Dante, the priest.

"Sorry I took so long." He shrugs. "My dad can be a pain in the ass when we have large functions. He has staff here to sort everything out, but he still has to be in charge."

"Like someone else I know."

Ramon takes after his dad more than he realizes.

"You met everyone, right?"

"I did."

"Good, good." Ramon is nervous around me, which is new.

"What's wrong?"

He won't meet my eyes as he scans the room.

I take a step into his personal space, watching his eyes widen in surprise.

"Fuck. Sylvia was outside and asked why I didn't have a date. I told her I did and that I'd introduce her later." He tugs at his hair, which has started to grow back—thank God.

"I don't see the problem. I thought she was into Eric." I'm confused. I seriously don't see a problem with what he's saying.

"She is, but I hate that I have to tell everyone. Why can't we just be together and be done with it? Why does it matter what others think as long as we're happy?"

You're overthinking it. I hear you, and I agree. If these people didn't mean something to you, then I'm guessing you wouldn't care, but since they're family and close friends, you feel like you have to open up. I wish I could help, but I'm certainly willing to be with you when you do."

He smiles and starts to relax. "Shit, I didn't realize how stressed I am."

"Feel better now?" I raise a brow.

"For now, I do." He glances around again. "Have you spoken to Mateo and Caprice?"

"Not really." I grab a glass of wine from a passing server, take a long sip, and prolong it when I see the intense need on Ramon's face.

"You?"

He clears his throat. "That was unfair...and no. She tried to flirt with Sebastian when she first arrived." He chuckles. "Sebastian couldn't get away quickly enough. He's keeping his distance."

"I seriously don't know why he's with her," I say.

"Their wedding has been postponed, so maybe Mateo is having second thoughts." Ramon shrugs. "Anyway, the wedding is starting soon." He chuckles. "Ruben looks ready to hurl."

"Ruben doesn't look the nervous type."

"Oh, he's nervous, all right. Rosie is the only one to ever get that reaction out of him." With all the amusement leaving his face, Ramon adds, "He loves her, and she loves him. That's all there is to it."

Is he telling me that he loves me, and that's all that matters?

Trusting my instincts and making sure we're not being watched, I grab the bottom of his vest and pull him closer, whispering into his ear, "I'm not exactly sure what you're saying, but you're mine and have been since we first met."

Straightening up, I walk away to cool off. Being close to him, inhaling his scent, and being in this situation with Ramon is starting to get to me—more than I thought it would.

11

Ramon

WEDDINGS ALWAYS TAKE MY BREATH AWAY WHEN THEY involve one of my brothers. Watching my brother Ruben now has me fighting back emotion. When the bridal music starts, most people turn to the back of the room to catch a glimpse of the bride in all her finery. Not me. I watch my brother's face when he catches a glimpse of the woman he loves. I've done this with Michael, Sebastian, and Lucien. Today, I'm doing it with Ruben.

I watch Ruben swallow back his emotions as he watches Rosie walk toward him. Then she's in my line of sight, and she's breathtaking. I wipe away a stray tear and rapidly blink to prevent the others from falling.

Noah nudges my hip and offers me his hand. Without hesitating, I entwine my fingers with his and hold tight.

When Rosie stands beside Ruben, his eyes shining with love, I really look at the dress, rushed to be finished in time. She's beautiful. The bodice of her dress resembles a corset, and it's the same deep purple as our cravats. Tiny cream and gold flowers adorn it. The gold chiffon skirt floats around her legs. Rosie didn't want the traditional white dress, and seeing her in her choice, I'm glad.

As Dante welcomes everyone here today, I let my mind wander.

I imagine that it's Noah and me getting married. I smile at the thought. I really want that, and until today, I had no idea that I wanted a marriage and to exchange rings. The idea popped into my head while I was watching Ruben fuss and worry about Rosie. Those thoughts made my heart ache. I had never thought about marriage before. I thought it was only for my brothers. But not anymore. It's something I want, eventually. Gay marriage is still illegal in Kentucky, so we'd have to go out of state, but it would be worth it in the end. We could go to New York. The company owns an apartment there, and it's registered in all of our names. I glance at Noah and decide that, after today, I'm not going to worry about what anyone thinks about us anymore. We still have to tread carefully on the site until this whole mess is sorted out, but after today, no more hiding.

Noah tugs on my hand, turning my head to meet his gaze, which is full of humor.

"I can't believe you switched off in the middle of your brother's wedding," he whispers, chuckling.

I blush because, yeah, I did.

With the wedding over, the guests stand as Dante says, "I would like to introduce Mr. and Mrs. Ruben McKenzie."

I laugh and clap along with half the guests, feeling as though a huge weight has lifted from my shoulders.

I squeeze Noah's shoulders, and it takes everything in me not to lean forward and kiss him. After today!

Once my brothers have led their wives down the makeshift aisle, I follow, feeling the heat of Noah's body against my back. He presses close, and my head spins. Wanting to press my ass into him, I move to the side and bump into Sylvia, trying not to give in to my desire.

"Wow," I say, my eyes widening when I really look at her. "You look gorgeous, Sylvia."

She offers me a soft smile. "Thanks, Ramon. You look handsome. Purple suits you."

I grin. "Why, thank you, ma'am."

She giggles and nudges me. "I've missed you."

My heart sinks. I told her that I didn't want to lose her as a friend. What have I done? I've ignored her for weeks.

Taking her by the elbow, I suggest, "Let's go talk. I think we have five minutes before I'm needed for the photos."

"Okay."

We slip through my family, but not before I notice the amusement on Mateo's face. He thinks I'm trying to disappear with Sylvia for less-than-honorable reasons. He couldn't be more wrong. The sooner I tell Sylvia, the sooner I won't have to hide.

We round the corner of the marquee. It's not exactly a private area, but it will have to do.

"Ramon—"

"Sylvia—"

We both laugh as we try to talk at the same time. I need to speak first, partly because I'm worried about what she'll say next.

"I'm gay," I blurt out, shocking Sylvia.

"You are?" Wow... I mean... just wow." She laughs. "I never saw that coming." She tilts her head to one side. "But I think I should have." I mean, that explains so much. As you know, I've made it clear on a few occasions that I wouldn't have put up a fight if you had wanted to take me to bed. But you never took me up on that offer. I guess I should be glad you didn't want me because you're gay and not because you didn't want me."

"I'm sorry, Sylvia. I should have been completely upfront with you from the beginning. It hasn't been easy, but I'm getting there."

"Yes, you should. Is this why you've been avoiding me? Because you didn't know how to tell me?" Sylvia starts to chew her bottom lip, and I can tell she's nervous.

"I didn't know what to say to you. I lied by omission all along, and it made me feel uncomfortable."

She wraps her arms around my waist, resting her head on my chest. I return her embrace, resting my chin on the top of her head.

"Thank you for telling me now." She pauses. "So, is it okay if I admit that I can't stop thinking about your missing cousin?"

I sigh and place a kiss on the top of her head. I hold her at arm's length so I can see her face. "Sylvia, I wish you'd find a sweet guy instead of my hard-as-nails cousin."

She blushes. "No one else has ever made me feel the way he does."

I smirk.

Sylvia shoves me in the stomach.

"Stop being a dick," she laughs.

I wrap my arm around her neck and guide her back toward my family and friends.

"If you're really into Eric and he reappears, I'll make sure to sing your praises."

"Make sure you do," she says, digging her elbow into my ribs as we separate. "I'm going to go say hello to Hunter's girlfriend, Gia. She doesn't know any of us."

I frown. I had no idea Hunter was here.

"When did he arrive?" I ask, following Sylvia's gaze.

"Just before everyone was seated. They hit traffic due to an accident and only just made it here on time."

"Okay, let's go."

It's been a while since I've seen or heard from Hunter. He went off the grid after helping Rosie and

Ruben. I spent a few nights drinking with him at the pool table back at Kenza when he was around.

I never felt attracted to him. It just felt good to hang out with someone who figured out my sexual preference almost immediately and accepted it completely. There was never any judgment.

Seeing me, Hunter smiles and offers his outstretched hand. I take it, and find myself pulled into a hug.

"It's good to see you again, Ramon," he says, slapping me on the back. Pulling back, he turns to smile at the woman beside him.

He wraps his arm around her shoulders and introduces her: "I'd like you to meet my girlfriend, Gia." He keeps her by his side.

I smile. "It's nice to meet you, Gia. I hope you don't feel overwhelmed with all my family around. It can be exhausting sometimes."

"Not at all. It was a lovely wedding, and your mother is delightful."

I throw my head back and roar with laughter. "Delight" is one way of describing my nosy mother.

"She is that."

I notice Sylvia frowning, and I remember that she's with me.

"Um, sorry." I wrap my arm around her shoulders. "You've met Sylvia, right?"

"We have. She very kindly showed us to the wedding marquee," Gia offers.

Hunter looks between us. With my arm around Sylvia, he must think I'm claiming her as mine.

"Ramon, do you have a minute?" Dante interrupts. After the introductions, I move away with him.

"What's wrong?" I ask as soon as we're out of earshot.

"I was walking past, and you looked uncomfortable. Plus, Noah was watching you and looked angry. And," he sighs, "my sister, Emelia, is annoying."

I chuckle and tease, "Glad I only have brothers. All those guys after my sister would give me gray hair." I shudder.

"That isn't funny," he mumbles under his breath. "She doesn't date."

"Hmm." I stop and turn him around to look at his sister, who is currently helping herself to another glass of champagne. "She's beautiful. There's no way she doesn't date."

"She doesn't—leave it."

Taken aback by the sharpness in his voice, I look at him in surprise. He runs his hands through his hair and winces.

"Sorry. She's a sore spot with me right now. Let's change the subject to you."

"If we must."

He smirks. "Oh, we must...Noah?" He raises a brow and waits for me to elaborate, but what can I say when it's obvious that he's figured everything out?

So, the truth, then?

"You guessed right." I smile. "He's Carla's brother."

"So you said when he was introduced." His eyes are full of amusement.

"Bastard," I mutter.

"Ramon, it's me you're talking to. Do you seriously think I'd give a damn?"

"You might be family, but you're religious. I didn't think the church approved."

Suddenly, Dante looks sick. His complexion has paled, and the pain in his eyes causes me to pause beside him.

I reach out and grab his arm. "What's wrong? Don't fob me off."

As long as you're happy, that's all that matters at the end of the day."

Dante recovers, but something is off with him. I haven't seen him that often over the years, but he's acting strange.

"If you need to talk, I'm a good listener," I offer.

With a wry smile, he responds, "I'm okay." He glances toward his sister and frowns when he sees her having an animated conversation with one of the male servers. "Not everything is as it seems," he adds. "I'll see you later."

Dante is going to annoy me until I figure out what's going on with him. I hate not knowing exactly what's wrong. But it will have to wait.

Talking to Noah takes precedence.

Noah

As I watch Ramon head toward me, my heart beats faster. His dark hair is ruffled by the slight breeze, probably from him shoving his fingers through it. I'm so glad he's growing it out again. But, as he gets within five feet of me, his dad drags him away.

If I didn't know better, I'd think his father was trying to keep us apart today. But I know better, and his father looks too stressed to be thinking about his son's relationship with me.

I just wish Elias had waited until I'd spoken to Ramon or even touched his hand. I just needed something to show me that Ramon was really there with me. I'm not a clingy guy, but I need Ramon's reassuring touch while surrounded by so many of his family and close friends. If we weren't so preoccupied with the trouble at the site and Ramon telling his family, I wouldn't feel so damn insecure.

Shaking the dull thoughts from my head, I force a smile. The last thing I want is for Pippa to catch me frowning. She'll pounce on me and demand to know what Ramon's done. I smile naturally at the thought. She blames him for every frown, smirk, or smile she's ever seen on my face.

"Don't you like weddings?"

I turn around, hiding my worry, and see a heavily pregnant Lily standing behind me.

"I love weddings. Shouldn't you be sitting down somewhere?"

"Oh, pooh. I've had enough sitting to last me a lifetime." She smiles fondly. "I love Michael completely, but he won't let me sit down. I know he's only thinking about me, but I need to stretch every once in a while. So, do you want to tell me why you and Ramon have stayed apart all day?"

"You'll have to ask Ramon that question."

"Ah." Lily moves closer and wraps her arm around mine. "Walk me toward the marquee."

"Subtle," I comment with amusement.

"I knew you'd see it my way." She grins. "I think he's nervous about being around so much family. He always seems confident, so I'm not sure what his deal is today. Just don't worry too much. Anyone can see that he only has eyes for you."

"Even when he has his arms around Sylvia?" I ask, letting the bitterness seep out.

Lily frowns. "I missed that. Really?"

"Yeah." I look off into the distance, not really seeing anything. "Are the photographs finished?" I change the subject.

"Mostly. We're taking a family picture before going into the marquee, which is why you're coming with me."

"Ah."

"Oh, God. Save me," Lily whispers as Mateo and Caprice intercept us.

"Michael was looking for you a minute ago," Mateo informs Lily.

Lily chuckles. "He'll find me soon enough. I'm not exactly easy to miss these days," she says, gesturing to her stomach, swollen with pregnancy. She gestures to her pregnant belly.

Mateo offers her a soft smile. "When is the little McKenzie due?"

"Three weeks. The same as Sabrina, give or take a few days."

"Shouldn't you be in the hospital or something? I mean, you're huge!" Caprice waves her arms out in front of her.

I glance at Lily, who appears startled by the insult. It's clear that Caprice's words weren't meant to be gentle or concerned.

Mateo hisses between his teeth. "Please excuse my fiancée. She doesn't always think before she speaks."

Lily offers a tight smile. "Certainly. If you'll excuse me, I see Michael." She reaches up and kisses my cheek, whispering, "Good luck."

Lily is a naturally beautiful woman, and she is even more beautiful now that she is pregnant.

"Oh, look...the wild one." Caprice glares at me from behind.

I turn and watch Emelia, Mateo's sister, approach.

"If you can't say anything nice, then keep your mouth shut," Mateo hisses between his teeth.

Obviously, there is trouble brewing between the two of them.

"Hi, Noah, Mateo." She ignores Caprice.

"Emelia, are you enjoying yourself?" I smile and offer her my arm.

Emelia is a beautiful young woman who seems

annoyed with her brother, Dante. The glares she keeps casting in his direction haven't gone unnoticed by me or him.

According to Ramon, her twin Diego is a fire-fighter in New York and couldn't get time off to come to the wedding. Neither could their brother Aiden, who is somewhere in Europe on the Formula One circuit. The family is full of athletes, including Mateo, a wide receiver for the Dallas Cowboys, and Kasey, a right winger for the New York Rangers.

"I'm enjoying myself just fine, thank you, Noah." Her eyes narrow as she glances at her brother's fiancée, then meets Mateo's stare. "You and Noah are wanted over there for a picture."

"What about me?" Caprice asks, obviously not wanting to be left out.

"Unless you've had a sex change operation and now have a penis, you're not wanted," Emelia bluntly points out. She smiles. "It's the bride and groom with all the men."

She winks at me before walking off as quickly as she arrived.

I clear the lump of laughter from my throat before it bursts forth and look at Mateo. I'm pleased to see that he also finds his sister amusing. "Shall we?"

I won't be long." Mateo untangles himself from a

disgruntled Caprice and walks away without looking back at her.

I step in line beside him and hear him let out a soft sigh.

"Exhausting," I comment.

He pauses. "Yeah."

That one word says it all. After our brief conversation upon my arrival and hearing about him, I hope he gets rid of her soon, before she really drains him.

Caprice is an attractive woman with a tall, slim body; perfectly smooth skin; and perfectly proportioned features, but she has a mouth like a viper. She seems to have a mean streak, too. I don't understand why she's so hostile when she hasn't even met any of us. Surely, she'd want to be the loving fiancée and show support to be accepted. Not likely, though!

At least my problems don't involve such a woman.

The minute Mateo and I catch the photographer's eye, he directs us to the group that has already gotten situated.

I'm unsure where I should stand, though. I can't see Ramon, and although I'm with him and my sister is a McKenzie, I'm not related to them. This begs the question: Should I be in it?

As I'm propelled forward, I immediately realize

it's Ramon doing the propelling. "You're with me," he tells me, not asks, and I like it.

It's not him publicly claiming me, but he's showing me that he considers me part of his family. Ramon obviously doesn't care if people talk, even though there are only a few people around who don't know about us.

But whatever!

It feels good to have his hand wrapped tightly around my arm, keeping me with him.

"I wish my father would let everyone get on with what they're supposed to be doing," Ramon groans. "He can't stand someone else doing something on his land without his involvement."

"Your father isn't one to sit back and relax. You know that."

"Yeah, but it gets annoying when he drags me into it every time I try to see you." He glances at me before looking away again. "If I didn't know better, I'd say he was trying to keep us apart, but that isn't my dad. There's no way he's doing that after what he said when we told him about us." He sighs and glances toward where his dad is standing. "I don't know why, but it just seems that way."

Ramon shakes his head and smiles when he turns to face me. "I'm with you now," he whispers in my ear, sending shivers down my spine. "Let's get up here," he says, indicating the fence. "Before my mom starts shouting orders."

I straddle the fence with the others. I'm behind Ramon as he climbs up, and the view leaves me wanting more, wanting to touch what's mine because he is mine. He's mine, and I'm his. I just wish being together wasn't so damn complicated.

Ramon steadies himself and looks back at me. The fire in his eyes nearly makes me fall from the fence flat on my face.

Ruben clears his throat and looks up at us, grinning. "You two ready?"

I laugh when Ramon gives him the finger.

Brotherly love at its finest!

We both straighten up and let the photographer get on with his job. The sooner he finishes, the sooner I can drag Ramon off somewhere for a quick kiss, even if only.

The way the photographer has us positioned will surely produce an amazing keepsake. Lucien, Michael, and their father, Elias; Sebastian; Ramon; and I are positioned with our right legs over the recently painted white fence, and the bride and groom are in front of us. A few shots later, the photographer signals for Emelia, Dante, and Mateo to join us.

A few minutes later, we're asked to stay put while Pippa, Lily, Sabrina, and Carla join the group. After some reshuffling, more photos are taken.

I've never liked having my picture taken and have always shied away from it. But now, I realize how much these photos will mean to Ruben and Rosie in the future. It would be nice to have something like this to look back on with Ramon.

I focus sharply on Ramon as his hand lands on my thigh and raise a brow in question.

"Me. You. Barn. Now."

Before I can respond, he jumps down from the fence, avoiding his father as he dashes off.

I jump down and catch Carla's gaze. They're filled with amusement as she watches me. I move toward her, pinch her straight out of Sebastian's arms, and wrap her up in mine. "I love you, sis." I kiss the top of her head and look into her searching eyes.

"I love you, too." Her eyes fill with unshed tears, which I wipe away with my thumb.

"I'm here to stay. Stop worrying." I kiss her forehead and smirk at Sebastian over her head.

He's eager to get his hands back on his wife. If I weren't so eager to see Ramon, I'd hold on to her longer to tease my brother-in-law. But my man is waiting.

"I have somewhere to be."

"So I heard." She smirks.

I grin, pass her back to her husband, and ignore the snickers coming from the two of them as I walk toward the barn.

12

Ramon

I PACE BACK AND FORTH IN THE BARN, FRUSTRATED BY the day I'm having. At every turn, someone pulls me in a different direction. That's what it's been like for a while now, being the youngest without a partner. Now that I have Noah, though, my family is going to have to give. Even if my dad seems upset today about my relationship, if he wants me to stay with the family, he'll have to get over his hang-up.

When I hear footsteps approaching, I turn toward the door and feel a huge weight lift from my shoulders when Noah slips inside.

I grab his hand and pull him toward the back, toward the small office. I don't want anyone to catch us because we're about to have sex, although I suspect it won't last very long.

My dick has been sensitive all day long with Noah looking so handsome in his suit. But, truthfully, it's the fit of his slacks that has been getting to me. He has a mighty fine ass.

I slam the office door shut and aggressively shove Noah up against it. I immediately unbutton his vest, and quickly remove his vest and morning coat, throwing them onto the desk.

Mere inches from his mouth, I admit, "I've wanted my hands on you all day. I can't wait any longer." I clasp his head in my hands, and before he can take his next breath, I kiss him.

Noah groans, and his groan is trapped between us as our tongues touch and fight to take control of the kiss. Passion with Noah is unlike anything I've ever experienced. It's a fire that consumes us, shifting to a liquid warmth that is as fulfilling as it is comforting.

Our hunger knows no bounds as our mouths stay locked together, our tongues entwining and our teeth bumping.

Noah's hands squeeze my ass before pulling me flush against him. Our cocks are hard as fuck as they rub together, but there's too much material between us.

I force my mouth away, inhale, and catch my breath when I feel Noah's hand slip to the front of my slacks. He slides the zipper down and pops the button.

His fingers search and find. He wraps them around my throbbing erection, then shoves my slacks and underwear down past my hips. My eyes roll back in pleasure as his thumb caresses the bulging head and his finger rubs along the slit, releasing more pre-cum in excitement.

"Does Sylvia make you feel like this?"

It takes a minute for my lust-filled brain to register his words. When it does, I answer, "Fuck no. Where's this coming from?" I think I know, but I need him to tell me.

Not wanting to have this conversation with his hand on my dick, I knock it away. I hitch my shorts and slacks up; my frustration is clear on my face.

Why does he have to start this now, when I know he was just as involved as I was? This is so fucking annoying.

"Don't get defensive. I saw you outside with her." He holds his hands up as I try to interrupt. "I know you went to talk to her, but you kept putting your hands all over her."

He's jealous!

Smiling, I step into his space and kiss him.

I catch him off guard, but not for long. He clenches his fist in the back of my hair, tugs my head back, and breaks the kiss.

"You didn't answer," he growls, his breathing uneven.

"You're jealous."

"Answer me, Ramon."

"Do we really have to do this now, when we're both hard as fucking hammers?" I shove him away and tug at my hair in frustration.

"Okay, you want to know what I'm jealous of? Then I'll tell you." He's getting angrier by the second. "I'm pissed that you'll openly touch Sylvia, but not me. I'm pissed that you spent most of today with others instead of with me, your date. I'm pissed that I'm still working on your site with no end in sight and that I have to stay away from you during the week. Fuck!" He turns and drops into the chair, hanging his head as though he has too much on his shoulders to hold it up anymore.

Uncertain whether my touch would set him off again or calm him, I moved forward. When I'm standing toe-to-toe with him, I thread my fingers through his hair and lean forward slightly. His forehead drops to my chest as I continue to caress the nape of his neck.

Resting my chin on the top of his head, I admit, "I told Sylvia that I'm gay and with you. I really do consider her a friend, but only a friend. I was interested in her when we first met, but that interest fizzled out before it could even begin. As for touching her, I never gave it a thought. I'm sorry." I kiss his bent head again and smile softly into his hair when I feel his arms move around my waist, holding me close. "This whole thing with the building site and us having to live separately during the week is getting to me as well. I want it to be over. I want to be able to come home from work every night and relax with you."

Noah tilts his head up to meet my gaze. "I want that too, and I'm sorry I'm taking out all my frustration on you. It's just today and weddings. How can they commit to spending their lives together when our life is so up in the air right now?"

Leaning down, I tenderly kiss his lips. We both sigh with pleasure at the gentle touch of our lips.

"I'm also sorry for not introducing you as my boyfriend to the wedding guests. I've never really been in this situation before. It's all new." I offer a wry smile. "Just because I haven't held your hand or stolen secret kisses doesn't mean you haven't been on my mind all day. Just so you know."

Noah stands and slides against me when I refuse to give him space. "I've been thinking about you as well." He starts to blush, causing my brow to arch in question. "I should feel secure with you like I did before, but I want so much more with you now than I ever did in the past. It scares the shit out of me. With you keeping your distance, I'm on edge. It's as though I'm waiting for something big to happen, something that will make you walk away from me forever."

I swallow the lump in my throat. Noah and I need to talk more often because I had no idea he was carrying so much worry around with him. I have my fair share of worries, but hearing Noah's confession makes my heart hurt.

"Noah, when you left me, it felt like my heart had been torn out. I never want to feel like that again, so you can forget about me walking away from you. It won't happen. I promise." I pause and then ask, "Can you promise me that you'll never walk away from me again?"

"I already have. It won't happen," he adamantly agrees.

I kiss his forehead and smile against him when he

spreads his thighs wider. He pulls me closer for more intimate contact.

"One more thing: give me a break on the public displays of affection. You know I don't have a problem with it when it's just us, my parents, and my brothers. It's just with everyone else. I'm so used to hiding it that I don't even notice when I am." I offer him a wry smile. "But when the shit on the site is cleared up, you'll be claimed."

He grabs my ass and nuzzles his face into my stomach, causing my blood to thicken with desire.

"Lift your shirt."

I don't need to be told twice.

My stomach quivers as Noah's tongue licks around my navel before dipping inside. The bulge behind my zipper feels like it's about to punch straight through the fabric.

I release my hold on Noah's head and slip my hand between us. I unfasten my pants and shove them down. If I'm not careful, the excitement leaking from my cock will show through the material.

"Someone's excited," Noah observes.

I chuckle, not feeling embarrassed. "I'm always excited when I'm with you."

Noah caresses my ass while continuing to lick around my navel. My dick nudges him under the chin, sending shivers of pleasure through me. My hips have a mind of their own and start to rock. The feel of Noah's fingers searching my crease and his slow movements on my body have me throwing my head back in uncontrollable desire.

"I love having you at my mercy."

I grunt in response, but Noah's tongue tickling my sac leaves me speechless. My dick is so hard that I'm afraid it will burst if I don't get immediate relief.

"Suck me," I beg, as his tongue slowly makes its way up my length to swirl around the bulging head.

Chuckling, he suddenly takes me into his hot, wet mouth.

"Fuck," I hiss.

My hips rock as pleasure ripples along my spine and centers at the tip of my penis. But as soon as Noah starts rimming my ass with his fingers and rubbing between my legs, the ball of fire explodes. The air gets trapped in my lungs as Noah sucks me to completion—and he fucking sucks.

My legs quiver, and I'm seconds from dropping to my knees when Noah starts cleaning me up with his tongue.

I can't take it anymore, so I push him back and break our connection. "No more." I gasp.

He smirks. "Spoilsport."

I drop forward and catch myself on Noah's shoulders.

He laughs. "That good, huh?" Pushing me away slightly, he reaches down and pulls my shorts and pants up. He fastens them and shoves my shirt back inside.

From this position, I can't avoid looking at his groin, and I'm happy to see how affected he is. In fact, it looks painful as hell.

I drop to my knees, grab his hips, and pull him forward. I unfasten his pants, and Noah's hard cock springs free. I nuzzle my face into his groin; the springy hair tickles my nose.

Bang. Bang. Bang.

"What the fuck?" Noah jumps to his feet, almost knocking me off balance. "Sorry," he chuckles.

He quickly shoves his heavily swollen dick away and winces, but manages to straighten up as the door opens.

"Hello, brother," Carla drawls, leaning against the doorframe.

Noah groaned, looking slightly embarrassed as he started laughing.

"You're wicked," he says, shaking his finger at her.

"It was either me or Pippa, so I figured you'd

rather have me catch you than Ramon's mom," she chuckles, nodding toward me.

"That wouldn't have been the first time," I grumble.

Carla freezes mid-step on her way to Noah. "She hasn't."

"She has." I smirk. "But that's a story for another time," I add, seeing the curiosity on her pretty face.

"I'll get it out of Noah when he least expects it..." Her eyes sparkle with uncontained mirth. "Oh, wait! The hot tub, right?" she announces with glee.

"Ha, she's got you there," Noah says as he pulls Carla into his arms for a hug. "I presume we're wanted."

"Dinner is about to be served, and everyone was wondering where you two had gone. I volunteered to find you both when I saw you disappearing in the same direction," she says, wiggling her eyebrows.

Chuckling, Noah says, "You don't miss much, sis. You never did."

Carla has been like a sister to me since I first became involved with Noah. I love seeing the teasing imp come out in her; it reminds me of the man she married—my brother, Sebastian. They're well suited. Until he showed interest in Carla, I'd never seen my brother so besotted with a woman. She caught him hook, line, and sinker.

Noah

After a day of socializing, I just want to go back to Ramon's cabin and relax with him on the back porch. A hot tub sounds even better right now. I don't even care if we don't have sex. It'll be nice to just lie in bed and cuddle in the quiet. I only need words from Ramon when I overthink things and need reassurance.

But after our break in the barn office, I'm feeling pretty good and confident in our relationship. Even Carla interrupting us before Ramon could finish hasn't dampened my happiness.

I'm walking toward Ramon now. He's standing with his brother, Lucien, and Lucien's wife, Sabrina. My heart fills with love for Ramon.

Throughout dinner and the speeches, Ramon sat beside me. By the time the meal was finished, I'm sure everyone in the marquee—or at least those in close proximity to us—had figured out our relationship.

Nothing was said. Mateo looked surprised but shook his head with a smirk.

I felt ten feet tall knowing that Ramon had arranged the seating so that we could sit together.

After reaching his goal, Ramon turned and smiled. He gently caresses my back with his hand before removing it and continuing to talk to his brother. I didn't pay attention to what they were talking about as I looked around the marquee.

Lucien's wife, Sabrina, is just as pregnant as Lily, and she glows with happiness. Lucien is clearly in love with his wife and hardly lets her go anywhere without him.

"How are you enjoying being back in Lexington?" I ask as she smiles at me.

This is the first time I've had a chance to really talk to her. I've met Lucien a few times, but Sabrina has always been back at the apartment resting with her mom.

"To be honest, I'm missing the house in Denver. But we'll be heading back soon."

Lucien wraps his arm around her shoulders and pulls her close. "We'll be heading back out there as soon as our baby makes an appearance." He kisses Sabrina on the forehead. "I want Sabrina to have family around her when she gives birth."

"That's understandable," Ramon adds. "I'm glad you're doing that. It saves us money as well," he smirks.

"On your niece or nephew?" Lucien queries, knowing full well what Ramon meant.

"Your child will be spoiled by his or her uncles. Which you knew already." Ramon places his hand on Sabrina's belly and gently rubs it. "I can't wait to meet this one and Michael's third."

"Michael's third what?" Michael asked as he walked up.

"Baby? You're not usually so slow. What's going on?" Lucien questions him.

Michael has practically been glued to his wife's side all day, so his sudden appearance without Lily and his frown have me worried, even though he isn't my brother.

"We need to talk," Michael admits.

"I think I'll go inside and leave you four alone." Sabrina gives Lucien a quick kiss before heading toward the house.

Before she makes it inside, Lucien demands, "Talk."

"Always so impatient," Michael mumbles, still distracted. "A name has come to mind." He rubs at his temples. "Brendan Griffin."

I see Ramon flinch when the name is mentioned, but he doesn't show any other signs that it has affected him.

"Griffin Construction is the only one to benefit from the McKenzie name being dragged through the mud in the newspapers," Michael continues.

"Why now?" Lucien asks. "Why have you suddenly thought about them when the shit on the site has been happening for a while?"

"I just read the business section in Friday's paper and saw the name. I may be wrong, but they've been our competition for a while now. They've always undercut our bids, and there have been a few times when we've had to go in and finish a job they started. Obviously, that pissed them off. It's worth thinking about," Michael finishes.

"Do any of you know him?" I ask, curiously. I can't help but wonder what came over Ramon when the Griffin name was first mentioned.

"Not personally, although I think Ramon went to college with his son, Andrew," Lucien offers. "He died about eight to ten years ago."

Looking at Ramon, I realize there's more going on than he wants made public. He makes eye contact with me, but then tries to look anywhere but at me. His eyes find me again.

I'm on the verge of questioning him further, but I hold back. They can wait until we're alone because I sense that he doesn't want to talk in front of his brothers.

"I'll go talk to him. Try to get a feel for whether you're on the right track," Ramon says, running his hands through his hair. "I'll get Jackie to make an appointment tomorrow." He looks at me. "We're going to say our goodbyes. I'll let you know the outcome of the meeting."

"Let me know the time, and I'll come with you," Lucien offers.

Ramon looks surprised but hides it quickly. "Don't worry about it. I can handle Griffin."

Lucien looks at his younger brother as if he can see straight through him, but he agrees. "Okay, but call me if you change your mind."

Ramon smirks. "I'm not five, Lucien."

Lucien grinned. "I know," he sighs.

"God, we're outta here."

13

Ramon

THE WALK BACK TO MY CABIN WAS SILENT. I KNEW Noah wanted to ask about my reaction to hearing Brendan Griffin's name. I'm just glad he kept quiet in front of my brothers.

It wasn't so much the mention of Brendan's name as it was the mention of his son, Andrew. I went to school and college with him.

"You're thinking too much," Noah interrupted my thoughts. "We'll talk after we've showered and changed. I, for one, would love to get out of this suit and into my sweats first."

Noah always prioritizes comfort.

"I agree." I do too, but I'm also glad to put off our conversation.

There isn't much to tell, especially since I didn't know Andrew when I was with Noah. My heart still aches when I hear his name. I wasn't in love with him, but I did have strong feelings for him, and I was devastated when I found out he'd died.

"Ramon?"

I slam into Noah, not realizing that he'd stopped and turned to face me.

"Perhaps you should tell me now and get it all out. I hate seeing you so distracted." Noah reaches out and starts to massage my tense shoulders.

Having his hands on me feels amazing and helps me relax. That's why I blurt out, "Andrew was the first guy I slept with."

Shit.

Keeping the groan inside at my callous statement, I risk looking up at Noah, whose hands have stilled on my shoulders.

He's thinking, letting the words roll around in his head.

"Let's go sit on the porch," I suggest. "It isn't a long story."

Maybe after I tell it, we can retreat inside and relax or do other things.

Climbing the porch steps with my tired legs, I walk over to a rocking chair and sit down. I'm glad I let my mom talk me into buying rocking chairs for the porch. Most of the time, I curse them when I trip over one of the legs.

Noah joins me, and I try to look relaxed, but I'm anything but. It's been a long time since I've thought about Andrew. He'd pop into my mind every now and then, but since I met Noah, he's been scarce.

"Talk to me, Ramon."

I sigh and tell Noah about Andrew: "We were friends all through school and college. Best friends, I guess, although we didn't hang out at each other's houses much. We kind of just hung out at school, and then in bars after college."

One drunken night, things came to a head. One thing led to another, and in the morning, we woke up naked. The events of the night before came rushing back too quickly for me to comprehend. I tried to get up, but Andrew wouldn't let me until we talked. He's the one who made me realize that I prefer a dick to a pussy," I chuckle. "He was relentless and wouldn't let me walk away."

Glancing at Noah, I see his fists clenched on the arms of the rocking chair. I don't like that I'm causing his tension.

Fearing rejection, I slide my hand into his and bring his hand up to my lips to caress it. I shift in the rocker and rest his palm against my thigh, keeping my fingers entwined with his. His not pulling away gives me the courage to carry on.

"I dated women recklessly after that night because what happened terrified me. Andrew's feelings for me were much stronger than mine for him. To me, he was just a friend. Yes, I probably loved him, but not in the way he wanted or needed. Between women, I'd choose Andrew. I'm not proud of that. Because of my actions, Andrew thought I would eventually need only him. He eventually left me alone and started sleeping with anyone who offered. The fact that I didn't get jealous only made things worse. He died in a car accident. Drunk driving. Luckily, he didn't take anyone else with him. Apparently, his father had found out about his sexual orientation, and they'd gotten into a huge argument about it. Brendan had also found out about Andrew's feelings for me, and I became the one to blame for his drinking and subsequent death.

I settle into the rocker and close my eyes. Noah hasn't commented, but he still has his hand on my thigh.

"That's the first time I've spoken about Andrew.

The first time I've trusted anyone with that story." I need Noah to realize just how much I trust and need him.

Noah clears his throat. "I did wonder whether you two had been together. But I wasn't expecting all that. Do you think your involvement with his son has him gunning for the McKenzies? Could he be causing the trouble on the site because he knows you're in charge of it? There hasn't been any trouble elsewhere, has there?"

I nod. "But it's been so long. I'm not sure why he would start up now."

Noah nods in agreement, then says, "Now that I know your relationship with his son, it makes sense that he isn't gunning for the McKenzies but for one in particular. We need to pay him a visit, let him know we're on to him, and tell him that if he wants to keep his business, he needs to let the ghosts rest. What he's doing could result in criminal charges if someone gets seriously hurt. We need to point that out to him."

"I hear you. I'll go see him and lay it all out. I'm so damn tired today. All I want is to shower and then curl up in bed with you," I admit.

"I like that idea. I'll shower first so I can read some more of my book while you shower." He smirks. "You take a while."

I laugh. "Only when I'm thinking of you and need to take the edge off."

Noah's grin couldn't get any wider. "Is that a fact?"

"Yeah, but not tonight. I need to touch you and show you just how much you're mine. I want you to know that everything between us is different from anything before." I admit this, already feeling my arousal grow.

Noah stood and pulled me up with him. He places his hand on my jaw covered in whiskers and slowly presses his lips to mine. The kiss ends before it even begins, but I don't miss the tenderness behind it. I want the rest of my life with Noah to be like this— tenderness when needed and hard-as-fuck passion in between.

"I need a shower," he whispers against my lips.

With a slight tug on my hand, he pulls me inside the cabin.

Noah

I'm lying in bed reading a book that Carla told me was good and hot. There was a twinkle in her eye when she said "hot," so, of course, I swiped it from her once she had finished it.

I've read about three pages, and I reckon I have about five more minutes before Ramon shows up. The image of him masturbating in the shower to take the edge off is stuck in my head. Sometimes I wish he'd keep his mouth shut so I wouldn't have these images in my head.

When I hear the shower switch off, I continue reading about Morgan DeLuca and Race True in a particularly steamy scene that has me engrossed.

I only shift the book when I feel the bed dip. I watch as a naked Ramon slides up the bed toward me.

"Good book?" he asks, settling next to me.

"I'm not into women, but this is one fucking hot book." I throw the covers off my lap. "It has me hard as fuck."

Ramon smirks and pushes my arm to allow him to read with me.

After a few minutes, he makes a gurgling noise in the back of his throat. "What's this called?"

"Sinful Intent. My sister's a fan of the author, Chelle Bliss. Why?"

Ramon turns and rubs his erection against my hip. "Because," he whispers into my ear, sending shivers down my spine, "I think we need to get the rest of her books."

With that, he takes the book from my hands, climbs on top of me, and settles in. He uses his feet to push the covers off the bed, and suddenly, there's nothing between us.

Ramon slowly moves up my body until he can rest his elbows on either side of my head. He looks down into my eyes and says, "I love you."

I'm so choked up with unshed tears that I have to blink them back. The love I see in his eyes and hear in his voice catches in my throat, preventing me from telling him what I want to say. His soft smile presses against my lips, and he tastes like happiness. His tongue presses forward, and as soon as it meets mine, I can't hold back any longer.

One of my hands slides into Ramon's hair, and with a slight tug, he growls and deepens the kiss. I caress his ass with my other hand until I need more and press him against me. His dick twitches against my belly, causing a similar ache in mine, which rests along his groin.

Ramon trails his mouth along my jaw, his teeth scraping my skin as I try to catch my breath. It's soon sucked out of me when he moves slightly and wraps his hand around my leaking shaft.

He straddles me, and I feel him smile against my chest as he works his way toward my nipples, which beg for his tongue.

His hand squeezes my thickness, and his thumb rubs the sensitive nerves around the mushroom head. My legs shake with need. I want to take over and flip Ramon onto his back, but I'm curious to see what he's going to do next, so I play the good boy, albeit a dirty one.

I put both my hands on Ramon's firm ass. When he bites down on a nipple, I grip him so hard that I spread him wide.

Ramon growls, pushing the head of his cock between my thighs and along my sac. The head of his thick shaft presses against my taint—my favorite spot between my balls and my ass. My eyes roll back in my head as my dick jerks and leaks in Ramon's hand.

"God, I'm trying to go slow," Ramon says, closing his eyes. Keeping my dick in one hand, he uses the other to wrap around his own cock. His eyes snap open as he guides the bulging head of his cock to that special spot and rubs it.

"Fuck...fuck." I grip his ass, pulling him closer and letting my fingers rub around the rim of his asshole.

"I'm going to come if you keep doing that," I groan.

"You're not the only one."

I've wanted Ramon all day, and having him naked and horny in my hands is driving me crazy with lust.

"I need to be inside you," Ramon says.

The loss of his hand nearly makes me weep, but his weight feels good as he leans over to open the bedside drawer.

I wrap my arms around his waist. When Ramon meets my gaze, I admit, "I love you."

He swallows a few times, and I'm glad I waited to say those words tonight. I wanted them to mean more than just returning his sentiment. From the look on his face, I did.

He drops his forehead to mine. "Thank you," he whispers before slowly sliding down my body and settling on his knees between my spread thighs.

"You have a beautiful cock," I chuckle, but it turns into a groan when his hand strokes mine from tip to base, giving my sac a slight massage.

Smirking, Ramon dips his head and swirls his tongue around my slit, lapping at the leaking crown I can't control. My legs tremble, and my belly quivers with need the more he tongues me.

I love his hair now that it's started to grow out. I grab it and press him down on me, needing more.

He loves having his hair tugged during sex, and

now is no different. As I tug, he growls and takes me deeper into his mouth.

"Fuck no," I say, quickly yanking him off me. I pant, trying to catch my breath and control the rush I'm feeling with Ramon in that position. "Inside me."

"Yes."

Ramon

Having Noah at my mercy and on edge is thrilling for me. No matter how we start, he usually takes over quickly. The fact that he's fighting his instincts speaks volumes.

I wanted to draw tonight out, but I think it's been drawn out enough.

I reach across the bed for the bottle of lube and condom that I dropped when Noah declared his love. I quickly suit up. I flip the cap and pour some lube onto my hand, wrapping it around my dick.

My eyes nearly roll back in my head at the feel of my dick being stroked, even if it is by my own hand.

"When you're done playing with yourself, I'd like some attention."

I laugh at Noah's comment.

"I'm getting to you."

"Looks like you were trying to get off."

I smirk. "I was just making sure I'm lubed up."

With a quick stroke of his cock, I pull him up onto my bent thighs, giving myself perfect access to his hole.

As I squirt more lube into my hand, Noah gasps as I rim him and slip a finger inside.

Noah groans and grabs his dick.

I knock his hand away and growl. "That's mine."

"Hurry up," he groans as I add another finger.

"Just fuck me, Ramon. Fuck...please."

Who am I to argue? He wants me where I need to be.

I toss the lube to the floor and guide my hard-as-fuck cock to Noah's ass. I slowly start to push through the wall of muscle. Sweat breaks out on my brow from the intense pleasure I feel as I enter him. He's so tight, and with the lube, he's warm and wet, too. Having him surround me sends my orgasm spiraling through me, but I bite it back and breathe to gain control.

Clenching my teeth, I'm finally all the way in. His balls are tight and heavy against me, and his dick lies swollen against his stomach, looking painful.

I rub the liquid from my finger over his stomach, teasing him further by tracing the length of his shaft to his balls.

"Move," Noah grinds out between his teeth. "Please."

His hands slide along my thighs, gripping my hips, as he urges me to move on him.

Ending the tease, I slide out and slam back inside.

Noah throws his head back, groaning in pleasure. However, he nearly shoots off the bed when I change the angle of my thrusts, hitting his gland with each downward thrust.

My own release is creeping up on me, and I'm more excited than ever with Noah under me. With his ass undulating around my thick, hard shaft, I know my release is going to hurt.

The fire has started to roar through my blood and is now centered in my balls. Very slowly, it starts to trickle outward.

"No," I hiss between my teeth, ducking and sucking the head of Noah's dick into my mouth. I take as much as I can, feeling his ass tighten and strangle my dick in a vise-like grip as he releases in my mouth.

I can't hold off any longer. His cock drops from my mouth as I roar through my own release. The pleasure doesn't stop; my hips pump slowly as the ripples in Noah's ass drag more cum out of my dick.

Finally slowing my hips, I glance down and realize that Noah came just as hard. The small amount I took in my mouth pales in comparison to what's on his belly. It's fucking everywhere.

I chuckle, run my finger through it, and watch as Noah's eyes darken.

"Don't get any ideas. That took everything out of me," I say.

"I might be aroused, but I'm too exhausted to do anything about it."

I slowly withdraw from Noah and collapse on top of him. "You felt so fucking good," I mumble, rubbing my spent dick against his. The jizz sticks to us, but I don't care.

Noah's arms wrap around me, holding me tight before he kisses my brow.

This is home. It's not just about sex, but honestly, I've never experienced a connection or heat like that before. I know this sex is different because we love each other. I've certainly never experienced it before, and I doubt Noah has either.

Tomorrow is a new day, and I'm more determined than ever to solve the problem at the site because I no longer want Noah to sleep anywhere but in my bed with me.

14

Ramon

AFTER LAST NIGHT'S TENDER LOVEMAKING, I FEEL MORE confident about dealing with Brendan Griffin. There's no reason he should bother me, but he does.

We've crossed paths before but haven't spoken much since Andrew died. Every time I see him, he reminds me of Andrew. Yes, I feel guilty for not being able to reciprocate Andrew's feelings for me. In reality, though, there is nothing for me to feel guilty about. I hadn't seen Andrew for months when he got drunk and got behind the wheel. He'd tried to get in touch with me before the accident, but I was evasive.

I want to believe that Griffin isn't behind anything

that's going on, but my heart knows that Michael is right. I only wish I'd thought of Griffin sooner. If something isn't done, someone is going to get seriously hurt. With that thought in mind, I enter the ground floor office of Griffin Construction.

His office resembles the McKenzie office in downtown Lexington. It has the same modern look with floor-to-ceiling windows. There's lots of glass, chrome, and white walls with murals that he no doubt paid a fortune to have painted especially for his office.

It's not what I expected. A long time ago, I went home with Andrew when his parents were on vacation. Their home was Victorian, and the pieces on display matched the time period.

But looking around now, I can't help but wonder why his office is so different from his home.

The sound of a throat being cleared pulls my gaze to a dark-haired woman sitting behind a chrome-and-glass desk. She's groomed as you'd expect of a personal assistant. Her dark hair is piled in a neat bun on top of her head. The makeup she's wearing is flawless, as is the button-down blouse she's wearing. She's in her late twenties, but she looks too young for her clothing style. But who am I to complain?

Her raised eyebrow tells me she knows exactly what I was doing and that she doesn't find it amusing.

"I'm sorry," I begin, offering an apology. "I see Brendan is around."

"He's busy," she interrupts before I can say another word.

"I have a feeling he'll make time for me. Tell him Ramon McKenzie is here to see him."

Her eyes widen in surprise, and she pushes away from the desk. "One moment."

She stands with her back ramrod straight before quickly disappearing, her high heels clicking as she walks.

The sound reminds me of a clock counting down the seconds, making me wonder when I'll get out of this place. Feeling uncomfortable, I fuss with the collar of my shirt, which feels like a noose tightening around my neck and choking me.

When I hear the door to Brendan's office open, I quickly straighten up and make sure I look relaxed before turning to face whoever has just appeared.

It's him—an older version of Andrew. Why am I only seeing this now? Brendan has aged a lot over the years, though, and he looks like he has a darkness hanging over him.

"I thought you'd be knocking on my door before long." Brendan turns and heads back into his office.

I follow.

When I close the door behind me, I'm taken aback. His office is what I expected the entire company to look like—Victorian, such a contrast to the reception area.

"You better take a seat," Brendan says, sounding forced.

"I will, thank you." I take the seat he offers, and while we size each other up, I decide that the direct approach is best. I open my mouth to speak, but Brendan interrupts me.

"This is an unexpected visit. It's been nine years and four months since Andrew died, and this is the first time you've visited me."

He's trying to rattle me, which makes me wonder what kind of reception I would have received if I had asked Jackie to set up an appointment for me. I'd decided this morning that a surprise visit would catch him off guard.

His bitterness has lasted a long time. I've always wondered about the night Andrew was drinking and ended up driving for the last time. Was it an argument with his father that sent him spiraling out of control?

"This isn't a social call," I say angrily. "Why are you coming after me?"

His eyes dart away before he hides his reaction to my words.

So Michael was right.

"You do realize that if someone is injured, or worse, killed, you'll face charges—possibly murder charges?" All I'll have to do is point the finger at you, and they'll pick apart every aspect of your business, including your financial records. They'll trace every dollar you've spent in recent years. Why the hell would you risk all that you've built just to cause trouble for me?"

I know he blames me for Andrew being gay. Apparently, if it weren't for me, Andrew would be happily married with a couple of kids. That isn't true, and we both know it.

"You don't know what you're talking about," he sneers.

"Oh, I know good and well what I'm talking about. People talk," I bluff. "This is your one and only warning to leave McKenzie alone before you get someone killed and lose everything when you wind up in prison. I'm telling you now: If someone gets injured because of something you planned, my family won't stop until you're behind bars. Legally."

I hate this. I hate that I'm sitting here threatening another businessman, knowing he's trying to shut us down for good. I'm surprised he would risk all his wealth, as well as that of his wife and daughter, to make me suffer for something I had no control over. When Andrew killed himself, I hadn't seen him for over seven months. That is one of the reasons I feel guilty about his death. Maybe if I had been around, I could have prevented it. Maybe I could have prevented him from getting behind the wheel that fateful night. Maybe he would have had someone to talk to about his dad, but I can't let the "maybes" weigh me down. I stopped thinking along those lines a long time ago because it wouldn't have changed the outcome. Andrew still lost his life.

Brendan still hasn't said anything. He's sitting behind his large mahogany desk, lost in his thoughts.

"What would happen if your family knew you were gay?" Brendan suddenly asks. I have no clue what he's leading up to.

"My family knows I'm gay and fully supports me."

He flinches as though he's been struck by my honest reply. This is telling.

"You knew Andrew was gay," I continue, "but you didn't support him, did you? You tried to make him someone he wasn't, which is why he turned to drugs and alcohol. It was your fault, wasn't it? Did you have an argument? Did you call him names? Did you try to bully him into liking girls? What was it?" I quickly stood and rested my palms on his desk, leaning closer to the man responsible for destroying his own son. I have no sympathy.

"You need to leave." He matches my stance.

"I'm not leaving until you tell me that whatever you have planned isn't going ahead. We're both businessmen, and there's enough room in Lexington for our companies to coexist. You know that."

He nods. "Leave."

I clench my fists, not believing he'll back off, but knowing I have no choice.

"I'll leave... for now. But if anything else happens, it won't be me knocking on your door; it'll be the cops."

He smiles. "They won't touch me," he says confidently.

"Oh, you won't know the ones knocking on your door. I can assure you of that."

With my parting shot made, I turn and walk out of his office. I feel like slamming the door, but I manage to hold my anger in check.

I can't help but feel like I've missed something, though I have no idea what. It's a nagging feeling at the back of my mind. Everything is probably okay, and I'm going to chalk it up to my frustration with the whole situation.

My family is amazing, and I seriously don't know what I would do without them.

I relax into the seat of my car, inhaling deeply as I close my eyes. After all these years, I can't believe that Brendan would risk it all for what he considers revenge.

I feel drained and can't wait to return to the site for a glimpse of Noah. That's all I'll get. A glimpse.

Wanting to get away from here, I start the engine and pull out of my parking space to head back to the site, to see Noah again.

I'm going to give him two weeks, and after that, he's no longer working the site. I plan on keeping him around, though, in a more managerial position. I certainly have no plans to keep him hidden. We've worked together as a team before, and I plan on that happening again soon.

Some of the guys working for me might cause trouble when they find out about Noah and me. Not just because he's gay, but also because he was there to keep an eye on everyone. Hopefully, with a brief explanation, things will smooth out. I can hope, at least. I'm not going to worry about how they'll react when they find out about my sexual orientation. That can wait, and, quite honestly, I don't see it as any of their business. It doesn't affect my work, so it shouldn't be a factor.

The call coming through puts my thoughts on hold as I press the button to answer it hands-free.

Noah

It's hotter than usual for the beginning of October today. Many of the guys have stripped down and are using their T-shirts to wipe the sweat from their brows. I joined them about ten minutes ago, and I can already feel sweat trickling down my back.

Deciding that now is a good time to take a break in the shade, I head out of the building we're working on toward the coolers.

The building is a twelve-story apartment complex for wealthy people. The luxury bathrooms will probably cost more than I'll earn in three months.

I stop at the blue cooler that I shoved up against

the wall a few hours earlier, flip the lid, and grab a bottle of water.

I unscrew the cap and guzzle nearly half the bottle when I hear a whistle from the side.

I turn and inwardly cringe when I see Jackie walking closer. She's pretty, but she's a piranha. Her curvy body would attract anyone with a pulse if she weren't so aggressive.

Until Ramon told me about her, I would have said that guys were knocking at her door all the time. Apparently, though, she turns nearly everyone away because she won't settle for anyone unless they're loaded. I know the McKenzies are fed up with her, which is why she's working in the site office. Given her personality, I presume she had a hard start in life, which is why she's looking for security now.

As I watch her eyes settle on my naked chest, I hold the smile in. She's certainly on the wrong track with me. Not only because I'm one hundred percent gay, but also because I'm not rich.

"You look hot," she drawls, her eyes on my chest as she stops within feet of me.

I decide to ignore the innuendo in her voice and finish the bottle until it's drained. "I am," I finally reply. "Did you want something?" As I ask, I hear a car engine and look up just as the car appears. Ramon pulls up outside his office.

He doesn't get out, but I can see and feel the intense look he's throwing my way.

Knowing his eyes are on me, I feel my dick thicken behind my zipper. Jackie might get the wrong idea if she notices.

Wanting to make Ramon hot and bothered, I bend over to the icebox, shove the empty bottle inside, and snap the lid in place. Out of view, I quickly adjust my belt to a looser setting. It's enough time for Ramon to watch the denim stretch over my ass. Standing up straight, I feel the denim slip now that the belt isn't as tight. As I stretch, the denim slips even further.

Jackie makes a strange noise in the back of her throat, which draws my attention.

Her mouth hangs open, and her eyes are glazed and fixed on the waist of my jeans. I glance at Ramon, who is leaning against his car with his elbows on the roof. His eyes are molten, filled with lust he's trying to hide.

After a quick glance at Jackie, he holds my gaze. "My office," he demands. With his back to me, he ascends the steps to his office and looks pained.

I smile.

He's just as affected by my little show as I am, and so is Jackie, by all appearances.

I grab my T-shirt and hold it in front of my groin to hide the evidence of my arousal. I follow Ramon inside his office, ignoring Jackie. She can think what she wants. Right now, I'm so hard for Ramon that I need to be inside him.

Lust clouds my brain the minute I walk in and see Ramon looking smug with his ass on the front of his desk, his legs crossed at the ankles, and his tie undone. He holds up two packets—a condom and lube.

I step inside, slam the door shut, and pull the deadbolt closed. As an extra precaution, I grab a chair and shove it under the door handle.

"This is going to be quick."

"Then what are you waiting for?" Ramon grabs his erection through his pants, and my head spins.

I dive forward, knock his hand away, and after a quick, hard kiss, turn him around.

I make quick work of my jeans, shoving them down my legs. I quickly rip open the condom and smooth it down my pulsing cock. Hard as steel.

I push up against Ramon. He sharply inhales, but curses when I snap open his pants to let his dick spring free. It isn't free for long, though, as my hand wraps around his hard length and pumps back and forth a few times. My thumb caresses the crown, rubbing in the pre-cum as though it's cream. He pushes into my hand as I slow my strokes before releasing him.

"Shoes and pants off. You're about to get messy."

I don't need to tell him twice. In one quick move, he takes off his shoes, pants, and shirt.

With his back to me, naked as the day he was born, I rip open the packet of lube. I apply some to my cock and some to Ramon's ass.

I waste no time stroking between his ass and slipping a finger inside. I quickly follow the first finger with another, and then another.

Ramon gasps for breath as he pumps his own dick while I align myself and slowly start to push forward. Once inside, I can't do anything but move. I can't go slow. Only fast.

I knock his hand off his dick and take hold of it, working it well in time with the pumping of my hips. My other hand rests on top of his on the desk.

I'm so fucking excited that my legs are shaking from the intense feeling running through me. Then, I feel Ramon's cock swell, causing the same reaction in mine.

He starts to groan, so I quickly cover his mouth

with my hand. As I feel him release, I drop my head to his back to smother my own groan.

His ass is so tight that, as cum shoots out of his dick, his ass spasms. This causes my dick to quiver as it's milked dry.

Both of us are spent and neither of us moves. I'm in heaven. I always am when I'm with Ramon.

I move my hand and grasp Ramon's hip, slowly withdrawing from his tight heat.

Still wrapped up in him, I move my hips enough to remove the condom.

"Ramon?"

Bang. Bang.

"Fuck," Ramon hisses. He quickly moves away and starts to pull on his clothes.

All I have to do is pull up my jeans.

"Ramon? Are you in there? I know you're in there. Where did Noah go?" Jackie continues bashing on the office door.

"Let her in."

I look at Ramon, who is dressed but needs to straighten up. "In a minute." I walk toward him, stand in his space, and place a tender kiss on his lips while straightening his hair.

He flinches away, then catches himself.

What the hell?

I freeze.

"Ramon, you have me worried," Jackie shouts through the door.

"Jackie has bad fucking timing," I say, not taking my eyes off Ramon.

He turns away first.

Clenching my jaw in anger at his rejection, I remove the chair from beneath the door and unlock it. As Jackie starts to open the door, I hear Ramon whisper, "That should never have happened."

I turn to face him and see regret written all over his face.

I'm too pissed off and upset to stay right now. "I'm leaving."

Even as I storm out of his office, I fight my instinct to turn around and go back to him. The need to know how his conversation with Griffin went this morning is killing me as I walk further away. I yank my shirt back over my head and ignore the apartment I'm supposed to be renting. I head toward the park. I need clear, open space right now. Somewhere where nobody can find me and start asking questions.

Questions like, "Why are your eyes red?" or "Do you have allergies?"

He shouldn't affect me this much, but he's my

heart, and every time he pushes me away, it feels like a knife to the chest.

My cell buzzes in my pocket. I take it out and see Ramon grinning up at me. My finger hovers over the green button, but the ringing stops before I can answer.

Then, I receive a text.

"Emelia has asked us to meet her in Poles at nine tonight."

I stare at the phone incredulously. No apology. Just a time and place to meet his cousin.

I know I'm probably being unreasonable. I also know that when he said, "It should never have happened," he meant it shouldn't have happened in his office with his staff around. I'm too sensitive and took it the wrong way. I know that now that I'm starting to calm down and think clearly. He was embarrassed at nearly being caught. The fact is, anyone would be embarrassed at nearly being caught having sex in their office.

My phone buzzes again.

"Please be there."

I quickly reply.

"Okay."

Why Emelia wants to meet at Poles is anyone's guess. It's a dance club that caters mostly to men. It's more upscale than most because the men aren't allowed to touch the women. I've met the owner once or twice at the gym he owns. He isn't one to be messed with and seems to be a savvy businessman. However, I don't think anyone who sees him working out would think so. He's like a human destroyer.

Shaking my head, I return to my thoughts about Ramon. I need to improve my working relationship with him before I ruin everything.

15

Ramon

POLAND IS A LOT DIFFERENT THAN I EXPECTED. I MEAN, a lot. I cringed when I received the text from Emelia, asking Noah and me to meet her here tonight. I also used it as a peace offering to Noah. I messed up; I didn't mean my throwaway comment the way he took it. I should have called him back to explain, but I was also upset that he automatically assumed the worst.

With a heavy sigh, I turned and continued looking around Poles. I thought there would be so much nudity that I'd be disgusted. Surprisingly, though, the women are dressed provocatively yet stylishly, which matches the ambiance of the club.

The stage, where I assume the dancers perform, is

on the right side of the bar. There is a piano and a singer on a slightly lower platform. Circular booths cover the rest of the main floor. The dim lighting creates a relaxed atmosphere, enhanced by the woman sitting beside the piano, singing a blues tune.

"Ramon, this is a surprise?"

"Yuri, it's good to see you again." He accepts my outstretched hand and gives it a firm shake. "I'm surprised."

Yuri pauses mid-drink, throws his bald head back, and roars with laughter. He's a tall, muscular guy with one hundred percent Russian blood—a great man to have on your side but lethal if you're on the wrong side of him or his family.

I've sparred in Yuri's gym—or should I say ware-house—enough times to know he wouldn't take offense at my words. He lives to surprise.

"Smeshno, moya podruga," he chuckles. "Funny, my friend."

I grin, unable to hide my amusement at his reaction.

"I like you, too."

"Yes." I hide my smile by turning away and looking around to see if I can spot Emelia.

The only reason I can think of for her being here is to piss Dante off. For some reason, the two of them were throwing daggers back and forth at Ruben's wedding.

I feel a hand on my back and turn, feeling relieved when I meet Noah's gaze. As I was about to step into his space, the sound of a throat being cleared prevented me.

I glance over my shoulder and frown at Yuri, who raises an eyebrow in question but smiles.

Shaking my head, I introduce the two and place my hand on Noah's lower back. I needed to keep him close and feel him against me.

I was a jerk earlier and shouldn't have said what I did. I knew how he would take my words, and it was a low move on my part.

Although he fucked me well, the tension I felt had still been palpable. The need to be alone was intense, which is why I blurted out those hurtful words.

Yuri barks something in Russian at a passing waitress. I have no clue what he said.

Her dark glare and abrupt "Da, nachal'nik!" causes Yuri to laugh, his eyes full of amusement at his angry waitress. I understood her: "Yes, boss."

Yuri laughs and slaps me on the back. "She'll bring your drinks. Come sit down, my friends." He led us to a booth at the back of his club that was already occupied by Emelia.

She quickly got to her feet to greet us, and my surprise showed.

"I was early," she explains, "so Yuri kindly showed me to this table." She offers Yuri a dazzling smile.

I'm not even sure she knows what she's doing to him with that smile, as she has an air of innocence about her—a "no touch" quality.

"I did not think she would want to sit out in the open," Yuri offers. "Now I must leave. I have business. Goodbye, moi druz'ya."

He disappears through a door at the back of the room.

After we take our seats, Emelia looks nervous. It can't be Noah or me who has her this way. Although we have only recently connected, Emelia is a friendly and confident person, so something must be going on with her.

Unable to watch her twitch any longer, I cover her hands with mine. "What's going on, Emelia?"

She fights back tears before looking at me. "Dante told me that I'm not allowed to travel to Denver and stay with him." She swipes at a wayward tear. "All my brothers travel. Well, my twin—although I love Diego—has a revolving door of women, so I don't want to stay with him. If I don't stay with Dante, I'll have to go home." She tugs her hands away and takes a long swallow of her drink. "I'm twenty-seven. How many twenty-seven-year-olds live with their parents?"

She has a point.

"I texted you because you're closest to my age. I figured you'd be more understanding. Plus, you're the easiest to talk to."

I feel good knowing she came to me, but I don't know how to help her. I've never been good at giving advice.

Noah leans in and, placing his palm on my thigh, saves me from answering. "Ramon's terrible at giving advice, but I'm not. First, though, tell me what was going on between you and Dante at the wedding, because I felt the daggers from where I was sitting."

I haven't given it much thought, but I've wondered once or twice what was going on.

"He's an ass, but now that I'm back from Europe, I want to spend time with him, see his church, and meet his friends. He says it's not the right place for me. How can Denver not be the right place for me? He's so infuriating. Ugh! He isn't my keeper, so nothing is stopping me from traveling to Denver on my own." She smiles, but her heartbreak slips through, and it's clear to all. "I'd travel with Dante, though."

There's certainly more to this than she's letting on.

I need to focus on the problem. It feels like I'm missing something, but Noah's caress of my thigh is distracting. It's even more distracting when he rubs his knuckles down the bulge forming behind my zipper. Thank God for dimmed lights. I'm also assuming that I'm forgiven for earlier.

I still need to explain to him why I pushed him away. I need to tell him why I felt the need to be alone instead of letting him stay and comfort me. I know he would have done so without question if I had let him. I hurt him with my words, and I need to make it right.

He really doesn't want me there, and it hurts. He's my brother. We're adults, so the age difference shouldn't matter. I mean, I can understand it years ago when I was growing up, but now he's just being an idiot."

I consider stopping Noah and his wandering hand, but I don't. I like the feel of it on my thigh; he's heightening my arousal. He's coming back to my apartment tonight. I can't let him go back to that apartment across from the site. No more. This is it.

Feeling as if a weight has lifted from my shoulders, I rest my palm on Noah's thigh and squeeze.

"He makes me feel like a teenager all over again,"

Emelia continues, oblivious to our arousing caresses under the table.

"I'm not difficult to live with, although Dante seems to think I will be. He says that he's a priest and can't have women's panties all over his home. I mean, I wasn't planning on displaying them. Besides, what about his shorts? He's not innocent either."

I choke on my drink. "Emelia, he's a priest, for God's sake."

She rolls her eyes. "I meant he's a guy, and he's going to have guy underwear lying around, so I don't see the problem with my panties."

Noah bursts out laughing. I can't help but join in. Emelia looks so disgruntled, and her talk of panties is hilarious.

Noah

I clear my throat and watch the amusement finally spread across Emelia's face. She's so cute! With her dark hair flowing down her back in soft waves and her curvy, petite frame encased in an elegant, short cocktail dress with minimal makeup, she is stunning. Yuri noticed that, too.

"Okay, well," she coughs. "I guess I know where he's coming from with that, him being a priest." But really, I'm his sister. All he has to do is announce at Mass that I'm staying with him for a short time. It's not difficult, and the problem would be solved."

She's not going to give up.

Smiling, I place my palm back on Ramon's thigh and slide it along until my knuckles graze his crotch. He still has a bulge, and as I rub over the ridged length, my own dick answers with a vengeance.

It's dangerous out in the open, but I need to remind Ramon that he needs me as well as wants me.

After calming down earlier, I decided to be more reasonable tonight, which is why I'm all over him. The relief I saw in his eyes when he saw me was worth a lot to soothe my aching heart.

Ramon keeps his hand on my thigh, resting it against my groin. He doesn't move his hand; he just teases.

He smirks because he knows this move is driving me crazy. Without missing a beat, he turns back to Emelia.

"I know where you're coming from," Ramon says. "I think you need to talk to Dante and find out if there's another reason he doesn't want you to stay with him. He might just be trying to put you off when there's a bigger issue." Ramon shrugs. "It's just a thought."

"Maybe. I hadn't really stopped to think. I'm not sure he's going to be happy when he reads the message I sent him when I arrived." She gives us a naughty grin. "I told him where I am."

This doesn't sound good.

"What did you tell him?" I ask, probably seconds before Ramon does.

Emelia grins. "I told him my location and that there are lots of sexy Russians here." Leaning closer, she whispers, "I actually asked him if he thinks they're part of the Bratva."

Ramon makes a weird noise in the back of his throat before he can speak. "He's going to lock you up and throw away the fucking key. Are you serious?"

Emelia's eyes fill with heat at Ramon's words, and I wonder at it before it disappears as quickly as it appeared, making me wonder if I imagined it.

"Yes, I am. If he thinks I'm going to get in trouble by myself, then he'll take me with him."

She has it all planned out.

Feeling Ramon's erection harden with each stroke through his jeans, I pull back. My dick is uncomfortable behind my zipper, and soon, I'm going to need more—a lot more. Having sex in Poland isn't such a good idea with Yuri owning the place. Plus, I'm too old to resort to public restrooms.

"I think we're about to have some trouble," Ramon mumbles, distracting me from thoughts of him naked.

I glance at him before following his line of sight. Dante.

"Um, he looks angrier than I thought he would," Emelia moans. "Perhaps this wasn't the best idea."

For a priest, Dante looks awfully angry.

"Ramon, Noah," he says, barely greeting them before focusing on Emelia.

"Dante," she nervously whispers.

"Emelia." He sighs and holds out his hand. She takes it and lets him pull her up from the booth. "We really need to talk."

Dante turns to us. "Thank you for taking care of her. I'll be in touch."

With those words, he pulls Emelia close and leads her out of Poles.

I turn to Ramon and smile when I realize he's already looking at me.

"I didn't mean what I said earlier," he apologizes quickly. He takes hold of my hand, entwining our fingers, and continues, "After what we did in the office, the earlier part of the day came rushing back, and I thought I wanted to be alone. I was wrong to let you think what I did. If there's ever a next time, I'll just come out with it, because I assume you'd rather have bluntness than what you got. I'm sorry."

I move closer to Ramon and kiss his cheek. "Once I'd cooled down, I realized you hadn't meant it the way it came out. Next time, I'd prefer honesty. If you need to be alone, just tell me."

He shakes his head. "That's just it. I thought I wanted to be alone, but as soon as you left, I wished you were still there. I needed you."

Part of me feels good hearing him admit that his words meant nothing, but I can't help feeling sad that he needed me and I left. I had just taken his words as gospel instead of confronting him.

"Say something." Ramon tugged on my hand.

"Let's forget about what happened after I came to your office," I smirk. "Tell me what happened when you went to see Griffin."

His eyes dim, and a tired look washes over him.

"I think he's behind it. He didn't admit it, but when I confronted him, he didn't deny anything. At the end of the day, he still blames me for Andrew's death. I think Brendan drove his own son to drink, and then his son got behind the wheel of his car that night.

He'd never been supportive of Andrew since he realized his son preferred men. I overheard some awful things during Andrew's telephone conversations with his father." Ramon releases my hand, stretches out, and places his hands behind his head as he leans back.

"I'm tired of this whole thing, but tonight it stops." He meets my gaze. "As of tonight, you are no longer living in that apartment. I don't give a fuck anymore. Why should I let him rule my life because of things I had no control over? I think we still need to be vigilant on the site, though. Hopefully, my threat of pressing charges and the possibility of losing everything will sink in, and he'll give up once and for all."

I'm not sure I heard much after Ramon said that I wouldn't be sleeping without him anymore.

"You listening?" Ramon kicked me under the table.

"Oh, yes. Especially the part about our living arrangements from now on."

He pauses, then starts to laugh. "I'm trying to have a serious conversation with you, and all you can think about is getting your dick sucked."

I smirk. "Well...if you're offering."

"Jerk," he counters. "I can't decide whether I need to call a meeting tomorrow morning before everyone starts work to inform them just how serious the consequences will be if anything does happen on the site or if I should just let everything take its course. Thoughts?"

My thoughts are X-rated, but Ramon will have to wait until we're back at the apartment to hear them.

"I think we should go home. Then, you need to have a conference call with your brothers because they'll want to know how you got along with Griffin. It might help you decide what to do about the crew tomorrow."

"Okay, we'll do that. I'm so fucking tired of all this shit."

"Me too... But I know ways to relax you." I smile softly, knowing he's imagining my hands massaging him.

"I'm up for that." Ramon strokes his length, causing an answering twitch in me.

"We need to leave and make that call." Once I'm on my feet, I wince and quickly shove my hand into my jeans to adjust myself.

"I'm sorry we're not in the same car; otherwise, I could have put my mouth to use on the way back."

"Fuck...that was unfair," I moan. He loves tormenting me. "I'm going to fuck you the minute we walk into the apartment, and you know it!"

Nothing like having the last word.

16

Noah

WORKING ON THE SITE TODAY IS KILLING ME! IT FEELS like every muscle in my body has been torn and twisted during torture. Well, it kind of has. I smile at the memory of having Ramon on his hands and knees while I fucked him. His bronzed, muscular body was taut beneath me as I pumped into his tight ass. Ramon was hard as hell, jerking himself off until I knocked his hand away and finished the job myself. He came as soon as I touched him, which made my balls ache with need and caused my dick to spasm as I came.

"Fuck." I adjust the bulge in my jeans, willing it to

deflate before it becomes obvious to the crew around me.

Ramon does that to me. He distracts me terribly, and on a construction site, I need to be focused on the present. Otherwise, accidents can happen.

Chris, one of the electricians, approaches, and I hear his distinct, heavy footsteps before I see him. His sidekick, Rick, drags his feet when he walks, and he isn't close. This makes me wonder what he's up to, because they never work alone.

Everyone on the crew had heard Ramon's words this morning, but only a few disagreed. However, Ramon's warning about taking legal action against anyone he discovers "assisting" Griffin didn't go over well. After a twenty-minute conversation, everyone seemed to calm down and realize that they had nothing to worry about as long as they minded their own business and got on with their jobs.

The old-timers, the ones who'd worked for McKenzies the longest, were offended that Ramon could think they'd do something to jeopardize their jobs. Ramon and I both knew where they were coming from and had discussed it over breakfast that morning.

There was no easy way around it. Ramon had to

make a point, regardless of whose toes he stepped on —and that's what he did.

I feel uneasy as I glance around the site. I'm not sure if anything will happen, but I can't help but worry about the guys. One of them might have a problem with Ramon—well, more of a problem than before.

During Ramon's announcement, I stood at the back as I watched for anything unusual. Nothing unusual happened, and everyone listened to Ramon. A few shuffled around when they didn't like what they heard, but other than that, nothing happened.

"Are you going to stand around all day daydreaming, or are you going to let me get past to work on that wall over there?" Chris asked.

I get the feeling he's trying to be polite, but he'd rather shove me out of the way.

"Fine. Where's Rick?"

He passes me, mumbling, and drops his toolbox when he reaches the wall he's apparently going to work on.

I'm not sure I believe that.

I'm not going to get anything done this morning.

I'm usually not so distracted, but the thought of Ramon in his office is wreaking havoc on my concentration. I'm probably acting like a five-year-old today. It's as though I have an itch that needs scratching, and knowing it can't be scratched makes it itch more.

I grin because that's damn accurate; that itch is Ramon.

"Fuck this!" I drop the hammer back into my tool belt and take the stairs down. There is an elevator, but it's enough to give me nightmares. Elevators on construction sites are temperamental at the best of times.

As I'm clearing the last set of stairs, someone yells, "Look out!" We all look up, and in a split second, I tackle a kid out of the way as two steel girders crash to the floor.

That was too fucking close for comfort. I also have no idea where the hell they came from. The steel girders for the higher floors were taken up there by crane two days ago. They're too heavy for one or even two men to maneuver without the support of a rig.

"What the fuck just happened?" Ramon yelled as he rushed through the gathering crowd.

His eyes focus on me, sitting on the floor with my foot about six inches from one of the girders. He looks momentarily stunned before quickly dashing over and hauling me to my feet.

I turn to help the shell-shocked kid up, but Ramon's brief touch of my hand makes me turn back to him.

"Are you okay?"

I nod. "Yeah. I wouldn't have been, though, but for the shouted warning."

His jaw tightens with anger and stress. "The site is closed for the day. Everyone will get paid, but for now, grab your things and clock out. Be back here tomorrow morning, unless you hear otherwise. You will be paid tomorrow unless you are called back. That means everyone." He runs his hands through his hair, and the slight tremor I see tugs at my heart. Without looking at me and amid the noise of everyone leaving, he whispers, "Follow me to my office. Now." Ramon turns and heads out of the construction mess, expecting me to follow.

I do. I'd follow him anywhere, and I hope he realizes that.

My stomach is still in knots about what nearly happened. Seconds. That's all the time we had to get out of the way.

After holding on to my guy, I plan on going back up there to figure out how they managed to fly through the air.

Ramon

I jumped up and raced to the entrance of the building with my heart in my throat when I heard the commotion from my office.

I was worried about Noah, but I was also concerned that one of my crew had been injured or worse.

I was shocked to find Noah sitting on the ground next to the child he had presumably pushed out of the way. Noah's foot was mere inches from the girders.

Even now, as I ignore Jackie and enter my office, my hands are still shaking. The fear of losing Noah tears my insides apart. I want to tear off our clothes and claim him. I need to feel him to know he's alive. I need him to claim me so that I can feel him hard and solid in my ass.

"Ramon, talk to me." Noah closes the door to give us privacy, and seconds after hearing his tool belt drop and the deadbolt slip into place, I can't hold back anymore.

In two paces, I reach him and pull him into my

arms. His arms wrap around my waist, and he holds me as tightly as I hold him.

Slowly moving my hands from behind his neck, I cup his face. While caressing his cheeks with my thumbs, I hover my lips above his before kissing him. It isn't the hard kiss of lust that we usually exchange. It's a soft kiss of love. I nearly lost him, and now I need to be tender. I want to show him how much he means to me. That's why I'm frustrated that we're in my office. Perhaps we need a new memory of being in here.

I slow the kiss down and ignore the throb at my zipper. Gently easing up on Noah, I nibble along his jaw and nip his earlobe while my hands roam over his naked chest. Noah moans and pushes his groin into me. Oh, he's ready for me.

I give him a quick kiss and pull away to quickly undo his belt and jeans. I shove them down his legs, and his beautiful cock appears—hard and thick.

"Touch me," he hisses.

"I will," I groan at the sight.

I quickly turn a chair around to face us, grab Noah, and keep him upright as I push him down into the chair.

"Umm, this feels good," Noah whispers as he strokes his dick. "It would feel better if you were down here." He points to the floor between his spread knees. His ankles aren't that far apart because his jeans are wrapped around them.

I smirk and drop to the floor. "This okay?"

"No, closer."

I keep my eyes on his cock as he strokes it, drawing more pleasure out of the bulging head. My own cock is fit to burst, but he isn't getting his hands on it right now. This, right here, right now, is about Noah.

"I want to see your cock."

"What?"

"You heard me, Ramon. I want to see your penis in person. You're teasing me with the bulge you have going on right now, but I love looking at you."

His words catch in my throat, and I find I can't refuse. I can set my own rules, though. "You don't touch my cock or my ass. This is about you."

He growls. "Do it."

I toss my shirt over my head and yank at my belt and fastenings, sighing in relief when my erection hits cool air.

"That's much better, but if you don't do something soon, I'm going to take matters into my own hands." Noah strokes his cock, keeping a tight hold on the base and his scrotum.

"Don't move," I hiss.

I caress his thighs and rub where I can reach between his legs, smiling when his cock twitches. I watch as more of his essence trickles from the slit, and then I use my tongue to taste it.

Noah catches his breath. I delight in my power over him when I feel a slight tremor in his legs. Knowing that I am doing this to him heightens my own arousal, making my dick tingle.

Needing to ease the ache between my balls, I wrap a hand around my shaft and start to fist back and forth.

Wanting more of Noah, I knock his hands away and use mine to massage his balls and cock. When I take him into my mouth, his "Fuck, fuck, Ramon" has my balls pulling up so tight that I'm afraid they're going to burst.

My hand plays with his scrotum while my fingers search between his legs for the spot that usually sends him into orbit. His whole body tenses when I find it.

I lightly stroke it with my finger while my mouth works him over. I take him deeper as his fingers slide into my hair and gently tug.

Feeling the tingles of pleasure gathering at lightning speed in my own dick, with my orgasm fast approaching, I glance up at Noah. His eyes shine with love for me.

I can't hold back any longer. I press between Noah's legs and take all of his cock into my mouth, humming around him.

His cum splashes against the back of my throat and triggers my release. I suck and massage Noah while he releases inside me and pump my own dick in a pleasurable release.

By the time we're both satisfied, Noah pulls my head from his lap, hissing, "I can't take it anymore," and seals our lips together in a brief kiss. "I can taste myself on you." He kisses me again and again and again. "I can't get enough."

I gently squeeze his scrotum, watching as Noah throws his head back and pushes into my hand. "There's no fucking way we're going again in your office."

Sad but true.

My hand is sticky as hell, not to mention Noah's jeans.

I sit back on my heels and laugh. Noah raises an eyebrow questioningly.

"My jizz hit your jeans. Sorry. I forgot they were there." I look around for my shirt, grab it, and use it to clean my dick and Noah's jeans.

I smirk. "You're truly claimed."

"Wiseass," Noah grumbles. "You feeling better now?"

"I should be asking you that question." I pull my pants back up and rummage through the small closet where I keep extra clothes. Unable to find another shirt, I pull out a T-shirt, a pair of work jeans, and my boots. I might as well make it look like a complete change.

While I'm getting dressed, I keep glancing over at Noah. I need to make sure he's really okay. He looks okay, but the frown on his face tells me that something is bothering him.

"Talk to me," I tell him as I change from my pants to the jeans. "Please." I fasten the jeans.

"What the hell happened up there today?" Those are too heavy for fewer than four people to lift, and there weren't four people up there. As far as I know, no one was above the third floor, where I'd just come from."

"So you are okay? You're fine inside and out?"

Noah quickly kisses me on the lips before taking a step back. "Yes, I promise you that I'm fine. I'm just concerned about how that happened."

I sigh in relief. "That I can handle."

Noah quickly glances at me after I respond.

"Let's go upstairs and take a look around."

He nods and starts to unlock the door, but then my cell phone starts vibrating on my desk.

"McKenzie," I answer.

"Ramon, Sabrina had a baby boy about an hour ago," Carla announces. Her voice is thick with emotion, and I'm sure she's crying and laughing at the same time. "I tried to call you earlier, but you weren't answering. I think your brothers have tried as well."

My heart sinks. "I'm sorry. I'd forgotten to turn the volume back up this morning." I mouth the news to Noah, who's waiting patiently by the door. He smiles.

"Is Sabrina doing okay? Lucien? Baby?"

Carla laughs. "Sabrina is doing well, but she's exhausted. Lucien was green and white not too long ago, but now he's wearing a grin as big as Canada. Alexander Lucien McKenzie is a beautiful seven-pound, five-ounce little boy. He has a great pair of lungs, too, as Lucien informed us. Are you going to come now or wait until tomorrow?"

I'm eager to visit my nephew, but I don't want to tire Sabrina out. "Let Lucien know we'll come visit later this afternoon."

"I will." She hangs up before any more words can be exchanged.

I grin like an idiot at Noah. "We're uncles... Alexander Lucien McKenzie."

His eyes fill with tears at my words, but he blinks them away.

I move into his space, cup his jaw with my hand, and slap a hard kiss on his mouth. "We're in this together forever, so yes, we're uncles."

"I never said otherwise," he counters, his emotion clear.

17

Ramon

NOAH AND I STILL HAVE NO CLUE HOW THE GIRDERS ended up the way they did, going from the top floor to the bottom. We've given up trying to solve the mystery, at least for the time being. Right now, we have a nephew to welcome into the world!

I have a feeling that it's going to entail more than just showing up at the hospital, if Sebastian has anything to say about it. We'll probably end up at Kenza to celebrate in style.

"You are not going out and getting your brother drunk."

Or not, with Mom's words echoing down the hallway:

"Mom, we're not teenagers anymore. We can handle the liquor. Don't worry," Sebastian tries to soothe. I could have told him to save his breath.

"Mom," I interrupted, much to Seb's relief.

"Oh, you're both finally here." She reaches up and hugs me before turning to Noah. "Your sister is with Lucien and Sabrina. Go see them." She pushes Noah in the direction I presume we need to head.

"I'll show you," Sebastian offers, moving in front of us.

"I'll see you boys on Sunday." With that, Mom disappears.

"What did you say to set her off?" I ask my brother.

"I opened my mouth before I thought better of it. She was giving me a hard time about getting Carla pregnant, so I changed the subject and ended up with a lecture about getting Lucien drunk."

"Why won't you tell her that you want to wait?" Noah asked.

I didn't know that was the reason.

"Because it's no one's business but ours." He sighed. "We want children, but for now, we're being selfish. We've decided to spend another twelve months or so on our own before we try." I just want her to myself a bit longer. I don't see what's wrong with that."

I put my hand on his shoulder as he stops at the door. "There's nothing wrong with that. I'm glad you aren't rushing into something for once. Just tell Mom so she'll stop hounding you." I grin. "She'll start on Ruben instead."

He laughs. "That's something to think about. I just wish she'd let up without us having to explain why we aren't having a baby."

"I get it. Anyway, open the door. We want to see our nephew."

Sebastian pulls the door open, and I grin. Carla is sitting beside the bed, cuddling Alexander. Sabrina is leaning back on the bed with my brother, who looks more exhausted than his wife.

As we enter, I chuckle at the scene before us. Sebastian crouches down beside his wife. Lucien just observes us with eyes that refuse to stay open.

"Who gave birth?" I ask, leaning over to kiss Sabrina's cheek. "Congratulations, beautiful mama."

"Hey, stop sweet-talking my wife," Lucien grumbles.

Noah briefly kisses Sabrina on the cheek, then kisses his sister and crouches down to look at the baby in her arms.

I turn back to Sabrina.

She smiles and snuggles more against her husband. "We're both tired, but I'm high from all the drugs they gave me. I think Lucien is ready to sleep for a week."

"I'll sleep when you're both home with me."

"Now, Lucien, you need to rest," Sabrina admonishes.

My brother rolls his eyes, and Sabrina notices. Her frown is short-lived, though, as he kisses his way out of trouble.

I ignore the cuddling duo on the bed and shove Sebastian out of the way so I can see my nephew.

He's like any other baby—small. I'm terrified to hold babies. I'm always afraid that I'll drop the little bundle. I never do, but they are so damn small!

"Here, Ramon, take him," Carla offers. Sebastian, knowing my fear, starts laughing.

Carla's scowl soon shuts him up, or rather, dims the noise.

"Let me up, guys."

Noah helps Carla up from the chair. With her eyes, she directs me into the chair she just vacated. "Now, hold your nephew." She grins.

Alexander is placed in my arms, and the air leaves my lungs. He's so precious, and I'm thrilled that

Lucien has the family he never thought possible. I take off the small white mitten from Alexander's hand and look at his wrinkled fingers. I smile in delight when he grips my offered finger. "He's perfect," I whisper, close to tears.

Noah sits on the arm of the chair next to me and slides his arm around my shoulders, caressing Alexander's head with his other hand. "Beautiful," he says, and I hear the smile in his voice.

Getting my emotions under control, I finally meet Lucien's gaze. "I don't have the words to tell you how happy I am for you."

Lucien nods, swallowing back his emotion at my words, as I turn to Sabrina. "Thank you for making my brother's life whole."

Sabrina openly wipes the tears from her face. "I love him and Alexander. They're my world."

"I know. Tell me, how has Mom been?" I ask. Sebastian snorts, and Lucien laughs.

"She forgot her own name earlier when she was here. Dad had to remind her." Sebastian shakes his head. "Come on, woman," he says, sliding his arm around Carla's waist from behind. "It's time to go." He kisses her neck and drags her toward the door.

"God, Sebastian," Lucien laughs. "Can't you wait until you get her home?"

"Nope," Seb replies with a smirk. "We'll see you all later." Sebastian opens the door to find Dante on the other side. He pauses briefly before entering.

He dashes out with Carla, not giving her time to say goodbye to anyone. Meanwhile, Dante climbs on the bed beside Sabrina.

Lucien frowns at Dante, who smirks. I get to my feet and let Noah take the chair before placing Alexander in his arms.

Noah

As I hold this sweet baby in my arms, I ignore the others in the room and enjoy the feel of him against me. He's heavy enough to feel his presence, yet he's also light and precious.

My sister looked perfect wrapped up in Alexander when we walked in, and I can't wait to be an uncle to her kids. Until then, I hadn't realized how much I wanted to be a dad—to have a son or daughter to come home to every night. Ramon and I would only be able to have a family through adoption, but I'm not even sure if that's an option for a gay couple. It's something to think about, and one day, I'll talk to Ramon about it. For now, I'm just happy he accepted me back without pushing me away. I would have deserved that, but I'm so damn relieved he didn't.

"—Sylvia," I overheard Dante say, which brought my attention back to the others in the room.

"I didn't know Eric was back." Ramon frowns and glances at me.

"What did I miss?" I need to know why Ramon looks the way he does.

Ramon offers me a wry smile. "Eric was with Dante. They bumped into Sylvia on their way in. Apparently, Eric dragged her off to talk while Dante came up here. I actually believe that Sylvia has Eric tied in knots."

"My brother almost walked into a closed door because he was distracted by Sylvia when he first saw her." Dante frowns. "It isn't like him to be so distracted by a woman, so I'm not sure how to take it."

"That's why I'm worried. He's never been in a serious relationship."

I find that hard to believe, considering he's in his thirties. "Are you sure about that?"

"Yes," Ramon, Lucien, and Dante answer together.

Okay, then!

"The thing is, I'm not sure what they have, but it isn't a relationship—at least not yet."

"Lust," Sabrina offers and shrugs when we all look at her. "Oh, come on. You're all guys; haven't you been in lust before?"

"All the time," Ramon admits.

I snicker.

Dante makes a gurgling noise in the back of his throat, and Lucien roars with laughter.

Sabrina starts to chuckle. "Well, he wasn't always a priest."

"That I wasn't," Dante agrees. "On that note, I'll leave you to it. I need to check on Eric and that young woman, but I'll be back before I leave. I need a cuddle from that little bundle."

After sitting back while they went back and forth, I finally started to laugh. "You sounded about ninety with that comment."

"Sometimes I wish I was."

I pause in thought.

Why would he wish that?

It makes no sense.

When Dante leaves, I focus on the squirming child in my arms. He's starting to wake up, as evidenced by his searching mouth.

I stand and pass him to Sabrina, who is already reaching for her child. They make a perfect picture.

I quickly grab my cell phone from my back pocket, point, and click a few pictures. One is so perfect that I message it to Lucien.

Ramon spent twenty minutes one morning programming everyone's numbers into my phone so I could always get in touch with his family.

When Lucien receives the message, his eyes widen in surprise at the photo. It shows the love between him and his wife as they cuddle their son.

"Thank you," he whispers, showing Sabrina.

Ramon slips his hand into mine, and our fingers entwine.

"We're going to give you some privacy to feed Alexander." Ramon smiles. "A beautiful name for a beautiful baby."

Lucien moves away from the bed and comes over to us. "Thanks, guys. We'll be at our parents' house on Sunday, maybe." He glances at Sabrina. "It depends on how my wife is feeling." He smiles.

"I think you should skip this Sunday and come next Sunday instead. Our family can be over-whelming at the best of times, and you guys are going to need your rest. Mom knows where you're supposed to visit, and she'll be doing that."

"That's what I told Sabrina." Lucien absently caresses Sabrina's hand as he sits on the bed.

"I guess we'll see you in a couple of weeks, if not sooner," I say, knowing Lucien will get his way.

Ramon tugs on my hand as we move toward the door.

We say our goodbyes, and before I know it, we're in the elevator, and Ramon pulls me close.

"Tonight, I want to lie in bed with you wrapped around me. No sex. Just us lying together."

I slide my fingers through his longer hair and return his embrace, relishing the change. His words go straight to my heart, where I want to keep them—and him—forever.

18

Ramon

WAKING UP WRAPPED AROUND NOAH MAKES MY HEART flutter. I've only experienced this feeling with Noah, and I'm glad it's back. This time, it's back to stay.

Last night, after visiting our new nephew, we ate takeout and then snuggled up in bed together. It felt nice to be able to relax with him. He knows all my quirks, and I know his. Sometimes I think I know what he's thinking, but then he surprises me. I love how it feels to have his naked body pressed completely against mine.

As I lie against him with the sunlight starting to breach the shutters, it's becoming increasingly difficult for me to stay unmoving.

The mere sensation of him has my morning wood twitching for closer contact, which I get when Noah shoves his ass tighter against me.

Biting back a groan, I rub his ass and hip and feel my dick surge with an overwhelming need for Noah.

Last night, we explored each other, but we didn't have sex. All we wanted was that intimate connection with each other alone. This morning, however, I need him with my heart, soul, and body.

Wanting to check Noah's readiness, I slip my hand over his hip, delighting when he gasps as my hand closes around his erection.

I gently bite his earlobe. "How long have you been awake?" I whisper.

"Not long." Noah places his hand on my hip and pulls me close.

I stroke his back and hips while grinding against his ass; my dick nestles between his cheeks, warm and snug.

"I want you." I kiss the back of his neck, moving along his shoulders. I feel him shudder under my mouth and hands.

"Then have me. I'm yours."

No sooner do the words leave Noah's mouth than my phone starts vibrating on the bedside table.

"Answer it," Noah commands.

"If I answer, this is over for the time being. You know that, right?"

"Yeah, but it could be important at this time of morning. Get it."

He's right.

I watch Noah climb out of bed and head into the bathroom while I grab my phone.

I frown when I see Sebastian's ugly mug grinning at me on the caller display. I have no idea when the fuck he set that picture as his profile.

Shutting off the noise, I growl, "Everything okay?" as I rub my temples.

"Why do babies appear at night?" He grumbles.

"What the hell are you talking about?"

"Lily."

He's giving me a headache.

"Look, I haven't had coffee yet, and I have no idea what you're trying to tell me, so just get to the point."

"Well, look who woke up grumpy," he complains. "Lily had her baby during the night."

I smile at his words.

"Mom just called and told me to call everyone so she could go see her new granddaughter. I'm not sure why she couldn't wait a few extra hours."

I chuckle. "Because she's excited, and she expects you to be as well, you idiot."

"I am."

"Stop whining and tell me about Lily and the baby." I lean back against my fluffy pillow.

"Sirena Louise McKenzie was born about an hour ago, and both mom and baby are doing fine." Not sure about Michael, though. From Mom's description, he looked as bad as Lucien did."

It's another little girl. I wonder if she'll look like her siblings?

"We'll go by later. Are they in the same hospital as Sabrina?"

"Yeah." He yawns. "I'm going back to bed with my wife. Catch you later."

After hanging up, I notice Noah, already dressed for his day on the site, smiling at me. He's obviously heard my conversation about the new baby. I add, "Sirena Louise was born about an hour ago, and both are doing fine."

"Uncles again."

I nod, the new baby temporarily forgotten.

His jeans hang loosely on his hips, and he isn't wearing a belt. His T-shirt fits him like a glove, and the pinpricks of his nipples show through it.

"If you keep looking at me like that, I'm going to climb back into bed with you and you'll miss your meeting."

Hearing Noah mention my meeting, I glance at the clock on the wall beneath the TV.

Fuck!

"I'll go start the coffee," Noah offers, and he disappears.

I smile because I'm not blind—I noticed the large bulge behind his zipper.

Sighing, I reveal my own as I quickly go through my morning routine, desperate to join Noah in the kitchen.

It doesn't take me long to finish getting ready. Once I'm dressed in dark gray pants, a pale gray shirt, and loafers, I let the tie dangle around my neck as I head out to find Noah.

He makes me stop at the edge of the kitchen, where I see breakfast laid out on the table: bagels, cream cheese, jelly, coffee, and juice.

"What?" he asks, blushing.

I don't think I could smile any wider. I move over to him and cup the back of his head as he tips his face up to mine. Leaning down, I kiss his beautiful lips. "Thank you."

I take my seat opposite him and sip the coffee before spreading cream cheese onto the seeded bagel. I'm not too health conscious and can eat pretty much anything at any time of day, so I dig in.

Having Noah prepare this for me brings a smile to my face.

"I don't think I want anyone else to know about the security cameras that were installed overnight."

Noah nods in agreement, his mouth filled with food.

I had initially intended to let everyone know about the cameras in the hope that nothing else would happen. However, as Noah said, if they know they're there, then what's to stop them from taking them out first? After some discussion, I decide to try the secretive route first and see what happens.

Nothing seemed amiss when we checked the floor from which the girders had fallen, which begs the question: How the hell did they fall to the ground floor?

Frowning, I suggest, "See how it goes, and try not to worry too much. I'll get through my meeting, and then we can talk about hiring security guards."

"You think that's a good idea? Having men traipse about the site who don't know anything about the construction process?" Noah makes a good point.

After finishing chewing a piece of the toasted treat, I answer, "It's one way to keep everyone safe, but you do have a point about their safety. If I knew how else to sort this out, I would do it. I thought going directly to Griffin would stop everything, but the falling girders were more serious than anything before. Let's see what's going on today and take it from there. I don't want to fall behind schedule if we can help it."

"I hear you. You know where I'll be if you need me." He winks.

I chuckle and finish my bagel. "Thanks for breakfast." I stand up and quickly clean the dirty dishes and put everything else away before meeting Noah by the front door.

We stand side by side and look into the hall mirror. I'm dressed for my meeting, and Noah is dressed for manual labor. Inside, we're the same, but outside, we're so different. When we first met, though, I was dressed similarly to Noah, in jeans and work boots. I prefer to work alongside the men, and I never ask them to do a job that I wouldn't be willing to do myself. That's why I work as a site manager instead of at the McKenzie building in downtown Lexington. Seeing Noah dressed as he is today, though, is making my head spin. All I want is to rip off my pants and shirt before replacing them with jeans and a T-shirt.

"What are you thinking?" Noah turns me to face him and fastens my tie. It's something I hate doing.

"I'm thinking about how much I'd love to wear jeans and work by your side all day instead of attending a meeting and catching up on paperwork." I smile and lean forward to steal a quick kiss.

The quick kiss turns into anything but as Noah seals his mouth over mine, and my breath catches in my throat.

He tastes of Colombian coffee and that unique taste that is completely Noah.

The kiss stays gentle. By the time he pulls away, our breathing is uneven, and I'm fighting to not finish what we started in the bedroom.

"Later," he says, pushing me away. "You have a meeting."

I growl, wanting to forget our commitments and stay here.

Noah laughs. "Let's get things settled, and then we can take a vacation. Just you and me. Somewhere without cell phones, girders, babies being born, or people bugging us at all hours. It'll be just us."

I sure as fuck like the sound of that." I slam my lips down on his in a kiss that is much too brief. "Let's go."

Noah

Since Ramon was away at a meeting most of the morning, I was able to concentrate and got more work done than I have all week. Now that he's been back for a couple of hours, my concentration is shot to hell again. I shouldn't find it so difficult to focus, but damn if I don't.

I've seen Jackie go back and forth between her office and Ramon's so many times that my head is spinning. Even from the fifth floor, I can see the frustration on Ramon's face whenever he looks out. All the windows and blinds in his office are open, giving me a perfect view. No doubt he'll have a story about her when we get home tonight. I hate not knowing things, so his day with Jackie will come up in conversation.

Every now and then, I check around me to make sure no one who shouldn't be here is here, and so far, so good. Still, it makes me feel uneasy being up here. The others are working below, which is one reason I chose to start laying the groundwork for the fifth floor.

Most of this floor is exposed to the elements, so the wind whips around me. It's unsafe to be up here without a harness attached to one of the safety hooks.

I find them damn inconvenient, but while working alone and away from the edge, I don't see the need for them. Ramon wouldn't see it like that, but what the hell.

I find it easier to work alone, and the quiet lets me think. Lately, I've been thinking a lot. About anything and everything, but mainly my future. Every time I think about that, Ramon is always in the picture. Until we visited Sabrina in the hospital and I held Alexander, I'd never considered having children of my own. I'm not sure if adoption is even an option for us since we're a gay couple.

I sigh. What am I thinking? Ramon has never mentioned marriage or kids. He's talked about spending forever together, and I guess I should have asked him what he meant by that so we were both on the same page about our relationship.

What's stopping you from mentioning it?

I hate my conscience sometimes, but it's right. Why can't I bring up the conversation? For all I know, Ramon might be thinking the same way I am about our future together. Maybe he's waiting for a sign from me that I'm interested.

Hopefully, if all goes well on the site today and after we visit Lily and Michael and meet Sirena, I'll bring it up or say something to lead to the conversation. But what should I say?

A gust of wind nearly blows off my ball cap, so I turn it around and firmly put it back on my head. I try to think of an easier way to find out Ramon's thoughts about us.

Nothing comes to mind, so I push the idea from my thoughts as I move closer to the open section, which is just a skeleton right now, and I feel a chill in the air unlike anything I've felt lately. If I were a betting man, I'd say there's a good chance of snow. That means Ramon and I could hit the slopes on our snowboards. It's been a long time since we've enjoyed the winter months together. Up in Canada, we had a blast, and I was sad when we moved to Lexington. Ramon did promise me that there was plenty of snow during the winter months, so we'll see. I'm really looking forward to it. Maybe we could stay in a mountain retreat with a fire to keep us warm.

As I'm starting to like this idea more and more, I turn to catch my cap again and have the fright of my life. I trip and end up on my ass, but quickly jump to my feet again.

"Surprise," she snarls.

How the hell did she get up here without anyone seeing her? Or did they?

"You can't be up here." I move toward her, but she backs away, moving closer and closer to the unsealed edge of the building.

"Hey, now." I freeze, not knowing how to proceed. "Don't keep walking; you're going to fall."

"I don't care," she mumbles, and I'm not sure she's actually here.

She has a slim build and blonde hair cut into a bob. Her delicate features and petite frame make her look like a fairy. I almost expect her to throw fairy dust at me.

I have no idea where that thought came from.

Shaking my head to clear my mind, I ask, "What's your name?"

She ignores me.

"How did you get up here without being seen?" I slowly edge closer to her, but she watches my every move.

"I'm used to being on a construction site. They're all the same when it comes to safety precautions and alternate routes in and out." She smiles before quickly running onto one of the beams jutting out into thin air. She sits astride it and watches me.

My heart is in my throat. What the hell is her deal? Surely someone saw her.

I drop to the ground and return her gaze.

"Why does he love you?"

Is this about Ramon?

"I don't know who you mean," I bluff.

She chuckles, calm as pie. "You know who I mean. Why does he love you when he didn't love my brother?"

Brother?

She can't miss the confusion on my face. I have no idea who her brother is.

"He was in love with Ramon, you know. Young love. First love."

I let the name, Andrew Griffin, fall from my lips and wonder why no one else considered her as the one behind the McKenzie problems.

There's no way she's been working alone because the stolen items and girders are too heavy for her to handle.

"Yes, my brother. He had his whole life ahead of him, but he chose to take his life because he knew that Ramon would never be his. Ramon killed my brother," she spat.

"Like fuck he did. They were each other's experiment, and your brother got too attached. Talk to your father. Ask him what he said to Andrew the night your brother drove drunk."

Her eyes narrow. "You're lying," she accuses, getting back to her feet in one fluid motion.

I hope she moves from the ledge before she falls. No matter what she's been doing or paying someone to do, she doesn't deserve to die.

So as not to startle her, I slowly stand up and edge closer.

Her eyes suddenly snap to me. "You weren't even around when my brother and Ramon were together, so how do you know what happened?" She takes a step forward before stopping herself.

"Ramon went to see your father the other day," I admit. "He accused your father of pushing Andrew to drink that fateful night, but your father wouldn't meet his gaze." I move closer still. There are now about two feet between us. "What do you think that means, huh?"

I know I shouldn't antagonize her, but her accusations are making my blood boil. It's because of the evil her father has fed her over the years.

"You don't know what you're talking about." Now, she won't meet my gaze.

I try to change the subject. "Why won't you tell me your name now that I know who you're related to?"

She shrugs, reminding me of a lost little girl. Someone who craves love but has never received it.

"Angelina," she whispers.

I barely catch her name as another gust of wind whips through the building. My ball cap goes sailing through the open space, distracting me momentarily. Angelina's cry makes me turn around to face her as she wobbles on the steel girder.

Watching her lose her balance is one of the most frightening things I've ever witnessed. Without thinking of myself, I throw myself forward into nothing.

19

Ramon

SIGNING MORE AND MORE PAPERWORK HAS BECOME A chore I could do without. I love the construction aspect and getting my hands dirty, but after a few days, everything else starts to piss me off. Today is one of those days.

Nothing is going right. Jackie has been in and out of my office every five minutes with one problem or another. I'm sure she knows the answers to half of her questions. I feel like screaming in frustration.

"Ramon!" Jackie screeches as she comes into my office again, as though her ass is on fire.

With my elbows on my desk, I rest my head in my hands and try to breathe through the annoyance.

Feeling as though I have everything under control, I lift my head and sigh. "Jackie, you're really trying my patience this afternoon. What now?"

She can't speak and looks panicked, but she can point.

I jump up from my desk, stick my head out the open window, and follow her finger.

After blinking a few times, I realize I'm watching Noah hanging on for dear life from a steel girder on the fifth floor. Dangling from his other hand is a petite person—obviously a woman.

"Sound the emergency alarm," I shout to Jackie, finally starting to act instead of standing there in shock.

As I run from the office into the building, I see that other workers are on their way out. I don't stop. I hear others racing up the stairs behind me and hope they're following to help.

All possibilities run through my mind as I see Noah hanging on for dear life on repeat.

Finally reaching the fifth floor, I see Noah being dragged back onto the concrete floor by one of the electricians. I can't remember his name in my panic, but I feel gratitude for the man.

Noah slowly gets to his feet and looks in my

direction as though he senses me. My heart stops before starting again.

He's safe.

Not thinking about anything other than holding Noah, I find myself moving toward him. When he's within reach, I take his offered hand and pull him toward me. I wrap my arms tightly around his neck and feel his breath on my neck seconds before he wraps his arms around my waist. He holds me tightly.

I'm not so wrapped up in him that I don't notice the gasps from the crew milling around. I didn't want everyone to find out this way because not everyone is comfortable around gay couples. But I guess our relationship is no longer a secret, and I don't care what they think. If they don't like it, they can leave.

Holding the man I love, whom I nearly lost, is causing my self-control to slip beyond anything before. It's going to be a long time before I can leave his side.

I inhale his scent, then ask the question that's bothering me. "Who is the woman?" I glance over to where one of the guys has her wrapped in his jacket while she sobs into her hands.

"Angelina Griffin."

My heart stutters. "What?" I turn my head again and look at her. It's probably been ten years since I last saw her. She looks nothing like the young girl who doted on her brother.

Over the years, I've often wondered how she was doing. From the look of things, she hasn't been doing well.

"I don't know what's going on. How did you end up out here?" I wave my arms around, unable to express the emotions and thoughts running through me. I couldn't wrap my mind around what had happened.

"I'm not sure. She suddenly appeared and started rambling. I thought she was going to jump, but then she seemed to be thinking, leaning toward me, when a gust of wind whipped through the site. It sent my ball cap flying, and she lost her balance. It scared the shit out of me." Noah's hands shake as he points around while telling me what happened.

The police and EMTs arriving put a stop to everyone standing around. I don't want to leave Noah, but I need to talk to the police and see if they can find out what's going on with her. Is she the one who hired the bastards messing with the McKenzies? If her father has been filling her head with lies all these years, then I suppose she blames me for her brother's death.

"Ramon, we need to talk," Jim interrupts. I glance

at him and nod. He's a detective, and he came here at Jackie's request.

It's about time Jackie took a look at who was right in front of her instead of searching for someone with money. Jim might not be rich, but he's been single a long time, and he only has eyes for Jackie. He turns into a bumbling idiot when she's around.

"I know," I tell him, nodding. Despite how he is with Jackie, he's a professional first.

The EMTs take Angelina away.

I look back at Noah and see the tiredness around his eyes. He's been through a lot today. I wasn't dangling from the building, but seeing him do so was one hell of a shock.

I slip my hand into Noah's and give him a slight tug to get him moving. I nod to Jim to follow us.

Progress is slow, as the place is crawling with rescue and emergency personnel. When we finally reach my office, I turn to Jim. "Can you give us five minutes?"

He nods.

As soon as the door closes, I wrap my arms around Noah again. I nearly lost him today. My eyes fill with tears as I hold him tightly. He pulls me in closer and keeps me locked in our embrace.

A few tears escape, and I try to wipe them away

before he sees them, but he knows me better than anyone.

Noah slowly pulls away, but keeps his hands on my arms. "I'm fine, Ramon." He offers a wry smile. "I'm probably bruised in one or two places, but I'll survive."

I turn away briefly and grab a tissue to dry my face. "I admit," I say, "I don't think I've ever been as frightened as when I saw you up there. I need a drink."

"You're not the only one." Noah sags into a chair and seems to deflate.

I need to get him home—and not to my apartment. I need to get him to the cabin—the cabin that I built with him and our life together in mind. He contributed as much to the plans as I did. I had always planned to move in permanently with Noah, but those dreams died when he disappeared. When he reappeared, however, they sparked to life again. With everything that has happened, I am not willing to wait to start my life with Noah.

"Let's talk to Jim and get it over with. Then, afterwards, we're going to the cabin. Eric is back in town looking for work, so I figured he could come here and be the site manager for a while. I just need to be alone with you."

Noah

"That's fine with me." I could hardly get the words out to Ramon.

Sometimes, I just want to pinch myself because I'm so lucky to have him in my life. I almost didn't, and it would have been my own fault. I don't regret leaving him to protect him. Sometimes I wonder if the threats would have been carried out if I'd stayed.

Not too long ago, I thought I'd be leaving him again—this time, forever.

I still have no clue why Angelina was up there with me or what her intentions were. It doesn't make any sense whatsoever. She didn't appear to be carrying a weapon, at least not from what I could see, and her dress was fairly transparent when the light was behind her.

Ramon places his hand on my shoulder in a gesture of comfort before opening the door and indicating for Jim to come in.

The detective is flushed, which makes me smile. From the glimpse I catch of Jackie, he isn't the only one.

Ramon clears his throat and says, "We have security cameras up there, so I'll send you the footage."

Jim nods and turns to me.

"Noah," Jim begins as he takes the seat Ramon offered. "Can we start with you telling me what happened up there?"

"We can."

I start by recounting everything from the moment I first saw her until I grabbed her when the wind caused her to lose her balance.

It was sheer luck that I managed to grab her and the steel girder. I felt as though my arm was going to pull out of its socket.

If Jed hadn't looked up from the floor below and seen what was happening, we both would have hit the ground and probably died. As it was, he came running up, clipped his harness to one of the attachments, and leaned over to grab Angelina from me. He shoved her at someone else who came running up before helping pull me up. Those five minutes were the longest of my life.

As I listen to Ramon tell Jim about the trouble that has been happening here at the site, I reach out and entwine my fingers with his. I just needed to feel his touch to keep me grounded.

When he finished talking, an awkward silence

stretched between us as we were lost in our own thoughts. I shake my head to clear it and ask, "Do you know what her intentions were?" Both Ramon and Jim stare at me. "I mean, she didn't appear to have a weapon, and I don't believe she planned to jump. So, I just don't understand what she was doing up there."

"I haven't spoken to her yet, but I will. It looks like I'll be speaking to her father as well." Jim gets to his feet.

Ramon offers his hand. "Thanks for coming out here."

"Anytime. I'll be in touch." Jim shakes Ramon's hand, and then he's gone.

Ramon sits behind his desk. After a few minutes of silence, he starts loading papers and his laptop into his briefcase.

"We're going to the cabin, so I'll do whatever work I have there. On our way, we can detour to visit Lily and our niece." Ramon smiles. "I'm itching to see how Michael is faring."

I raise a brow.

He chuckles. "He's such a wimp when Lily is in pain. You saw Lucien. Michael will be worse. Mark my words."

I don't know if I agree or disagree, but I love how

much his brothers love their wives. They love with everything they have. Just like Ramon.

Ramon stands up. "Let's go."

I chuckle as I get to my feet.

He knows what he wants: to be away from here with me.

I can't complain about that.

20

Ramon

I'VE BEEN AT THE CABIN FOR OVER A WEEK NOW. YOU'D think I'd be able to relax and let go of the tension, but some of it is still there.

Some of that has to do with my secret research into gay marriage. Even though we wouldn't receive any benefits as a married gay couple if we chose to continue living in Lexington, we'd still have the official document proving our marriage. I'm not sure what Noah's thoughts are on the subject, and I'm always nervous to ask him.

I keep hoping he'll give me some indication that we're on the same page. Sometimes he seems so closed off that I'm not sure of anything other than that I want to keep him here at the cabin with me for the rest of our lives.

"Hey, you," he whispers, wrapping his arms around me from behind and leaning into me. "You looked so deep in thought that I couldn't stay inside watching you anymore."

Leaning on the porch railing, I take Noah's hands and interlace our fingers. Holding his hands against my chest, I continue watching the trees surrounding the cabin. I watch a squirrel search for food amongst the fallen leaves.

"You going to talk to me?" Noah broke the silence before kissing the back of my neck.

Shivers of delight race through me, causing my dick to twitch behind the zipper. He loosens his grip and slowly caresses my chest, rubbing my nipples until they harden. The desire he's creating in me knows no bounds, and I have to fight the urge to turn around and strip him.

"I was thinking," I start, answering his question, "that I don't want to go back to the city. I don't want to go back to living in the apartment. I want to use this as our main home." I turn to face him, smiling at the delight on his face.

Noah leans into me as I caress the side of his face. He kisses my palm. He entwines our fingers and pulls my hand away from my cheek, closing it around his kiss.

"Then let's do that. I was being paid for working at the construction site, but now that's finished. I'll find another job because we're in this relationship together, and that means I contribute."

I open my mouth to disagree, but Noah covers my mouth with his hand.

"Yes, Ramon. I'm not sponging off you, even though we're living together. We used to have a shared account where we put in the same amount every month to cover food and household bills. We're doing that again."

"Can I speak now?"

He smiles. "Only if the words are what I want to hear."

"They are. The joint account is fine. It's still open. It's still open. But I don't want you to work with someone else. I want you to work with me. We've worked together in the office before, so we can do that again."

What about your brothers?" He frowns.

I laugh. "My brothers won't care. They've talked about creating a couple more positions due to every-one's workload, and as my brothers advance, they want to spend less time in the office and more time with their families."

"We'll give it a go and see what happens."

I smile, happy to hear the answer I wanted.

He smirks. "But you knew I'd say yes, didn't you?" Noah steps into my space and rubs his groin against mine.

"I did. Smug is the word I'd use to describe how I'm feeling right now."

"Hmm." Noah reaches between us, his fingers teasing the edge of my waistband. "And how are you feeling now?"

That's an easy one. "Horny as fuck." I push into him.

He shoves my sweatpants over my hips and lets them pool at my feet until I kick them off.

My dick thickens with arousal as the air hits it. Noah's eyes stay transfixed on my dick as he collects the pre-cum with his finger. He rubs it into the flared head, which bulges with need.

One touch from Noah and I'm ready to release. His touch excites me, and the shards of pleasure I feel from his fingers cause my legs to quiver and my breathing to grow heavier.

I growl as Noah kneels before me and find that I can't stop my hips from searching for his mouth.

"I love doing this to you," he says, licking me from base to tip. "It's a powerful aphrodisiac knowing what I do to you. Knowing that I can practically bring you to your knees."

His fingers work magic on my scrotum and between my legs as I widen my stance. I nearly lose my balance when Noah sucks the head of my dick into his mouth.

The sensation of having his warm mouth wrapped around me will cause me to climax too soon. Then, he releases me from his mouth, grabs the base of my cock, and tightens his hold to prevent my orgasm as he blows on the slit.

I see stars as I push against him, straining for more.

Glancing down, I meet Noah's passionate gaze and watch him swirl his tongue around the head. He smiles, then takes me deep into his mouth. Massaging my scrotum, he swallows and hums around my cock, which is as hard as fuck. That's all it takes.

My hands grasp his hair as my cock explodes. He swallows my cum as it releases. The sucking and licking feels so good that it becomes too much.

I pull him off me. "No more," I gasp.

He dips his head and licks me clean, then stands with his hands on my hips.

"I love you," he whispers just before his lips touch mine.

I taste myself on his lips and sigh in pleasure as the kiss deepens slightly—just enough to arouse me.

Noah

Two weeks have passed since my ordeal on the fifth floor of the construction site, and I'm relieved to have survived. So much could have happened when I jumped toward Angelina, and I'm still thankful for how lucky we were.

As it turns out, Angelina had no intention of harming me or herself—at least not that day. She eventually confessed to Jim that she'd paid a fortune to hire a couple of guys to cause trouble on the site. Ramon was sad, angry, and disappointed. He'd come to trust the two men she'd paid. They'd worked for the McKenzies for almost eighteen months before anything unusual started happening.

He still had a lot of anger toward Angelina's father. Even though he had nothing to do with the trouble. Brendan Griffin was responsible for filling

Angelina's head with lies. He finally confessed this once he realized what his only living child had been doing.

I can't help but feel bad for the family. Losing a loved one is never easy, and being partly responsible for what led up to the accident is something I'd never want to live with.

My only thoughts now are to move forward with Ramon.

We've been living in our own bubble these past couple of weeks, and I like it. The coziness I feel with him and in this cabin is tremendous. I know we have to leave in four days to head into the city, but the thought of coming back for good in the not-too-distant future keeps me going. We'll be commuters, but I can hardly wait.

Waking up beside Ramon every morning makes my heart feel lighter. I don't think I'll ever be able to properly describe the feeling I get knowing he's there. Knowing that, at the end of the day, we'll go home to each other, no matter where the day takes us, fills my heart with happiness.

That's what I want for the rest of my life. It's time I admit my feelings to Ramon. Hiding them is a worry I don't need, and Ramon deserves to hear them.

Over dinner, I'll bring up the subject and hope that he wants the same thing. He woke up this morning feeling something. His emotions have been a mix of worry, surprise, excitement, and joy, but they always come back to worry. I'd be lying if I said this doesn't bother me.

The dinner he's putting the finishing touches on in the kitchen will be eaten on the back porch. I set the table with the best china and candles I could find in the house. I hope the ambiance will help us talk about our future together. After all, a romantic dinner between two lovers really means he wants to talk, right? He certainly doesn't need to feed me to get into my jeans, and vice versa. My heart hopes that we will soon lay our intentions out on the table for each other.

"Dinner's ready," Ramon shouts, breaking into my thoughts.

My heart thumps in my chest, fearing what this evening will bring.

Deep down, I realize I'm being stupid. Ramon has talked about commitment more than once, so why should the prospect of marriage fill me with dread?

Shaking my head to rid myself of these thoughts, I walk around the porch to the back and smile in delight when I see the table set with pasta, salad, and bread rolls. A bottle of crisp white wine is uncorked and ready to be poured. Candles are lit, and my handsome guy stands to the side of the table, looking nervous as hell.

Wanting to put Ramon at ease, I smile as I move toward him.

I hold out my hand, and Ramon wraps his around mine, allowing me to pull him close.

Our lips meet in a soft kiss as I run my fingers along the buttons of his shirt. That's another thing. Ramon asked me to wear trousers and a shirt tonight. No shorts or bare chests.

Ramon looks good enough to eat in his pale blue shirt and dark blue pants, which is why I have to force myself to pull away from him.

Ignoring the fire in his eyes, I sit down and wait patiently for Ramon to join me. When he does, we start to eat in silence.

For the first time since I've known him, the silence feels uncomfortable. Usually, we can spend hours in silence, doing our own thing, and it's comfortable. But this feels strained.

I feel Ramon's glances and it's like he wants to say something but can't find the words.

It's like a small child who wants to make a confession but fears the parents' reaction.

I manage to stay quiet while eating the dinner before me until we put our cutlery down. Then, I can't stay quiet any longer.

"Spit it out," I abruptly demand.

I try to appear relaxed, but I'm anything but. My hands grip my thighs for dear life.

Ramon chokes, not expecting my abrupt words, and his eyes shoot to mine.

"I, um." He clears his throat and chuckles. "I'm acting like I'm about five." He smiles. "I want to talk, but I'm not sure how to broach the subject or if you'll want what I have to offer." Ramon blushes.

"You won't know unless you tell me." I smile because I think I know what he wants to talk about. At least, I hope that we're on the same page. "I'm here with you, Ramon. I'm not going anywhere," I grin. "Even if you want me to, I'm not going anywhere. Now, spit it out so we can get to dessert."

He frowns. "I haven't made dessert."

I roll my eyes.

"I knew what you meant." He clears his throat again, and his nervous energy rubs off on me.

"Ramon, you're worrying me."

He reaches for my hand, takes a deep breath, and tells me, "I've been researching gay marriage."

My breath catches in my throat when I hear the

words I've wanted to hear. Well, not exactly, but close.

"And?" I whisper.

"Damn, I'm making a mess out of this." Right before my eyes, Ramon drops to one knee in front of me and asks, "Will you marry me, Noah? Will you love me for the rest of your life, like I will you?"

My mouth opens like a fish out of water, but no sound comes out. I try again, but still nothing comes out.

Ramon moves closer and cups my face in his hands. When our lips are mere inches apart, he whispers, "Marry me," and I'm lost.

"Yes." I lunge at him, knocking him to the floor.

Within seconds, our shoes, socks, pants, and shorts are off.

I reach into my back pocket and bring out a packet of lube and a condom. I quickly suit up, drizzling some lube onto my hard cock. Making sure I'm coated, I rub the remainder on Ramon while rimming his ass with my finger.

He spreads his legs as far as they'll go while I drop on top of him. Our cocks rub together, and our lips meet. Our tongues twist, curl, and capture each other's as I enter his ass with my finger.

I can't wait.

I kneel back between Ramon's thighs and push his legs open wider and forward for ease of access. Then, I'm in heaven as I start to push into his slicked-up ass.

"Yes! Oh, fuck! Don't stop." Ramon pumps his own swollen dick as I fill him up. His muscles clamp down on me so strongly that, given my excitement to have him, I'm going to come the minute I start moving.

Ramon pants under me, gripping the base of his dick tightly as the crown bulges with need. He arches up, and I'm sure I see stars as his ass spasms along my shaft.

"So close," he growls.

I knock his hands away and growl, "Don't touch. That ass and dick are mine. You're going to spill your jizz with my mouth and dick pleasuring you, not your own hands."

Oh, fuck!

Ramon reaches forward, clamping his hands on my ass as he grinds against me.

"Oh, yes," he moans.

I clamp my mouth closed, slowly pulling most of the way out before sliding back inside him just as slowly. The pleasure wraps around me and builds and builds. Ramon's cock swells even more, and pre-cum trickles onto his belly as his arousal soars.

In a move not everyone can manage, I dip my head and suck the head of his cock into my mouth.

Ramon pounds the floor with his fists as curses fly from his mouth.

Feeling my orgasm build, I remove my mouth from his dick, wanting to watch him climax. I rock my hips back and forth as my shaft slides inside him. I wrap my hand around the solid length bouncing on his stomach. I pump my fist on his shaft, and within seconds, his hands cling to me as tightly as his ass clings to my cock.

My climax finally explodes as Ramon starts to come. His semen coats my hand, stomach, and chest, as well as his stomach. So fucking much. I grind my hips into him, unable to stop coming—it feels so good.

Unable to see straight, I slowly pull out of Ramon's ass and collapse beside him on the floor. I kick off my jeans, which are still tangled around my legs.

My muscles have all turned to mush, and the only thing I can feel is my dick as I remove the condom. I tie the end and drop the condom to the floor.

Finally, Ramon moves and grabs a napkin that must have been knocked to the floor when I lunged for him. After cleaning himself, he tosses the napkin away and rolls onto his side to stare down at me.

Seeing the love in his eyes, I reach up and bring his face down to mine so I can kiss his tempting lips. I don't stop there, bringing him fully on top of me. I let him settle with one of his legs between mine and his head resting on my chest.

"You said yes." I feel his smile against my chest.

"I did."

"When?"

I smile, knowing that Ramon is organized and won't be stopped now. He's also too impatient.

"New Year's. The first of January."

"I love you, Noah, and that's a date."

I smile, realizing that, for the first time in a long time, I'm happy. Really happy. "I love you, too."

EPILOGUE

Ramon

Sitting on the sofa at my parents' house, I watch Noah play with Michael Jr. and Charlotte. They're growing up so fast, and Lily can't turn her back or they'll climb on something they shouldn't. It reminds me of my brothers and me.

To this day, I'm not sure how my mom kept us in line and raised us right. She did a great job raising us.

Our new niece and nephew are around two weeks old, and they are beautiful. I've never seen my brothers so tame. Well, I have seen Michael tame before, when Lily gave birth to the twins, but never Lucien. This is all new, and one day I'm going to remind Lucien how he was when Alexander was born. But something tells me he won't care.

"My brother looks good over there." Carla joins me on the sofa.

I put my arm around her and pull her close. It won't be long before Sebastian appears, though.

"What have you been up to? I don't see you anymore."

She nudges me in the side. "Well, if you and my brother didn't hole up at your cabin all the time—which we've all been warned to stay away from when you're there—then you might see more of me. I've missed you both."

In my selfish desire to spend time with Noah, I hadn't realized how that would affect others, especially Carla, who holds a special place in my heart.

I kiss her on the forehead. "I'm sorry." Then I remember her comment about being warned to stay away. "What did you mean about staying away from the cabin?"

She chuckles. "Pippa warned us that it might be best to stay away from the cabin while you two are there."

Groaning, I drop my head onto the back of the sofa. "I can't believe my mom..."

She grins and interrupts, "Believe it. I think...

hmm, something about the hot tub keeps coming up... no pun intended."

It takes a minute, but then I roar with laughter, feeling Carla giggling beside me.

"Hey, what are you doing with your hands on my wife?" Sebastian asks, trying to keep a straight face, but the twitch around his lips gives him away.

"I like having my hands on your wife."

Carla chuckles as she stands up and wraps her arm around Seb's waist. "Don't be a stranger, Ramon."

"We won't. I promise."

All of my family is here today, even Sylvia, whom Mom invited much to Eric's annoyance. They've been caught in intense situations a couple of times, but this is the first time I've seen Eric give Sylvia such dark looks. Usually, he has a hard time hiding his lust for her, but not today. It makes me wonder what's going on.

After hearing Carla's words, I realized that she isn't the only one I haven't kept up with. I told Sylvia that I wanted to stay friends and that I value her friendship. Where have I been? I know it goes both ways, but maybe she's had more going on in her life as well.

I seriously need to start catching up with everyone before they give up on me.

Feeling eyes on me, I glance over at Noah and return his smile. His eyes kept dancing toward my parents, who were sitting on the loveseat by the window. It's his cue to announce our engagement. Initially, I told him it was his job to make the announcement because I did the asking. He wouldn't hear of it and pointed out that it's my family, so it's my announcement to make.

We could have argued about it, but I conceded—besides, I was looking forward to shouting the news to the world.

That's how I find myself moving to the center of the room, with Noah joining me. He slips his hand into mine and squeezes it encouragingly.

Michael is the first to realize something is going on, and he smiles when he thinks he knows what it is.

I clear my throat to get everyone's attention, and the nerves come back tenfold when Dad focuses his attention on me. It doesn't matter that everyone else is looking at me too. He's my dad, and I suppose no matter how old I get, his opinion always matters most.

"You obviously have something to tell us, son, so get on with it. You'll feel better afterwards."

Oh, fuck!

"We're getting married— Noah and I, last night." I clamp my mouth shut before I say anything else.

"You got married last night?" Mom gasps.

I guess that's how it sounded.

Noah

No matter how hard I try to hide my grin, it won't stay hidden. Ramon's blundered words have caused confusion. After a few minutes of everyone talking at once, I set everyone straight. I think Ramon doesn't know who to confront first. "Everyone, quiet!" A hush falls over the room. "What Ramon was trying to say, but couldn't because he was nervous, is that we decided to get married last night. If we can arrange it, the wedding will take place on January 1st."

Pippa sighs in relief. "I thought you meant you'd gotten married last night without me." Her lips tremble.

Ramon releases my hand and moves toward his mom. He pulls her up and wraps his arms around her, cradling her under his chin and resting his head on top of hers. "I'd never do that to you. I promise. You'll have to come to New York with us. Of course, we want you, Dad, and anyone else who doesn't mind traveling."

"Why New York?" Lucien asks.

"We have an apartment there, and it's legal for us to get married there. Lexington doesn't allow gay marriage," I answer.

"You don't need to go that far to get married," Michael offers, smiling. "It was on the news a while back that it's now legal in West Virginia. Huntington is only two or three hours away. That would be a lot easier for everyone, especially those of us with kids. We can drive instead of dealing with the airport. But if New York is where you want to get married, I'm sure we'll all be there." Michael stands and pulls Ramon in for a hug. "Congratulations, brother."

Eventually, all the congratulations are out of the way, and I find myself on the back porch with Carla.

I've missed her, and I've been a jerk for not spending more time with her since I've been back. I know she's missed me as well.

I pull her in tight to my chest and smile when her arms wrap around my waist. We both stare out at the mountain range. It's a beautiful view, but neither of us is really taking it in right now.

"Are you really happy, Noah? I mean, are you really, really happy?"

I don't need to think about her question. "I'm happy because I have a sister who's married to a good man who adores her. But more than anything, I'm happy because I'm finally going to marry the man who holds my heart and always will."

She sniffles into my chest.

"Hey, sis. Please don't cry," I beg.

I've never known how to deal with Carla when she's crying. She scares the shit out of me.

"I'm really happy for you, Noah. I love Ramon like a brother, so this is even more special." She sniffles again. "I love you, and I'm so glad you came back."

"I love you, too, sis. Thank you for always being there for me, even when I didn't realize it."

I hold my sister and let her cry softly into my shirt until I feel her tears stop.

"Is it safe to come out here?" Ramon asks.

Carla pulls away and accepts the tissue from Ramon to wipe her face.

"Have you asked her yet?" Ramon raises an eyebrow in question.

"Asked me what?" Carla looks between us.

I feel emotion come over me at what I'm about to ask Carla, and the words get stuck in my throat.

Ramon moves toward me. "Breathe. You've got this." He rubs my shoulders.

I offer my sister a wry smile. "Will you stand with me at our wedding?"

Oh God. Her tears are back, and this time they're stronger.

She nods and hugs me. I comfort her until Sebastian appears and takes his wife into his arms.

"She's standing for Noah at our wedding."

Now that he knows why his wife is in tears, Sebastian smiles. "I'll take her home."

"C'mon, babe." He lifts Carla into his arms and heads toward his truck.

"Oh, boy."

I sag into Ramon.

"I know it's been an emotional day for everyone." Ramon takes my hand and pulls me down beside him against the brick wall.

With quiet all around us, he looks out into the distance and whispers, "This is the beginning of a new chapter in our lives, and I can't wait to see where it takes us."

I wholeheartedly agree with Ramon's observation.

THE END

. . .

Turn the page to read about Ramon's birthday celebration before Noah disappeared.

Catch up with the McKenzies and join in the wedding celebrations for Ramon and Noah in "A McKenzie Christmas." Available now.

Love in Montana is book one in the De La Fuente Family Series. This is Sylvia Taylor and Eric De La Fuente's story, and a spinoff from the McKenzie Series. Available now.

RAMON'S BIRTHDAY
A SHORT STORY

RAMON. As I walk into my apartment, I stop in my tracks when I see Noah sprawled out on the sofa. One of his legs is bent along the cushion, and the other hangs from the seat. One arm rests above his head while the other rests over his belly.

I lick my lips as I continue to watch my sexy guy and notice his growing cock, hidden by the deep red robe he's wearing. Asleep my ass!

Swallowing, I clench my fists, resisting the urge to walk over to him. I want to do everything I've been thinking about today. After a shitty day at the office, all I want is to unwind with Noah. To celebrate turning thirty.

Normally, I would have worked from the site office, but my brothers wanted me at the McKenzie offices today so they could take me out to lunch and buy me drinks. The lunch was good, and I found it relaxing to spend time with my brothers. However, I felt as though something was missing. When I walked into the apartment and saw Noah, I realized what—or rather, who—had been missing.

I never expected to fall for a guy, but I have. Up until I turned twenty-four, I denied my attraction to men and always chased women. But that all changed after a drunken encounter—one I'd rather forget but can't seem to. From that point forward, I'd basically realized that I wanted to be with other men. Every now and again, however, I'd get an itch for a woman. Unlike Noah, who was one hundred percent gay, it wasn't like before.

"You planning on standing there all night watching me sleep, birthday boy?" Noah asked.

He grinned at me, his smile welcoming. He stands up from the sofa and drops his robe. I bite back a groan at the sight of his naked body as he starts to walk toward me.

I grin. "Nope. But I'm ready for the only birthday present you can give me."

"And what's that?" Noah asks, stroking his shaft.

"You."

Seeing the blaze of heat in Noah's eyes, I react by

yanking my shirt over my head and slipping my shoes off. Keeping my eyes on Noah, I unfasten my belt, button, and zipper. Before I can pull my pants down past my hips, Noah is on me.

His hands slide into my shoulder-length hair and pull me into his kiss. He holds my mouth against his, and our teeth clash and our tongues entwine. I place my hands on either side of his whisker-covered cheeks and deepen the kiss, needing more. Noah breaks off the kiss and caresses my back with his arousing hands. He slips his hands into the back of my pants and shoves them down past my hips, freeing my hard-as-fuck dick.

Noah shudders as he cups my balls in his hand, then strokes my cock. He squeezes my dick briefly before rubbing the precum into the bulbous head, sending shards of pleasure to my balls.

"Oh, fuck. You're going to make me come too soon," I groan.

Noah laughs. "You'd get hard again the minute I touched you."

I smile. With that statement, Noah has just acknowledged that he knows me well. I could have orgasm after orgasm all night when I'm alone with Noah. Nothing has ever felt as good as it does with Noah.

I pull Noah back into me and nearly come as our cocks slide together and our mouths meet. With his naked body pressed up against mine and his scent all over me, I'm about ready to climax. I've had thoughts of Noah in my head all day. I'd even go so far as to say I've had a permanent hard-on, wanting this man all day.

Growling deep in my throat, I wrap my arms around Noah, who places his hands on my ass and squeezes as we rut against each other. We're both leaking with excitement.

Noah slips a hand between our bodies and wraps it around both cocks. He starts to jack us off. The closer we get to climax, the more erratic our breathing becomes.

I nip around Noah's lips and bite the tender flesh softly as I move down his strong, masculine jaw toward his ear—Noah's trigger spot. We're seconds away from climaxing when I clamp my teeth around Noah's earlobe. He slides a finger into the crease of my buttocks and presses on my anus. We shout into each other's mouths as we climax. Our cum mixes and coats our stomachs, cocks, and Noah's hand.

It blows my mind, and I'm afraid I won't be able to walk. The orgasm took everything out of me. By the look of things, Noah is in the same condition.

"Shower," I pant, a slow smile spreading across my lips.

NOAH. I stand facing the wall with my arms stretched above my head and my hands resting against it. My legs are wide open, and I grit my teeth against the unbearable passion I feel for the man kneeling behind me. Hot water beats down on us, but I can only concentrate on Ramon cleaning the calf of my right leg. I hope he plans on moving further north, though.

He has the most talented hands I've ever experienced, and right now, they're moving in the right direction—toward my aching balls and throbbing cock. I'd never climaxed so intensely or for so long before I met Ramon. However, it's not just the hottest sex that makes me want to stay with him. I love his sense of humor and how he uses it. He's also great at solving problems. We can talk for hours about music, films, books, and sports, and we both support the Bruins ice hockey team.

I catch my breath as Ramon finally strokes me where I need his touch. My legs quiver as he spreads my ass cheeks and kisses my puckered hole. Groaning, I try to keep still while Ramon's fingers stroke between my legs, then cup my balls. I'm going to come before he stimulates my cock—I'm so close.

"Fist your cock."

I don't need to be told twice, so I wrap my hand around my shaft and start a shallow back-and-forth motion. But I nearly lose it when I feel Ramon spread me open with his fingers. He leans in and presses his tongue against me.

"Oh God, Ramon... I can't hold on."

"Shush. Don't come yet. I want my finger in you first."

My legs are about to give out on me in the shower.

I press down hard on the base of my dick and breathe deeply as Ramon slowly inserts a finger into my ass. His finger sinks deeper, and I nearly lose it when he rubs against my prostate.

A tingling sensation starts at the base of my spine as he keeps stroking my sweet spot. I can't hold on any longer.

"Harder, Ramon. Harder."

He doesn't say anything; he just slides two fingers inside me and fucks me.

If my balls pulled up any tighter, they'd disappear. I grab my cock again and start to fist myself. Back and forth. Back and forth. As the tension in my body builds, Ramon slows his movements until his fingers press against my prostate again. Gritting my teeth to hold on, I almost roar in ecstasy as he strokes against it. I ejaculate all over the shower wall and my hand.

Ramon gently pulls out of my ass and washes his hands with soapy water. He turns me around and watches me give in and slither to the shower floor. Grinning, Ramon settles between my legs, leans in, and sucks my cock into his mouth.

I pull Ramon's head away. "It's your birthday. I want to give you your birthday present."

Ramon grinned, his cock sticking out from his body. "Oh yeah. I'm not going to complain."

Before he can say anything else, I change positions, having him sit on the shower floor with his legs spread.

I caress his thighs, unable to take my eyes off his weeping cock. It stands long, thick, and proud, reaching toward his navel. So damn long. I love this part of our sexual relationship because Ramon's cock is beautiful. I've been with guys whose penises did nothing for me, but Ramon's is deliciously thick and elegant. It has my own cock rising again.

"We need a bed," I groaned, eager to see Ramon completely exposed.

I hold out my hand to him, and he takes it, allowing me to pull him to his feet. We quickly dry off.

RAMON. I lie on our bed and watch Noah approach, stroking my cock, knowing he's going to send me to heaven with his hot mouth. Precum leaks out of my penis, more than usual, dripping down along its length.

"Hands off. That's mine," Noah states.

Before I have time to think, I'm moaning and thrashing on the bed. Noah leans over me, licks up the pre-cum, and slides his tongue over my length and back to the head of my cock.

"You always taste so fucking good." Noah sucks as much of my shaft into his mouth as he can. He swirls his tongue around the head, knowing it drives me wild.

Without removing his mouth, he spreads and bends my legs so that he has free access to my balls and ass. His eyes shine as he sits back and admires the feast in front of him.

"I can't decide whether to suck you off or fuck

your ass. I want to do both," he tells me with a wicked look in his eyes.

I gulp, and gulp again. "Both." My hips arch and my dick jerks, leaking more with each passing thought. Thoughts of Noah's talented tongue and what he can do with my thick cock.

NOAH. I break out into a sweat as I grab the lube and condom. I smooth the condom down my shaft and pray that I won't come before I get inside Ramon. I coat my hands with the oily liquid and meet Ramon's lust-filled gaze. He always affects me like this. Like I'm an uncontrollable, horny teenager.

I wrap my hand around Ramon's cock, feeling my own expand at the shudder that wracks his body as my fingers glide over his cock. Unable to wait any longer, I slide my other hand between Ramon's legs and begin gently rubbing his ass.

Leaning over, I take Ramon's cock back into my mouth while inserting a finger into his ass. Ramon arches up from the bed when my finger hits the right spot.

Ramon's cock is leaking and twitching in my

mouth, telling me to hurry up before he comes too soon.

Once I'm sure I've prepared Ramon enough, I grasp my cock, push the bulbous head through the muscle, and stop. I need to catch my breath because I'm so close. I always am with Ramon. Being inside Ramon feels like nothing I've ever experienced.

"I want all of you." Ramon moves his hips, taking more of my cock inside him. "Now...before I come."

"Fuck," I curse, slamming all the way in, my balls smacking Ramon's ass.

Ramon clenches his fists in the bedding, tensing every muscle in his body and squeezing the hell out of my cock. "Move... Christ, Noah... Fuck... So fucking good."

Ramon arches up into me, sending pleasure to the back of my mind.

I catch my breath before leaning over and sealing my lips to Ramon's. I love kissing Ramon's rough texture; the spicy cologne he wears always fills my nostrils when I'm this close to him. As we kiss, I start to slide out and back inside Ramon just as slowly, rubbing against his prostate.

Ramon catches his breath.

I use my arms to hold myself up as I hover over Ramon, starting a fast-paced back-and-forth motion.

This causes us both to break out in a sweat. With one hand, I take hold of Ramon's erect penis and start masturbating him.

"Ahhh... fuck... I'm going to come," Ramon moans, continuing to twist the bed covers in his hands.

"Me too." I can hardly speak, the pleasure running through my body from the tip of my dick to the tip of my toes is so intense.

As I watch Ramon writhe under me, I see his beautiful cock enlarge even more in my hand. The sight causes my dick to swell and leak into the condom as I continue to fuck Ramon's ass.

I look up and meet his gaze before dropping my head to the tip of his long cock. I suck Ramon's shaft between my lips, and I'm satisfied when the man under me moans and gasps with pleasure as he orgasms.

I swallow everything Ramon gives me and finish just as he leans up and starts nibbling along my jaw. He nips my earlobe as he presses against my ass.

I orgasm. Cum shoots out of me into the condom as Ramon's ass tightens around me, prolonging my pleasure.

RAMON. After we're finished and have cleaned up, we find ourselves lying in each other's arms, watching a replay of an earlier hockey game. The leftover birthday cake sits on the bedside table, along with the tickets Noah bought me for my birthday.

Life couldn't be happier unless, of course, my family ruins it. I don't think they will, but I can't help but wonder how my family will react to my being gay or bisexual. Since I met Noah, though, and we started living together in Lexington, close to my family, I've only been with Noah. I don't want anyone else.

"What are you thinking about?" Noah asks. "You were happy and relaxed, and now you've tensed up."

Sighing, I turn and lie on my side, facing Noah. "I'm thinking about my family and how they'd take the news about us." There's no point in lying to Noah. He knows my mind as well as he knows my body.

"So that means you're thinking about telling them."

"I constantly think about telling them. I'm not ashamed to be with you, and I want you to join me at family meals and other family events. But every time I intend to tell them, I chicken out."

Noah moves in closer, so we're lying skin to skin. He says, "Knowing you want to tell them about me and that you aren't ashamed to be with me is all I need right now. You'll tell them when you're ready, and I'm good with that." Noah grins. "So, tell me. Did you have a good birthday?"

I laugh, then tackle Noah and loom over him. "I had the perfect birthday, and that was all thanks to you." The kiss I place on Noah's lips is as slow as my smile. "Thank you."

THE END

MCKENZIE
BROTHERS
HOLDINGS

DEAR READER

Thank you for reading *Playing with their Hearts,* and thank you for your reviews! It's really appreciated.

Subscribe with your email to be alerted about new releases, sales, and events.

http://lexibuchanan.net

Prologue

ROGAN - 9 years old

A twig snapped behind us and I slowly dropped back, allowing Leon and Chase to continue ahead to the river. I didn't want to draw attention to the fact Fallon had followed us. They'd just call my sister names—and me—even though they knew she liked hanging around with us. I always acted as though I didn't care one way or the other, but in truth, I did care. Fallon was my sister and my best friend. Not that I'd admit that little fact to the guys any time soon. They would never understand why I wanted to spend time with her—sometimes I didn't either.

Fallon was thirteen months younger than me, but she was also a lot smaller. She reminded me of a fairy with the freckles across her cheeks and nose. She used to hate them until I told her they weren't freckles but cinnamon sugar, her favorite pancake topping next to sprinkles.

Tall grass rustled as she got closer, but I knew Fallon, and she wouldn't be watching where she was going. She'd be watching us. My heart thumped hard in my chest while I quickly wondered what I could do to make sure Fallon wouldn't get hurt without alerting the guys she was behind us.

The decision was taken away from me when she let out a piercing scream. The hair on the back of my neck stood up as though I'd been electrocuted. Leon and Chase turned toward the sound, seconds before I turned and raced toward my sister; their footsteps pounded behind me.

I almost stumbled into Fallon when I found her dancing around in the tall grass. Her face was stained red and her eyes were puffy from the falling tears. She released her breath in big gulps and hiccups.

"Her legs." Chase gasped, pointing at the angry red blotches on her white legs.

"Poison Ivy," I mumbled, cursing. "Help her onto my back." I turned and waited for Chase to lift her up. "I'll get you home, Fallon."

I fastened my hands under her, taking her weight. "I'll catch up to you both," I told my friends.

They looked between themselves, and then Chase offered a wry smile. "Of course you will." He shook his head.

"It hurts so bad, Rogan," Fallon cried out. She

tightened her arms around my neck, nearly cutting off my air supply.

I ignored my two friends as I gave my sister a ride back to the house. For an eight-year-old, she was strong, as were her lungs, the sound ringing in my ears. I glanced down and winced at the red marks and white dots all over her legs. The sight spurred me on and I sprinted through the back gate and up the garden path, running straight into the house.

Both Mom and Dad appeared from different directions when they heard the ruckus.

"Poison Ivy!" I gasped, my breathing heavy. It had been far too long since I'd run so fast, and add Fallon's weight and my panic, and I was sweating like a pig.

Dad lifted Fallon from me and sat her on the kitchen table trying to calm her down. Mom grabbed the medical box for the magic cream she had in there. It worked on burns and stings.

Eventually, Fallon calmed down, and holding a hand out toward me, asked, "Watch a movie with me?"

I offered her a half smile and turned my back. "Climb on."

Dad chuckled and helped her up.

I carried her to her bedroom and placed her

gently on the bed, then I spent five minutes fiddling to get the *Goonies* to play. It was about one of the only movies we watched together—we'd seen it too many times to count. I didn't care because she was my sister.

Mine to protect.

My best friend Chase knew how close I was to Fallon, even if he couldn't understand why I would want to spend time with her. The thing was, Fallon and me, we'd always been close, especially with Mom and Dad working full-time, all the time. It had been the two of us since our parents had met and fell in love. I'd been three and Fallon two. Dad said he would love Fallon as his own daughter the day he married her mom. He even gave Fallon our last name —Scott. We were growing up the best of friends, and I wouldn't want it any other way.

Leon, my other best friend, teased me often about Fallon, which got my temper going. Chase had to get between us recently so I wouldn't punch Leon in the nose. It would have made me feel better for a short time, then, of course, I'd have felt bad.

At the end of the day, family was family, and I'd always have Fallon beside me. I hoped to always have Chase and Leon as friends, but that could change. My sister was different and always would be.

Turning, I found Fallon cuddled into the pillow with a picture of a beagle puppy on it. I chuckled and joined her on the opposite side of the bed. We stayed that way until the credits for the movie started to roll, and then I felt her hand slip into mine.

"Rogan," Fallon whispered, drawing my gaze to hers, "will you always be mine?"

Our foreheads touched together. "You'll always be mine, Fallon," I replied, hoping nothing would ever change between us.

FALLON - 13 years old

As my social studies teacher droned on about English colonization, I got lost in my thoughts wondering whether or not I could get away with following my brother, Leon, and Chase to the diner after school.

The center of Augusta, Maine wasn't far from school, but Mom and Dad told us we had to go straight home today. *Together.* I was slightly confused by that because Rogan always made sure I never walked home alone. He felt strongly about it. So it made me wonder what he was up to.

Ever since he and his friends turned fourteen they'd been into girls. Leon started to have problems with me hanging with them, but I didn't get why. They hung out with other girls, so why not me as well? I think it was Leon who put Rogan up to leaving me out. Rogan felt bad, I could tell by the way he looked at me with an apology in his gaze. It wouldn't have been Chase because he never really bothered one way or another.

Woolgathering, as my mom would say, took up most of my class time, but that left me with no clue of what I was supposed to do for homework.

And then I was saved.

"Here." Julia Quinn passed me a slip of paper. "I noticed you weren't really in class." She smirked.

Surprised, I took the paper and looked down to see the homework assignment written on it.

"Do you want to grab a coke after school?"

Her eyes shot up at my spur-of-the-moment question. "Really?"

I smiled. "Yes, really." I'd known Julia since first grade, and we sat together during second, but hadn't really become friends.

Rogan said I needed to make some friends with girls. He'd stressed the word *girls*, which I found amusing.

"Okay, let's go." Julia shouldered her backpack.

Rogan wasn't going to like me showing up.

"Let me just tell my brother."

Julia stayed silent as she followed me outside and

into the bright day. I started to sweat before we reached where Rogan, Leon, and Chase waited.

"I'll walk you home first," Rogan said.

"I'm getting a coke with Julia."

Rogan eyed my new friend and shook his head, a half smile on his lips. "Clever. Very clever."

"I thought so too."

"Let's go." Rogan turned and expected us to follow.

Julia moved in beside me. "Are we really getting a coke with them?" she whispered, and I didn't miss the excitement in her voice.

"Probably not," I admitted. "They'll go off and do whatever they had planned. They don't want Rogan's little sister tagging along."

I was right too, except I didn't understand why I was upset with Rogan for hanging out with a bunch of girls without me—but I now had a girlfriend.

Rogan, 17 / Fallon, 16

Chapter One - Rogan

"Why does she have to come?" Leon grumbled and pointed at Fallon, his face going an ugly shade of red. "For once I'd like to do guy stuff and not have your sister tag along."

I got in Leon's face. "Why can't she hang around with us? She's been with us for years."

"I don't like it now that we're older. What if we want to talk about girls or something? She's going to run off and tell them what we said."

I blinked a few times before I let out a long-suffering sigh. I got what Leon was saying, but I considered Fallon part of the group, or at least I thought she was part of the group. Maybe to me she was but to them she wasn't.

I turned to Chase. "Do you feel the same way about Fallon?" I tried to calm down and didn't, the flex of my hands as they tightened into fists was a giveaway.

"It's okay," Fallon whispered as she moved to my side and put her hand on my wrist. "I'll go."

I moved to hold Fallon with me, but she backed up, her eyes swimming with hurt.

"It really is okay. I'll go and hang out with Julia." Fallon insisted, before turning and walking away. Her shoulders drooped, which worked me up even more.

"I'm sorry," Leon said, and he loudly exhaled. "You have to admit we can't talk like we would if she wasn't with us. And I really need to talk about something."

Chase laughed. "What is wrong with you? We've

talked about all kinds of stuff in front of Fallon before. Why is now any different?"

"Because," Leon drawled, "I want to talk about her"—he pointed lower on his body and his cheeks went a bright shade of red—"um, you know?"

My heart stopped and I stared at Leon wondering if I'd actually heard him correctly. The silence was loud but that was probably the blood pounding through my head. Chase shoved Leon. Leon blinked and cursed under his breath.

"I didn't mean *hers*." Leon's eyes popped wide. "I don't know why I said it like that." He quickly amended. "I want to talk about a particular girl's…um —" He held his hands out and backed away from me. "I promise I don't mean Fallon's…um… Don't punch me in the face. I have a date."

"Date?" I frowned, his last words stopping me from moving closer.

"Yes…I have a date, which is what I want to talk about without Fallon listening." Leon walked away and I glanced at Chase, who shrugged.

"I don't know anything more than you do." Chase smirked. "I thought you were going to kill him for a minute there." He grinned and wandered off.

Chase wasn't wrong. When Leon had mentioned Fallon and her…*um*…I wanted to knock Leon's head off. No one thought about my sister in that way, let alone talked about her in that way.

Ignoring my friends—if one of them was still my friend—I headed home. Fallon wouldn't have gone to Julia's house, not when she was upset. She'd have gone home and locked herself in her bedroom. I knew her well, and it hurt that one of my friends had hurt her. Leon had needed to talk, maybe ask questions knowing Leon, but he could have said something on the side without Fallon having heard.

Pushing through the gate at the back of the garden, I spotted Uncle Frank helping Dad weed the garden. More accurately, Dad was weeding while Uncle Frank held a beer in one hand and the garden rake in the other. Sometimes I got the feeling Uncle Frank only came around for the free food and beer. My parents weren't what you'd call well-off, but they worked hard, even though it still meant living paycheck to paycheck. Uncle Frank was jealous of what Dad had with Mom. I didn't know why.

Uncle Frank's wife always seemed to do what he asked. And they had two kids who were five and seven years older than me. Fallon didn't really get on with either of them.

Shaking my head, I ignored Dad and Uncle Frank and rushed into the house. Mom was in the kitchen and gave me a look before nodding her head toward the stairs.

Fallon had locked her bedroom door and, unless she opened it, I wasn't getting inside.

"Fallon," I hissed, "let me in."

"No. I hate you."

Those last three words wounded me, and even knowing she didn't mean them, it still hurt deeply. I dropped my forehead to the door. "That's not fair, Fallon. You know I love you. I was standing up for you, but you were the one to leave." I pressed against the door with the palm of my hands. "Please let me in. You're all I have."

There was silence and then I heard the key turning in her door. I nearly fell inside when she opened it suddenly.

I pulled myself up short and snapped my eyes shut when I saw Fallon standing before me in a hot pink bra and panties. "Fallon!" I hissed in shock.

"What? You wanted me to open the door. So I did."

My eyes narrowed into slits as I glared at Fallon standing there without a care in the world, hands on her hips, glaring back. I knew she was hiding the hurt behind a devil-may-care attitude, but it was too much for me to see her in her underwear. It was probably more than girls wore to the beach, but *she was my sister!*

To keep my eyes from straying over her curves, I made myself busy and closed her bedroom door. "I'm locking it again so Uncle Frank doesn't walk in." Uncle Frank had done that on one or two occasions. He never respected a closed door.

"I'm sorry I was angry with you," Fallon whispered, blinking back tears. "I'm not really. I know you were on my side."

Not letting her state of undress bother me, I tugged Fallon against me and hugged her hard and tight. "I'll always be on your side. Leon was just being an idiot because he has a date and wanted to talk about...*things*."

Fallon tilted her face up to mine and frowned, then a slow smile appeared on her face. "He wanted to talk about the birds and the bees, huh?" Now her face split into a huge grin.

Embarrassment crawled up my neck. "Don't even say that." I covered her mouth with my hand while her eyes danced with amusement. "I mean it, Fallon. You are *never* dating."

Fallon rolled her eyes as she wiggled out of my arms and took a step back. "I'm sixteen, Rogan." She giggled and looked flushed. "Mom has already had *that* talk with me, so I know all about it."

Uncomfortable with the way our conversation had gone, I reached up and rubbed my neck. "Put some clothes on," I snapped, afraid of the way my heart raced when my eyes ran over her.

"Honestly?" She huffed, and shoved her arms into a pink robe. "Better?" She glared at me.

The robe did nothing to hide how beautiful she was. She was going to have to wear a sack to hide from all the boys who would get it into their heads to touch her. But I was the only one who knew how beautiful she was on the inside, and I hated that one day she would be with someone who'd know her better than I did. It bothered me more than it should, and I didn't know what to make of it.

Fallon wasn't only my sister, she was my best friend and the person I relied on the most, and I knew she relied on me just as much. She made me smile. She made me so damn mad I could spit fire. But heck if I knew how to separate those two emotions.

One day that was going to happen, maybe when I went off to college. Fallon was still going to be in high school for another year. Who would she have when I left? I knew she talked to Julia. Julia was her only female friend, although I was sure Julia only initially became friends with Fallon because of my friends and me. Julia pretended to be into me to get at Leon. It was so obvious it was embarrassing.

Fallon cleared her throat and smirked. "You went off into Rogan's world." Shaking her head, she stepped away. "I'm going to take a shower." She raised a brow when I didn't move, and then a teasing light entered her sparkling emerald green eyes.

She dropped the robe, and gave me her back. Reaching behind, Fallon unclipped her bra, letting it drop to the floor to my stunned disbelief.

It took a moment to get my brain working and realize I gawked at my *sister*, who grinned at me over her shoulder. I narrowed my eyes, and cursed under my breath when I felt a reaction below the waist.

I panicked and got the hell out of her bedroom.

The little tease!

Fallon had known I would run the moment she'd started stripping, but heck, she really had to stop doing that in front of me now that we were older. Plus I had to admit I was a regular horny seventeen-year-old boy.

No way in hell should I react to my sister like I had.

My sister!

I'm going to hell.

My thoughts had certainly not been brotherly when she stood before me, all that sun-kissed skin on display for my eyes, and I had looked—more than I ever should have.

Chapter Two - Fallen

My heart pounded against my breastbone as I closed the bathroom door. What was I thinking? I couldn't forget the look on Rogan's face when I took my bra off. He'd looked at me in a way that wasn't allowed—in a way that made my body tingle and caused blood to rush around and into places I had no idea could feel hot and swollen.

I stepped into the shower and let the warm spray pound down against me. I hoped the images on replay in my mind would disappear and I could go back to Rogan being just Rogan, my *brother*. My thoughts about him weren't sisterly, and hadn't been for a while.

The palm of my hands rested against the shower wall while the water continued to pound down, plastering my hair from the top of my head, and down my back.

Maybe there was something wrong with me— there had to be. Nothing made sense when I imagined myself with anyone else. The only time anything made sense was when I was with Rogan. We'd always been together and now that we were getting older, I was scared things would change beyond my control. Things had already started to change—the way Leon hadn't wanted me around, the way Rogan looked at me, the way I reacted when his gaze was on me.

I understood why Leon had reacted the way he had. It didn't mean it hurt any less.

With a flick of my wrist, I turned the water off and, wrapping a bath sheet around my shivering body, stepped out of the shower. In my bedroom, I quickly dressed in jeans and a T-shirt, my feet bare, then spread out on top of my bed with an old photo album I kept in my nightstand. It was filled with pictures of Rogan and me, taken over the years. I often got it out to look through, especially when I felt down or lost. Or when I needed a reminder of the history we shared and the reason why I should never think of Rogan in any way but sisterly.

One picture stood out in the book. It was taken three years ago at the beach. We had our arms around each other and Dad had made some funny comment that made us laugh. Rogan's smile lit up the picture, his eyes sparkling with amusement, his dark hair falling into his left eye, and his smile so wide that I traced his full lips with a finger.

A throat cleared. "I love that picture." Rogan took a hesitant step forward, and then with more confidence, crawled onto the bed. He settled alongside me, his eyes focused on the book in front of me.

I swallowed around the lump in my throat, unable to bring myself to meet his eyes. "It was a good vacation." I played with the corner of the book, and closing my eyes, I whispered, "I'm sorry about before. I never should have done that." My cheeks flushed with embarrassment.

"No, you shouldn't have," Rogan said in a voice so quiet I couldn't decide whether he was angry with me or not. "I think it might be for the best if we forget about it."

I quickly blinked back the unexpected tears to get rid of them, and nodded. "I need to pack."

I knew Rogan watched me from beneath his lowered lids as I moved from the bed and over to the closet. We should talk more about what happened; I really didn't like Rogan's suggestion of forgetting about it. But if we talked, I would end up in tears and that wouldn't do.

"I won't mention it again." I swallowed hard and hoped Rogan accepted my word.

"I guess I better go pack too." I heard, rather than saw, Rogan crawl off my bed and cross the room. As he jostled the doorknob, he said, "Just remember we're camping, not staying at a five-star hotel."

I gasped and quickly turned. Rogan ducked out of the way just as I sent a book sailing across the room. He laughed and so did I, and I felt like a weight had lifted from my chest.

"I happen to love camping," I shouted as Rogan smirked and closed the door.

Available now!

LOVE STRYKER
EXCERPT

Stryker (10 years ago)

"DAD, I'M NOT SURE this is such a good idea." My heart raced in my chest as though it would explode. My palms went slick as fear coursed through my veins.

I'd already thought Dad's late night plans were a bad idea…and they seemed worse the minute I saw the dark, deserted alley. It gave me the chills.

Nothing good was up that alley.

Even at fourteen I knew it, but my dad was determined so I followed him across the street. Something shouted for me to run, which gave me pause, but my legs had a mind of their own and followed him.

My dad turned, and then frowned when he noticed the slight hesitation in my usual eagerness to follow him anywhere. The nervous twitch in his right eye went crazy. "It isn't, but it's the only thing I can do."

Before I could work out what he meant, my dad grabbed my arm as though he was afraid I'd run. He dragged me to the mouth of what I considered a nightmare.

The stench of rotten food made me want to hurl. Every creak, even the wind howling around us, had my eyes constantly straining to see through the pitch black. I half expected someone to jump out brandishing a gun, or knife, or some other weapon.

Head down, my eyes landed on the hold my dad had on my arm. Something wasn't right. In fact, nothing about the evening felt right.

I knew my dad constantly bet on the fighters in the cage, winning and losing on a regular basis, but what that had to do with tonight, if anything, I didn't know. My dad never took me to the fights no matter how much I begged. I wanted to hang out with dad… wanted to be like the fighters—tough, strong, fearless. One day, that would be me standing in the cage with the crowds shouting my name. Then my dad wouldn't have any choice about keeping me away from that life.

I'd never understood the obsession my dad had for the fights, but they'd put him on a high for days afterwards…unless he lost.

Pulled to a stop, I felt the shake of my dad's hand as his grip tightened. He turned to look at me and the fear I saw in his eyes was something I'd never expected to see. My blood turned to ice and the wrongfulness of the night felt all too real as a large vehicle headed down the alley from the opposite entrance.

Caught in the headlights, my first reaction was to run and hide. The tension jumping off my dad was high. His breathing was frantic and sweat beaded on his forehead.

With my free hand, I shoved the black hood of my sweatshirt from my head so I didn't miss anything.

My pulse hammered in my neck and all I could hear was my heartbeat thrashing in my ears.

When my dad's only reaction was to stand and stare at the approaching vehicle, I knew then, that they where here because of him.

What had he done?

"Dad?" I turned and hoped he'd offer me an explanation as fear and anger knotted in my gut.

He didn't and wouldn't meet my gaze until the purr of the SUV's engine cut off. "Son, I'm sorry. If there was any other way I'd have taken it, but there isn't…I love you. You won't believe those words soon, but I mean them with every breath I take."

"What?"

Before he could say more, the doors of the SUV opened and a large man climbed out, moving behind us. Three other men emerged and stood in front.

The one in a dark suit stepped forward, his steely eyes on my dad. "Peter."

"Mr—"

"No names tonight…*Peter*." His gaze slid to me and my breath caught at the back of my throat. He looked me over—assessing. "He'll do."

What did he mean?

"Dad?"

My dad didn't explain and, seconds later, I felt his grip on my arm loosen as the large guy stepped closer.

None of this made any sense, but I'd known something was wrong the minute I'd stepped out of our apartment.

It was obvious that my dad had done, said, or agreed to something, but my brain worked overtime trying to work out just what.

Then I felt my wrists clasped tightly before they were pulled behind my back in a grip so strong that I knew even as I struggled that I wouldn't get free.

"Dad," I shouted, my eyes begged him to help me, but he just watched while they dragged me away.

The suit held his hand out and halted the guy who had me. He spoke with a threat inflected into his voice to my dad, "With this exchange, you can consider your debt paid in full. You stay away from him and me, and, you never step foot near the cage again…in any city. You won't like the consequences if you do." The man in the dark suit stepped in close to my dad, and threatened, "Am I clear?"

My dad's body quivered in fear and his eyes nearly bugged out of his head while the man threatened him.

Fear trickled from my belly and gradually spread throughout the more I listened to the conversation around me.

Until now, I had no idea just how serious my dad's gambling habit had become. I should have though. But surely he wasn't giving me over to the men to settle his debt. Was he? What did they want with me?

What... No!

The hold on me tightened as I started to struggle. The man behind me wasn't like the others. He was big and strong, and wore jeans and shirt as opposed to the others in suits. His scent was trouble, and even though I continued to struggle, I knew that he wouldn't release me.

My heart pounded as sweat ran down my face, mingling with the tears I couldn't control as my situation sank into my brain.

My dad, who I loved, who I thought loved me, had sold me in exchange for his gambling debt to be wiped clean. How could he do that?

My dad glanced at me one last time, pain in his eyes, before he turned and ran down the alley.

The man behind, tugged me toward a black SUV, but I struggled and tried to dig in my heels, my eyes still on my dad as he ran and left me with these assholes.

At the SUV, another man tried to grab my legs, but I kicked out and heard him curse as my booted foot slammed into the man's jaw.

"Hold that fucker," the man growled, grabbing me around the neck while more hands held me down.

My vision started to dim but then the man in charge forcibly removed the hands. "I don't want the fucker dead." He stepped back straightening his jacket. "Get him in the truck. *Now*."

No way!

In a last ditched effort to get away, I yelled, *"Dad! Help me!"*

My dad paused.

They all did.

Then my dad took one step toward me…hesitated. A bullet hissed from beside me—a silencer muffled the sound—and I watched as my dad disappeared around the corner seconds before I saw brick from the building fly off.

He did it!

He left me!

"I'm not going with you," I raged against everything. The fact of what my dad had done, the restraints holding my wrists, the hands gripping me. I struck out, blindly, as I struggled and kicked. My teeth sank into the soft flesh of the hand covering my mouth and I felt a moment of triumph as the man cursed in pain. Seconds later, the triumph was gone as the man's fist flew into my face. I felt the pain blossom, starting on my nose as my mouth filled with the metallic taste of blood. The pain ricocheted through me as I turned my head to the side and spat out blood. It felt like my jaw was on fire while I breathed through the pain.

I sucked in a breath to fight harder but my body tensed as fingers dug into my cheeks as a hand clamped around my face. The man in charge leaned forward, his eyes burning with anger as he loomed over me. "You're mine now lad. You're going to become my fighting machine. No more fucking nursemaids. I'm going to make you a man, and you're going to make me money to pay off your father's debt."

I couldn't talk with the hand clamped around me, but I memorized the man's face, and made sure that I would never forget it.

That close to me I noticed the scar to the right side of his face that ran a good few inches. I thought that he was an American at first, but now I wasn't sure. Something else was in him, and his accent, one I couldn't place, slipped with his anger.

I hoped that when I woke up in the morning the memory of tonight would still be there. Because one day, when I was a man—stronger—I was going to get even with everyone involved…including my dad, the one person I always thought would be there to love and support me—the one person who was supposed to protect me from evil.

How wrong was I?

Evie (10 years ago)

WHILE MY MOM AND dad were partying with friends, and supporters of my father, I was on the sidelines trying to pretend my life didn't suck. I'd tried to fake a headache so I'd be allowed to stay home but it hadn't worked. I'd been told to sit and sip water regardless as to how late it had gotten.

I was twelve years old and hated that my father had just been elected as a state senator. My mother told me that I was selfish for thinking about myself all the time; that I should be more supportive.

How could I be more supportive when the new job meant my father would be away from home even more than he already had been? I really didn't see me wanting my dad at home as being selfish. I loved him, and missed him when he wasn't home.

But now, he would be gone more and school would be even harder to deal with. The other kids loved to make fun of me because of my family and my father's ambition.

I wanted to be part of a normal family. I couldn't even remember the last time we all ate around the table at the same time. I would only have my dad for family vacations now. He'd promised more but I knew that wouldn't happen. He loved his work, and really I should stop being ungrateful because I had everything I would ever want...apart from the one thing I *really* wanted...my father home.

My one best friend, Millie, was the only one who truly knew my fears, and she was the only person to know how much I hated my life.

Over the past few months I'd spent so much time at Millie's house that it felt like my second home. I loved being there. Her father was larger than life and, although he'd scared me at first, I'd finally gotten used to him.

My mother still tried to keep me apart from Millie when she wasn't lost in a world of her own making, and actually paid more attention as to what I was up to.

Like now.

I sighed as I spotted her walking toward me with a sour expression on her face, as though she'd eaten a lemon. It soon changed to a smile when Mrs. Grant appeared to her right.

Mom certainly had something on her mind though because her path continued toward me. I hated being center of attention, which she knew so I hoped that I wasn't expected on stage or anything while my father made his speech, even though I knew I wouldn't get away without.

"Evie dear." Mom took the cup of water from my hand and tugged me up. "Straighten your dress. Your father is about to make his speech and we both need to be at his side to show our support." And then she had to go and ruin it all. "We'll be on the front page of the newspaper tomorrow."

My heart sank and I wanted to run. I would have except her grip around my wrist tightened…almost to the point of being painful.

"Just be pleasant for the rest of the night, and," her lips twisted with annoyance, "I'll let you go on the trip with Millie and her family."

While her words sunk into my shocked brain, I let her lead me across the room to where my father stood with his team.

Mom knew how to get her way but I didn't for one minute believe she'd just thought about that to get me to do their bidding. She'd have something else up her sleeve and need me out of the way so that she didn't have a child to supervise. I wasn't about to complain because I wanted to go to Chicago with Millie more than anything. When I'd brought it up to Mom, she'd scoffed at the idea because she considered Millie's family beneath her. I couldn't see why she couldn't treat everyone the same.

"Smile," she hissed between her teeth.

And like the world's most lifelike puppet, I did exactly what she wanted. My smile was full of love and support as we greeted Father.

"There she is." His smile was real as he enclosed me in his warm embrace and I felt a pang of guilt that mine wasn't. "My princess," he whispered against my ear before he kissed the top of my head.

Available now!

OTHER BOOKS BY AUTHOR

Hawke's Ridge

Maddox · Colton (2026)

Den Hollows

One of Six · Two of Six (2026)

Den of Filth (New MC Series 2025)

Reckless Wilder (2026)

Fifth Realm Series (Romantasy)

Quiver of Chaos · Wings & Arrows (2026)

Standalone Romantasy

Persephone Unchained

Tallulah James Mystery

*Dead and a Murder or Two · Dead and the Wedding Crashers ·
Dead and a Deadly Deed · Dead and a Best Friend*

Boston Bay Vikings

*Camden · Bennett · Ethan · Sutton · Carter · Bryson · Ivan · Theo
· Noah · Knox · Jericho · Roman*

Boston Bay Vikings Minor League

Lake · Rhodes · Nikoli · Dario · Madden · Bradford

Single Titles

Butterflies and Darkness · Come Back to Me · Indecent Villain · Lawful · Love Stryker · Tears in the Rain · Whispers of Yesterday

Holiday Season

Holiday Kisses in the Snow · Jingle Bells

Romantic Suspense Series

Twenty Eight Days · The Next Victim (2025)

Blossom Creek

Christmas at Emelia's · A Rake in Blossom Creek · Heatwave in Blossom Creek · Secret Love in Blossom Creek · Mischief in Blossom Creek · Runaway Bride in Blossom Creek · Naughty & Nice in Blossom Creek

Bad Boy Rockers

My Brother's Girl · Past Sins · My Best Friend's Sister · Never Let Go · Saving Jace · Silent Night (Novella)

Kincaid Sisters

Meant to be Mine · You Were Always Mine · Will You be Mine

McKenzie Brothers

Playing with the Boss · A McKenzie Wedding (Novella) · Playing with Fire · Playing with Desire · Playing with Trouble · Playing with their Hearts · A McKenzie Christmas (Novella)

De La Fuente Family (McKenzie Spinoff)

Love in Montana · Love in Purgatory · Love in Bloom · Love in Country · Love in Flame · Love in Game · Love in Education

McKenzie Cousins

(McKenzie Spinoff)

ABOUT THE AUTHOR

While Lexi is the author of the chick lit series, Tallulah James Mystery, and the fantasy/romance series, The Fifth Realm, she is also the author of over seventy novels. Based in Ireland, this British author has been writing since 2013.

Follow on social media:

Website: http://lexibuchanan.net
Email: authorlexibuchanan@gmail.com

facebook.com/lexibuchananauthor
x.com/AuthorLexi
instagram.com/authorlexib
bookbub.com/author/lexi-buchanan
amazon.com/Lexi-Buchanan/e/B009SPA94U